Natalie Tan's Book of Luck and Fortune

Roselle Lim is a Filipino-Chinese writer living on the north shore of Lake Erie. She loves to write about food and magic. When she isn't writing, she is sewing, sketching, or pursuing the next craft project.

www.rosellelim.com
 @rosellewriter

NATALIE TAN'S

BOOK OF

LUCK &

FORTUNE

ROSELLE LIM

OneMoreChapter

OneMoreChapter
an imprint of HarperCollins*Publishers* Ltd
1 London Bridge Street
London SE1 9GF

www.harpercollins.co.uk

This paperback edition 2020

First published in Great Britain in ebook format by One More Chapter 2020

First published in the United States by Berkley, an imprint of Penguin Random House 2019

A catalogue record for this book
is available from the British Library

ISBN: 978-0-00-836185-3

This novel is entirely a work of fiction.
The names, characters and incidents portrayed in it are
the work of the author's imagination. Any resemblance to
actual persons, living or dead, events or localities is
entirely coincidental.

PUBLISHER'S NOTE: The recipes contained in this book are to be followed
exactly as written. The publisher is not responsible for your specific health or allergy needs
that may require medical supervision. The publisher is not responsible for
any adverse reactions to the recipes contained in this book.

Printed and bound in the UK

To Daddy, who taught me how to cook.
To those who think you can't; you can.

Acknowledgments

The idea of this book began when I was at a concert listening to the erhu for the first time. The voice of the instrument moved and inspired me to write about an errant musician. I wrote a book I wanted to read: something magical, and full of food, that reflected my culture.

It took many, many people to make this book a reality.

I want to thank Jenny Bent, my incredible agent. I've learned so much from her and I couldn't have a better advocate in my corner.

A huge thank-you to Cindy Hwang, my excellent editor. The book wouldn't be in such phenomenal shape without her. To the wonderful team at Berkley: Kristine Swartz, Angela Kim, Rita Frangie, Vikki Chu, Pam Barricklow, Jessica McDonnell, Craig Burke, Fareeda Bullert, Roxanne Jones, and Tara O'Connor.

Thank you to Victoria Capello, Sam Brody, and Eliza Kirby at the Bent Agency. Another big thank-you to Sarah Manning for her efforts in making the book available in the UK.

A special thanks to my film agent, Mary Pender-Coplan at UTA.

Thank you to Beth Phelan, the creator of #DVPIT, and the

fabulous #DVSquad. This pitch contest is near and dear to my heart and the connection to other writers is invaluable.

To my husband, Robert: You've read this book one chat window at a time. You picked me up when I had no belief in myself. I love you.

To my daughter, Natalie: I named the main character after you. I hope that you will read this book one day.

To my close friends, Sneha "Fishie" Astles, Megan Hood, and Andria Bancheri-Lewis. Thank you for believing so much in me. I love you all.

I owe words of gratitude to Claire Morrissey, who helped take care of my mental wellness, and to Kelly Grenon, who kept me in great physical shape.

On to the village of fellow writers who helped me in my journey:

To Sonia Hartl, Kellye Garrett, Tamara Mataya, and Samantha Bohrman: you all inspire me and I consider you the closest of friends who happen to be writers. Sonia and Kellye, I love you both. We are the three ladies under the tree: we did it! Tam, you always believed in me and encouraged me to dream big. Sam, you are my guiding star: you know what I want to accomplish and always guide me to my destination.

To Kristy Shen and Karma Brown: You are my oldest CPs. You've been there for me from the very beginning.

To Helen Hoang: You are my sister from another mother. I can't thank you enough for your friendship, insight, and guidance.

To Sandhya Menon, Julie Dao, and Stephanie Garber: Sandhya and Julie, you've both been such wonderful mentors. I can't thank you enough for being so generous with your time and friendship. Steph, thank you for being the first person I spoke to when I began this journey by signing with Jenny. You're such a kind and positive person.

To Samantha Bailey and Rachael Romero: my agent sisters. You've been there with me and shared in my triumphs and struggles. Your kinship means the world to me. Sam, your optimism is absolutely infectious and underneath that is such brilliant resilience. Rachael, you are an embodiment of a fairy tale and I'm lucky to have your friendship.

To Jenn Dugan and Karen Strong: I met you both through #DVPIT and I'm so grateful. Karen, you are always so wise, practical, and inspiring. You help balance me and keep me laughing. Jenn, you are so generous with your heart and your time. I can't thank you enough.

To the large village of Betas and Cps: Jessie Devine, Tom Torre, Kasey Corbit, Jennifer Hawkins, Jeanmarie Anaya, Kendra Young, June Tan, Nafiza Azad, Kristen LaPionka, Judy Lin, JR Yates, Tasha Seegmiller, Rebecca Enzor, Kristin Wright, Farah Heron, Victoria Lee, Katie Zhao, June Hur, Becca Mix, Annette Christie, Andrea Contos, Kristin Reynolds, and Kelsey Rodkey.

The Canadian in me apologizes if I have missed anyone.

Chapter One

A horned lark perched on the concrete balcony outside my window, framed against the colorful paifang of Montreal's Chinatown. Ma-ma, who shared my love of birds, would have gasped at the sight of it. It was so still, I could study it closely: in the morning sun of steamy hot July, the smudge of gold on its throat seemed to have been created by a paint-dipped fingertip, and the dark markings along its collar, cheek, and crown inked by a calligraphy brush.

The lark stared back, its tiny black eyes studying me before it serenaded me. The melody transitioned from an ordinary song to one that was haunting and familiar: "Sono andati?"

My admiration of the feathered visitor turned to dread. Every person had a song humming under their skin to the beat of their heart. "Sono andati?" was my mother's. The only reason I'd hear it now was if . . . I lurched to my feet and shooed the messenger from my ledge before turning my back on the window, refusing to listen.

The rain came once my feathered vocalist had departed. It echoed the same tune, pinging against the gutters and metal roof, imitating timpani drums instead of the robust strings and brass of an orchestra, delivering the meaning with tiny percussive notes I couldn't ignore.

Ma-ma was gone.

Numbness traveled through my limbs, emanating from my heart, freezing me in place. Reeling from the loss of my mother, I could do nothing but stare out the window.

I needed to go home to San Francisco. By the time I packed my bags and left for the airport, the melody had followed me into the interior of the taxi. The sputtering vents of the air conditioner complemented the dancing raindrops on the car roof. The aria played on ordinary surfaces, a constant impromptu performance only I could hear.

The last time I heard this music had been on vinyl, spinning on an ancient turntable Ma-ma had once fished from a dusty flea market. Sesame oil sizzled in the air, popping out of a hot wok filled with stir-fried enoki mushrooms, mustard greens, baby bok choy, and strips of pork tenderloin. My mother had danced by the stove against snakes of smoke emanating from sticks of sandalwood incense stuck in nearby pots of ash. The scent filled our tiny Chinatown apartment.

Ma-ma had always predicted some sort of curse would claim her. She subscribed to superstitions as if they were horoscopes—welcoming their vagueness instead of recognizing them as worthless generalities. She avoided the number four because it represented death and misfortune, while seeking out lucky eights. She made no important decisions on the fourth day of the month but postponed them until four days later, on the eighth. Once she had mentioned that she made sure she didn't give birth to me on the fourth. I laughed when she told me. My birthday ended up on the seventh, a day short of her ideal date, seeing that Ma-ma could only control so much.

It didn't matter anymore, of course, because she was gone. What would I do now?

I thought about calling Emilio, but I had burned that bridge a long time ago. Tears slid down my cheeks. Tiny crystals sang a sorrowful melody against my skin before trickling down into a glittering pile on my lap. I gathered them in my hands. Such was the beauty of sadness: it transformed the hollowness of the heart into something as precious as the loss it suffered.

An unfamiliar number flashed across my phone's screen. It came from a San Francisco area code. My past called to me.

"Hello?" I asked.

"Natalie? Natalie Tan?"

I didn't recognize the voice. My skin prickled. "Yes, it is."

"This is Celia Deng. You gave me your number before you left in case of emergency. I'm sorry to call under such circumstances, but it's about Miranda."

Ma-ma. I knew why she was calling. A heavy weight sank to the bottom of my belly. Celia continued: "I don't know how else to put it, but she passed away this morning. I'm so sorry. It was sudden."

Ma-ma was the only family I had left in this world, and we hadn't spoken in years. As her daughter, I was expected to obey. By refusing, I'd caused an estrangement between us that was justified by our culture. She had called me a few times after I moved out. The conversations played like a broken record: a rehash of our arguments in the apartment, of two people talking over each other, not listening to what the other one was saying. After I left the country, the calls stopped. She must have realized that the miles between us represented the ones in our hearts.

I had left San Francisco in anger, and as time passed, silence became a habit. All of my unspoken words to my mother now hovered in the air, swarming in swirls of black until I could no longer see through them. I slammed my eyes shut, unable to tell Celia that I knew and was already on my way to the airport. How could I explain that hearing Ma-ma's song had already told me all I needed to know?

"The entire neighborhood is shocked. It was so sudden. I spoke to your mother last night and she was fine. Well, as fine as she could be with her various ailments. We were watching our favorite K-drama and were considering what to order in next week." Her voice went soft, lost in the memories she'd shared with Ma-ma. "I can't believe she's gone. I know you didn't leave on good terms . . . but Miranda loved you very much. She spoke of you often and told me the sweetest stories."

Although I had no right to resent her for her closeness with Ma-ma, a tiny ball of jealousy curdled inside my chest, nestled inside the numbness. "I'm heading home now. I'll take the next flight out."

"See you soon, Natalie."

I ended the call before I realized I hadn't thanked her.

I didn't want to go back home, but there were Ma-ma's affairs to settle—and what would I do with her apartment? I certainly couldn't live in it.

There was nothing left for me in San Francisco, no friends, no family. Our neighbors in Chinatown had known Ma-ma's agoraphobia meant she couldn't leave the apartment, yet when I was growing up they had never visited or offered aid. Even Celia, whom I'd left my number with, was a stranger. She'd always been my mother's friend, not mine. My father had abandoned our family before I was born, so I was tasked with the sole responsibility of taking care of my home-bound mother. While our neighbors' indifference had taught me the valuable lesson of self-reliance, their inaction contributed to the heavy burden of responsibility I'd carried as a child.

They were content to remain bystanders while I had become a caged bird, first as Ma-ma's helper, then her keeper. For as long as I could remember, my mother's dark spells had been a part of her, as day coexisted with night. I loved her all the same, though my memories of those times held a certain fuzziness at the edges like that of an old afghan. When Ma-ma's reservoir of sadness overflowed, she retreated to her bedroom: paralyzed, weak, speaking in endless whispers. I brought her cups of hot oolong. Food was ordered in until I was old enough to cook.

I would sit by her side, stroking her dark hair, threading the inky strands through my small fingers. My mother's cheek was smooth and decorated with rivers of tears. Nothing I did could banish the sadness, so I stayed with her, hoping my presence would ease her pain and that most of all, she would be reminded she was loved.

And things would have remained this way if she'd accepted my desire to go to culinary school. But she'd adamantly denied me my heart's wish, insisting on college instead. I didn't need her permission to pursue my dreams, but I had wanted her support and blessing. I realized then that I had to leave and go out on my own. I couldn't stand another day of fighting with her. She refused to acknowledge that I wanted a different path.

It took me two years to save up fifteen thousand in tuition for the first year of culinary school in the city while working three jobs. The glorified closet I'd lived in still sucked up most of my income. Rent in San Francisco was steep, even with three roommates.

When I started culinary school, I thought it would be easy, but the pressure of fulfilling my dream crushed me. Self-doubt suffocated me and made my hands shake. I ended up failing all of my courses, and I'd blamed Ma-ma.

But I'd refused to return home in defeat. I'd used the opportunity to travel, something I was deprived of while caring for my agoraphobic mother. I decided to go around the world and find a culinary education through other means. My dream had always been to open my own restaurant, and I couldn't competently do this without learning more first.

And so I'd traveled, funding my journeys with the humility to work any menial job. One stint as a painter had me dangling off the side of a building in Prague as the strings and woodwind section of an orchestra practiced in the courtyard below. As a dishwasher in Cairo, I'd snuck off into the night for a ride in the desert to see the pyramids. My peripatetic lifestyle hadn't allowed me to make many friends, but the practical education I'd received from working in kitchens was invaluable. I hadn't achieved my original plan of getting a degree in culinary arts, but I'd successfully defied Ma-ma and learned just the same. However, my dream of running a restaurant remained un-realized.

And now seven years had passed and Ma-ma was really gone.

After I settled her affairs, nothing would tether me to San Francisco. Perhaps when all was done, I could return to traveling, but to where? Now that my mother was gone, the world suddenly didn't hold as much allure as it once had.

Despite our falling-out, I had lost the only person in this world I cared about. It had always been just the two of us. My grandmother, Qiao, died before my parents were married. My father was gone. Ma-ma and I had clung to each other for love and survival until I'd left.

As strange as my mother had been with her quirks and supersti-tions, my memories of her and our time together were stitched into the thickest of blankets, ready whenever I needed comfort. And I needed it now.

While I was gallivanting across the globe, my mother had died alone.

Chapter Two

San Francisco undulated with hills against the blue of the bay. As the cab headed from the airport to my mother's home, the balmy summer breeze threaded its way through the open windows into the strands of my long hair, sending it flying like fluttering ribbons of black silk.

I couldn't shake the feeling that my mother had known she was going to die, but hadn't wanted me there when it happened. She had always told me, "Death is not meant to be seen. It's an immovable force that claims every living thing. Might as well strap yourself to a tree to witness a hurricane." Perhaps my mother meant to spare me some pain from the inevitable.

What do I do now?

I had planned on leaving Montreal soon. I had been there for a year and was searching for the next port, even while my anemic bank account urged me to seek stability. Most twenty-eight-year-olds had family, careers, a foothold in some sort of direction—wanted or unwanted. After all this time, I found myself yearning for the very same thing I'd sought when I left—a career doing the thing I loved most of all: cooking.

Now that I had worked in the kitchens of others, more than ever I wanted a restaurant to call my own. Something small and humble, serving authentic Chinese dishes. Massive establishments with armies of servers and kitchen staff held no allure for me. I craved intimacy, to know and see my customers and develop a relationship with them.

Ma-ma had been my first cooking teacher, helping awaken in me a lifelong fascination with food. It still cut me that she of all people had denied me what I'd desired most. She claimed she was protecting me from inevitable misery: she didn't want me to have the life of being trapped in a restaurant. Ma-ma had said I was destined to fail if I chose this path. During one of our fights about it, she finally revealed to me that my grandmother, Qiao, had run a restaurant and needed my mother to run it as well, but Ma-ma had refused.

The revelation about the family business excited me, and I grew more determined to pursue my dream, knowing that Laolao had done so as well. Ma-ma did her best to enforce her will. The old restaurant was below our apartment, but it was boarded up and had fallen into massive disrepair. And besides, Ma-ma told me, the kitchen would be my cage: no room for a husband, family, or a life outside it. She painted a miserable life of cooking for others while struggling to feed myself. She herself had never wanted the life Laolao had intended for her: in her eyes, the hours were far too long, the frequent interactions draining, and the thought of catering to the whims of others left her miserable and unfulfilled. The most hurtful thing she said to me? That no matter how hard I tried, I would never cook as well as Laolao. No one could.

Dreams, even modest ones, had a steep price. Mine had cost me my mother and given me the silence of seven years.

Now that silence could never be breached.

The taxi dropped me off by the Dragon's Gate at Bush Street. I saw it right away: the neighborhood was different. Dusk's veil failed to hide the increasing number of converted office buildings and upscale, big-name chains moving in where bodegas and apartments used to be. These buildings used to be small businesses that housed hives of families. I'd read that the boom in the real estate market in San Francisco, fueled by the tech industry, had created a housing crisis for those with low and middle incomes. Ma-ma had been lucky that she owned our building, otherwise she would have been prey to the mass evictions that occurred. Growing up, I was accustomed to an insular neighborhood where the faces were as familiar as my own, but more and more, the demographics were changing. Gentrification was devouring Chinatown. Even knowing this, however, I hadn't expected the neighborhood to change so much in seven years.

I pressed my hand against one of the stone lions guarding the gate. This symbolic archway at Grant Avenue and Bush Street marked Chinatown. I'd grown up seeing this beautiful monument outside my window. In the past, the paifangs were the magical doorways of my universe. My mother's reclusive ways had afforded me a sort of freedom: even as a small child, I'd had the run of the oldest Chinatown on the continent while performing errands for my mother that she wouldn't leave the apartment to do herself.

A gathering fog brewed at the base of the gate the way steam rises from a perfect bowl of noodle soup.

I was home.

I should have gone straight to the apartment, but I feared the finality of what awaited me there. Instead, I kept my head down, veering by my old front door, speed walking past the familiar shops of our neighbors, hoping the fog would thicken like salted duck congee to conceal my arrival. I should pay my respects and visit them after my time away, but I wanted to do no such thing. I rationalized to myself that, just this once, my grief justified dismissing these cultural expectations.

I headed toward Stockton Street, escaping my deserted block with its faded signs and dwindling businesses. My neighborhood was struggling, as it had been most of my life. However, rumors abounded of a golden age during my grandmother's lifetime. I had mentioned this to Ma-ma once and she dismissed it as a fairy tale, wishes of those who couldn't change their ill luck or destiny. She had been a firm believer in the Chinese adage of keeping one's eyes on one's own plate and swallowing one's misery. Even though this wasn't how I wanted to live, I feared I had internalized that proverb and made it my own.

I turned the corner to face Old Wu's restaurant, the Lotus. Since the main entrance and windows faced Stockton Street, it was considered outside of the neighborhood, remaining prosperous and seemingly untarnished from the decay that had gripped the residents on my street. Its facade showcased the old world with its curved tiled rooftops, second-story balcony, and golden Chinese characters raised high above the entrance. A string of red paper lanterns zigzagged across this section of the street, bobbing in the breeze like ripe cherries in a bucket of water.

I had an unpleasant history with this place and its owner, but after so many years away, perhaps Old Wu had retired. My growling, empty stomach, and sudden cravings for cheung fun, zhaliang, and yin-yang fried rice, overrode any misgivings.

Evening had fallen and, as expected, the restaurant was nearly full of Chinese clientele. The noise from the dining room crackled in my ears, and I plucked out bits and pieces of conversation like picking up kernels of rice with chopsticks. Ma-ma and I had switched between

Chinese and English at home. She was responsible for my fluency in Mandarin and Cantonese.

Old Wu, who'd always manned the takeout counter like a vigilant sentinel, wasn't there. I exhaled as the tension left my shoulders. An edition of the *San Francisco Chronicle* and the latest issue of *Scientific American* lay together wedged beside the cash register. No sign of the man, but his reading materials of choice remained, so he must be around somewhere. I chalked up his momentary absence to good luck.

The hostess greeted me at the podium, then led me to an empty table. Since Ma-ma had never left the apartment, we'd always gotten takeout, so I had never eaten inside the restaurant before.

I ordered our preferred three dishes and poured myself a cup of jasmine tea. I wished every restaurant had the customary teapot of jasmine or oolong waiting at the table. My stomach gurgled, impatient for the food to arrive. I'd purposely ordered more than enough for one person—the three dishes meant leftovers for tomorrow.

The server soon brought large platters of cheung fun and zhaliang along with various condiments for dipping. Cheung fun was a delightfully surprising dish: nestled within the flat, translucent rice rolls were plump prawns. Zhaliang were crispy, long fritters wrapped in rice noodle. This was a favorite because of the combinations of contrasting textures: tender steamed rice noodles and crunchy golden fritters. The taste of these two dishes was determined by its accompanying dressing: spicy if paired with hot mustard, salty with soy sauce, and sweet with the peanut sauce.

I helped myself to three each of the fritters and rice rolls. I first used the soy sauce on my portions, savoring the chewy noodle and prawns, then alternated between the peanut sauce and the hot mustard. Before I could dive in for a second helping, the last dish arrived.

Yin-yang fried rice was a feast for the eyes and the senses. Swirls of cream contrasted with an orange tomato sauce to form the iconic pattern. Underneath the sauces lay a bed of yang chow fried rice containing a bounty of minced jewels: barbecued pork, Chinese sausage, peas, carrots, spring onions, and wisps of egg. Slices of white onions and pork emerged from the tomato sauce while shrimp and sweet green peas decorated the cream. Which side I preferred depended on my mood. The tomato sauce was tangy and sweet while the cream was subtle.

I dipped my spoon into the cream side, heaping the rice into my bowl. This was comfort in my time of need, nourishment and a sense of stability when grief threatened to crumble the earth from under me. After this meal, I would face the emptiness left by Ma-ma's passing.

The steam rising from the fried rice dish obscured my view of the entrance, which meant I was completely surprised by the ambush I faced next.

"How dare you come in here!" Old Wu shouted as he walked to the edge of my table. The food in my mouth lost all flavor. I instantly reverted to the cowering seven-year-old girl I had once been, fingers gripping the sides of my seat.

He pointed at me, his index finger a thin dagger made of flesh and bone. Wu's reedy build had always reminded me of a malevolent grasshopper. "Natalie Tan. It was your fault that your mother died alone. What kind of a daughter are you?"

Chapter Three

I couldn't answer. His question had wounded me where he had intended it to—into my very being. He was right: I was guilty of the greatest transgression. Filial piety was sacred in my culture, and my mother had died while I was 3,100 miles away. I trembled, speechless from his judgment and my shame, as his onslaught continued.

"You left her alone for years. You knew she never went out. You knew this would happen! She raised you on her own and took care of you. This is how you repay her? You come back too late to be of use!"

I could say nothing to defend my actions. If I hadn't left her, Mama would most likely still be alive. I'd have been there all along to ease the strain, or at the very least been able to call an ambulance for her this morning, when she passed. Maybe that would have made all the difference.

"You're not welcome here. Get out of my restaurant."

I lowered my spoon to the plate without making a sound and reached for the handle of my rolling suitcase. Eyes downcast, I pushed myself away from the table.

"Mr. Wu, please," a familiar voice spoke, the same one from the phone earlier today. "Have some compassion. She just lost her mother." Celia Deng stood beside me, her firm hand resting on my shoulder, resplendent in a navy frock with a white hibiscus pattern. She was five years younger than Ma-ma at forty-eight, yet despite their age difference, they were close friends. There was no trace of gray in her curled hair. Her subtle perfume smelled like cut gardenias. She continued in firm but gentle tones. "She must have arrived from the airport and wanted to get something good to eat. You can't fault her for choosing your restaurant."

Blood rushed to my face, bringing a welcome heat. Why was she defending me? Was this an act of pity? Old Wu's harsh face softened. "If it was your idea, then I apologize."

"I'll take her home now. I'm sure she must be exhausted from her flight. I'll pay the bill." Celia squeezed my shoulder as a cue to leave. I reached for my suitcase and took my place beside her.

He cleared his throat. "No, it was my fault, Celia. Don't worry about the bill."

"No, no. Business is business, Mr. Wu. We all need to make a living." She reached into her purse for her wallet.

"I refuse to allow you to pay for my error. Put your wallet away, Celia."

"I'm one of your most loyal customers and I don't want to lose my standing. Please, I insist."

This was a familiar dance, and I'd have laughed if Old Wu were not involved. The tug-of-war to pay the bill was a common cultural occurrence involving everything from mad dashes to the till, to calling the restaurant or telling the server ahead of time who would be paying. In most cases, the end result required the server's patience in waiting for the resolution. The performance of paying the bill demonstrated the traits of generosity and hospitality so prized by our culture.

Celia emerged victorious and left two crisp twenty-dollar bills on the table before she linked her arm with mine and escorted me out of the restaurant. Old Wu returned to his post without further comment. My heated cheeks remained the sole trace of the old man's earlier tirade. The details of the incident might fade, but I would never forget the shame.

"I'm sorry about Mr. Wu," Celia murmured. "He's set in his ways and he doesn't understand your relationship with Miranda. He's probably still stinging from your laolao's death decades ago."

Old Wu was of the same generation as Laolao. Ma-ma had seldom spoken of her mother because their relationship had been complicated at best, but I'd always yearned to know more about my grandmother.

"He knew her?" I asked.

"Of course. Your grandmother's restaurant was once the jewel of Chinatown."

I unwound my arm from hers in surprise. Information about my grandmother had never flowed freely from my neighbors.

Celia smiled. "Qiao and Miranda loved each other, but both wanted very different things." She paused. "Miranda asked us not to mention your laolao to you. I have honored her wishes until now."

Ma-ma. I still couldn't believe she was gone.

"How did it happen?" My voice dwindled to a whisper. If Celia weren't in such close proximity, she might have missed it.

"It was the strangest thing. Anita Chiu found her outside your building, collapsed on the sidewalk. I still don't know why Miranda stepped out."

A sudden hope swelled inside me, mingling with the shame and guilt. Ma-ma's agoraphobia had kept her confined upstairs. The building could have been on fire, and if she had to walk across the threshold for safety, she still wouldn't have been able to. Had something changed over the years I was gone? "Was . . . She'd been able to leave the apartment?"

"No. It was so unlike Miranda. I saw her two nights before when I came for a visit. She looked fine then. A little pale but within the normal range for your mother."

Why had my mother stepped outside?

I was thirteen, on my way to the bus stop, when I tripped over a crack in the sidewalk across the street, opening a deep gash in my shin. Ma-ma had seen the whole thing, her face plastered against the glass of the window, but she wasn't able to come down and help me. The combination of sheer panic, anguish, and helplessness on her face was forever burned into my memory.

Why did you go outside, Ma-ma?

"It is a mystery to all of us. But the important thing is that you're here now." Celia paused to gather her breath before continuing. "Her body is at the morgue. I can go with you in the morning, and if you want me to, I can help you plan the funeral. Miranda wanted a traditional Buddhist ceremony. We can do a private one and rebuild your family shrine."

"Family shrine?"

"You had one. I saw it once, but Miranda put it away after your grandmother died."

Laolao died long before I was born. Ma-ma had only spoken of her as one would a favorite fable, presenting merely the morals of the tale and leaving the details vague on purpose. Guilt gnawed at me for wanting more than what my mother had given, but now that she was gone, the opportunity to know anything about my grandmother was lost. Regret flooded me: I should have pushed harder. Laolao was a part of me too.

"With your mother the way she was, I know you've never been to a Chinese funeral. Do you know what to do? Let me help you. It's the least I can do."

Celia's kindness crept in to surprise me. Such was the vulnerability of grief: every act of concern was felt more deeply, for the path to the heart was clear. It mattered not who was offering, this was what I needed now, and I was grateful.

"Thank you," I said. "I don't know what to do or how to even begin arranging this."

She patted my arm. "After having arranged the funerals for my parents five years ago, I know the ins and outs. I'll be your guide."

We stopped at the door to Ma-ma's apartment. Celia gave me a tight embrace. "I'm really sorry about Miranda. Would you like me to come in with you?"

I shook my head. "I need to do this alone, but thank you."

"I understand." She nodded. "Oh! And before I forget, beware of the cat."

"The cat?"

"I've been feeding the little piranha for Miranda. She picked it out a month ago. I was both delighted and supportive of her decision until Meimei drew blood. The kitten is very cute and only likes—liked— your mother. Don't be insulted if she hates you."

Meimei. Little sister. Ma-ma chose the name well. The idea of my mother having a companion made me smile. She should have done it years ago. My gaze drifted to the faded scratches on Celia's forearms, which I hadn't noticed until now. "Thank you for the warning and for everything else."

"You have my number. Call me when you're ready."

Celia returned to her building and left me standing alone by the door to the apartment.

By the time I turned the key, climbed up the stairs, and stepped into my mother's apartment, I was crying. A trail of sorrow followed me. When sadness made an appearance in my life, it always brought the weight of the ocean with it.

I locked the door behind me and set down my luggage in the foyer.

It was like traveling back in time—nothing had changed. From the bird figurines my mother collected to the small cracks in the pale lemon walls she had so carefully painted, it was exactly as I remembered. The layout of the apartment was modest by San Franciscan standards but generous compared to the closets I had lived in the last few years. Two bedrooms, one bathroom, a combined kitchen and living area, and access to a seldom-used rooftop patio. Three windows overlooked Grant Avenue and provided a clear view of the green tiles of the paifang, the ornate arch marking the edge of Chinatown at Bush Street.

I closed my eyes and breathed in the familiar scents of the apartment: oolong, jasmine, and tieguanyin teas held in vintage tins in the pantry; pungent star anises and red Sichuan peppercorns mingled with pickled ginger and dried chili peppers in the collection of spices above the stove; the musty scent of newsprint from the stacks of Chinese newspapers Ma-ma subscribed to; and the subtle perfume of phalaenopsis on the windowsills.

Home, but empty in a way I'd never experienced.

On the kitchen counter, a long envelope stuck out from one of the slots of the unplugged toaster. Ma-ma had never eaten toast in her entire life. She had bought the appliance for me because I'd loved peanut butter and jelly sandwiches on toast for lunch. The paleness of the crisp paper matched the shade of sliced bread. Ma-ma's elegant script spelled out my name. The pristine corners betrayed its age: this had been placed there recently.

Goose bumps rose on my skin.

I picked up the envelope and ripped it open. My fingertips

skimmed the rippled surface where the pressure of Ma-ma's pen had marked the paper. My heart clenched, squeezing inside my rib cage like a captured bird. Written on sheets of onionskin were my mother's last words to me.

Dearest Natalie,

I had imagined your homecoming to be full of joy, sugared fritters, and late nights listening to the tales of your travels. I wanted to hear your stories and all about the new dishes you've tried.

I attempted to write you this letter every year, and until now, I could never finish it. At first, it was because of pride: I wanted you to come to your senses and come home because you knew I was right. Then as the years grew longer, I didn't care anymore about who was right or wrong. I shouldn't have allowed the silence between us to stretch on for so long. I never reached out because I was afraid that you didn't love me anymore.

I love you so much.

I'm sorry.

I'm sorry for not understanding your wishes.

I'm sorry I tried to impose my will on you.

I'm sorry for all the hurtful things I said, that you would never cook like your grandmother, words uttered in desperation and spite.

These were my fears. I pinned them onto you, hoping you'd claim them as your own and abandon your dream. I wanted you to stay close to me. Instead, I lost the very person I loved most in this world.

I will always love you, dear heart.

Your presence in my life helped me forget its fractured state: my heart has been broken since before you were born. I fear it will be my undoing, but I have accepted this. It's my burden and mine alone to bear.

Before you came into this world, your grandmother and I quarreled, just as you and I have done.

She wanted me to be someone I'm not, just as I tried to do the same to you.

You should have the freedom to choose your own way. I understand this now. You are more like your grandmother than I was willing to admit. And that isn't a terrible thing by any means.

Your grandmother helped build this community. She came from China with nothing but her mother's wok and the cooking skills she had learned from her own mother. All by herself, she opened a restaurant, and her dishes brought people together: strangers, bickering relatives, newcomers, and old-timers alike. Her establishment welcomed all and was the jewel of Chinatown.

But I refused to honor my mother's legacy.

Because of this, I have watched the street die. The neighbors are struggling to keep their businesses afloat. They will lose everything they have worked so hard for. If your laolao's restaurant were still open, this would never have happened. People came from miles around to eat there. She kept the neighborhood alive.

I lied to you about the restaurant. I told you that it was in a horrible state of disrepair. I did this to dispel any illusions you might have had about running it. But I was wrong to turn you away from what you sought.

If you want to reopen the restaurant, you have my blessing. It is dirty and dusty but still operable. Perhaps it is your destiny to follow your grandmother and save the neighborhood once more. Follow your dreams, beloved daughter.

> *Love,*
>
> *Ma-ma*

The letter was dated yesterday. It fluttered to the floor as I braced my palms against the counter.

I wished her written words could have taken to the air and shattered the long years of silence between us. What she said about my cooking, all those years ago, had left lingering scars. I'd wanted to prove her wrong, and yet I still hadn't accomplished my goal. I'd been so angry that I allowed myself the luxury of reticence until it became a habit.

If only my pride hadn't kept me away from her while waiting for an apology that never came. If only I had treated her as if she were the fickle clouds dispersed by the winds, instead of the eternal mountains. Clouds were mutable, mountains immovable. If only.

I wandered into the living room and sank into the faded sofa.

You are more like your grandmother than I was willing to admit. My mother had seldom spoken of Qiao. For years, I'd yearned for any memory Ma-ma could afford to give. But I'd never begged, for thinking of her seemed to bring my mother pain, and I'd loved her too much to press.

Ma-ma had also seldom mentioned my father, but I never wanted anything to do with him. My mother's anger toward him had become my own, an inheritance I welcomed as a reaction to his abandonment.

My fingers dug into the cushion, squeezing the thinning foam underneath. And the restaurant. It had been boarded up on the first floor, forbidden to me because it was too dangerous to enter. But now I knew: my mother had lied when she told me it was ruined beyond all repair. My dream had been right beneath her all these years.

She wanted me to follow my dreams.

I broke into sobs, my chest heaving, gasping for breath from the pain of loss. My teardrops formed tiny crystals and fell hard against the linoleum. The ache within my rib cage swelled with every gulp of air.

As I cried, my gaze fell upon the wooden lotus-shaped bowl on the coffee table. Bought at a flea market, the bowl's subtle wood grain reminded me of melted chocolate. It served as a replacement for the ceramic bowl I had accidentally broken before leaving. I traced its rounded petals before dipping my fingers inside it, into a small sea of teardrop crystals. Ma-ma had collected my tears since birth: first saving them in silk pouches, then graduating to bowls. I hadn't understood why she'd wanted to keep them. She told me that she always wished to keep a part of me with her, and that there was beauty to be found everywhere—even in sadness. When Ma-ma cried, her tears took days to dry, leaving salt trails in their wake. The fragile salt disintegrated into nothingness.

Where was the piece of her I got to keep with me? Everywhere I looked I saw reminders of her presence, but nothing rivaled the power of her last letter lying discarded on the kitchen floor. I rushed to pick it up, pressing it tight against my broken heart. There was nothing I could do to bring her back.

When I finally stopped crying, I gathered the tiny crystals into my hands, pouring them into the bowl on the coffee table to join the others. A stray sunbeam struck the center, illuminating the ceiling with dancing prisms. I marveled at the display. Ma-ma always found the beauty in unlikely objects.

A soft meow interrupted my thoughts. A powder-puff-shaped creature emerged from the hallway. A pink rhinestone collar sparkled around her neck, complementing her glacial blue eyes. Meimei? I had almost forgotten about Ma-ma's kitten.

She approached me without hesitation and rubbed herself against my calves, weaving in and out of my legs until I bent down to scoop her into my arms. Her snowy fur was softer than I imagined. I carried her to the high-backed chair. Sitting down, I lifted her to my face so our eyes could meet. She batted my nose in defiance.

"Hello, Meimei. You and I loved her the most, and now we have to start grieving her." Sorrow swelled in my throat, cutting off my words. I held the cat against my chest and sighed. Purrs emanated from her tiny body, waves of vibrations that washed across my skin like the most comforting of massages. I held her closer and smiled when I noticed she had dozed off.

"Oh, little one. You have me now."

Perhaps a part of my mother remained after all.

Chapter Four

My mother had given me her blessing, which meant I'd left in search of a dream that was right here at home the whole time. The restaurant. I needed to investigate. The cat batted my ankles as if she concurred with my sense of adventure. I bent down to pick her up and take her with me.

The door to the restaurant was at the base of the stairs leading up to the apartment. I pushed the door open and fumbled for the switch. Light flooded the narrow galley, which was flanked by cupboards and counter space on one side and the stove, oven, and fridge on the other. Just as my mother had said, it looked to be in perfect working order, with enough room for one person—the cook. It was in many ways comparable to the cha chaan teng—tiny counter service restaurants— I'd worked at in Hong Kong.

This was where Laolao had cooked for her neighbors all those years ago. She'd spent most of her life walking up and down this galley kitchen. She was here.

She'd learned how to cook from her own mother and hadn't gone to a fancy culinary school. If she could do it, perhaps I could too.

This was what I'd always wanted. This could be mine.

The realization settled in between my shoulder blades, in a spot I couldn't reach or ignore. I'd thought that as long as I kept moving, working in kitchens, and traveling, I had a goal. But Laolao had had *true* purpose. She had known she wanted to cook, and she'd achieved great things. Ma-ma had had purpose too. She had embraced motherhood and become the sole parent I had needed and wanted.

I had always wanted to cook. What better way to pursue my dreams than to literally follow in Laolao's footsteps? Could my purpose be right here at home after all? Ma-ma had not only denied me this—she had concealed the restaurant's condition from me all along. But there was no point in being angry at ghosts.

My skin itched from the stale mustiness clinging to the air. A thin veil of dust covered every surface, reflecting ages of neglect; much like the patina on Ma-ma's bronze birds. Dust caked my fingertips when I skimmed them across the counter.

My initial excitement was soon replaced by doubts. Most new restaurants struggled to survive their first year. Even with the humble beginnings I envisioned, reopening the restaurant would still cost money I didn't have. I strolled toward the front of the restaurant, flipping the switches, turning on the pendant lamps. The lights continued to work after all these years, proving there was definitely more than a flicker of life left in this place. The dining area, annexed in part by the stairs to the apartment above, included four wooden bar stools and two square tables.

The space was bigger than I'd thought it would be: I had expected only counter service. I walked to the picture windows, covered by plywood, shuttered as if prepared for a hurricane. A chalkboard hung on the far wall where swirls of white marred its green surface, remnants from the damp rag used to wipe it clean.

Oh, to have been here to see what this place was like in its glory: to smell the aromas from the kitchen, to hear the roar of the hot oil and the hiss of the steamer against the chatter of the customers, and the sounds of the street in the bells of the cable cars and traffic zipping by.

If my regrets and wishes were fireflies, the brilliance of their dance would turn night into day.

I walked to the main door and removed the coverings from the glass.

The cat's meow drew my attention to the counter. She was batting a heavily draped object about two feet tall, sitting on the counter near the wall. I walked closer and unwrapped the woven striped runner rug that was tucked around this mysterious item. My fingers searched for the edge of the fabric, tugging to pry it loose without disturbing what lay underneath. The rough textile chafed my skin as I unraveled the rug.

It was a statue, dark with the discoloration that had set in over time. Unlike bronze figures whose tarnish only enhanced their beauty, this taint created a darkening cancer. Craters pitted the surface like the scars of the moon, pockmarks rendered in metal. The sculpture's sadness, and uneven features, were familiar. Guanyin: the goddess of mercy and compassion. A revered goddess shouldn't be treated this way.

It was odd that Ma-ma, governed by her superstitions, had done nothing about this.

Of course, I didn't believe my mother's fears or the many demons that rode on the back of them. Demons weren't real. They were ghost stories meant to frighten children. It was very sad that my mother hadn't been able to understand this.

Still, in her honor, I would make this right. I touched the gouged surface of the statue, my fingers tripping over the pits. Maybe one day I could see her restored.

Meimei meowed, hopping off the counter to stand by the door, where someone was waiting. It was nine in the evening and no one, aside from Celia and Old Wu, knew I had returned. An ash blond woman in her late forties rapped her knuckles against the glass door. She was too well dressed to be a burglar and too professional in her powder blue suit to be a lost tourist.

"Not open," I said in a loud voice, over-enunciating the words in case she failed to hear me.

She held something white against the glass with her palm. A business card.

I walked toward her to get a closer look. Melody Minnows, realtor. The picture on the card matched the woman at the door, right down to the shade of mauve lipstick and diamond hoop earrings. I repeated that we were closed.

She dove into her oversize purse, retrieved a sticky notepad and a pen, jotted something down, and pressed the note against the glass. *I'm sorry about Miranda. How is Meimei doing?*

This woman knew my mother. I let her in.

Chapter Five

Melody smiled and murmured her thanks.

"You knew my mother?"

"Yes, we spoke a few times. She invited me upstairs for a cup of coffee. That's where I met the cat." Melody crouched down and held her hand out to Meimei. The cat hissed before running into the kitchen. "When is the funeral?"

"Soon. I still have to figure out the details."

"Ah, of course." Her perfect smile never faltered. I wondered if she had trained herself in front of a mirror. "It's a lot bigger than I thought in here—the blueprints don't do it justice! The last time we talked, Miranda was contemplating selling. I told her the market was perfect, and I have several buyers already interested. I know I can sell it over asking. Everyone is looking for office space, and this is a hot location. We'll have to move fast before the planning committee changes the bylaws. This is prime commercial space."

Her blue eyes darted to and fro, the movement reminding me of archaeologists wielding flashlights in an undiscovered treasure-filled tomb. I could almost hear the cash register ringing in her head.

Melody didn't care about my mother—she was a vulture. My hands curled into fists.

"There's commercial property on Polk listed at three million. They got rid of the residential space upstairs and converted it to office space. It bumped up the value tremendously. I mean, if you want to convert it to a condo and business, that's also an option, but it needs to be upscale. Perfect for an affluent hipster couple with no kids."

I took a deep breath to steady myself. That was a great deal of money.

"Ms. Minnows, I'm not interested in selling right now."

Melody's smile never wavered. "Perhaps after the funeral, you'll reconsider. It's a lot of money to leave on the table. Why would you want to stay?"

"I may be reopening the restaurant."

"In this neighborhood?" She pressed her hand against the base of her throat. Her French manicured nails gleamed in the fluorescent light. "Bad idea. There's already five great restaurants within walking distance, and that doesn't even factor in the mediocre joints scrambling for attention. Besides, the businesses here are struggling. I've been trying to convince them to sell, but they refuse to. Something about roots, superstition, and family. I guess tradition is more important than bankruptcy. But you could all walk away as millionaires. For you, the money would mean you could open a nicer restaurant, with a bigger operating budget, and a better location than here. You'll have to act soon, though." She ended her pitch with a wink and a tap on the face of her platinum Rolex watch.

There were spikes under her immaculate veneer. We Chinese valued family far more than she realized. Even though she didn't understand this, she'd made good points, and I was torn. This was all so sudden. But I'd been given a gift: Laolao's restaurant. Would selling now be a disservice to my dream and to her?

ROSELLE LIM

"I'll leave you my info." Melody placed her business card in my hand. "Again, I'm really sorry about your mother. She was such a lovely lady."

Melody let herself out. I doubted that this was the last I'd see of her. The woman was a shark drawn to the blood in the water—after all, the neighborhood was bleeding money. And if I reopened the restaurant, I would be as well. The mortgage on the building had been paid off in Ma-ma's lifetime, but we'd been far from wealthy. Ma-ma had lived off some small investments, but there wasn't much, and if she had managed to save anything, it'd be a modest sum at best. I didn't expect a windfall; I only hoped it would at least be enough to cover the funeral expenses.

I locked the door and shut the lights off, gathered Meimei into my arms, headed up the stairs, and made the decision to contact Celia in the morning. Before I could decide about the restaurant, we needed to say goodbye to Ma-ma.

Celia arrived the next morning in a navy silk frock with a black cat pattern. Her gardenia perfume drifted from her skin, and her cheerful smile matched her rosy cheeks. She exuded the effortless kindness reserved for saints and fairies.

"Thank you for coming," I murmured. "Please come in."

I stepped aside and followed her up the stairs. She took her kitten heels off at the landing, donned a pair of guest slippers, and headed to the living room. In the meantime, I offered to make a pot of jasmine tea.

After leaving the kettle on the stove to boil, I headed into the living room. Celia and the kitten were engaged in a standoff. Celia kept her distance at the farthest end of the sofa while Meimei occupied the high-backed chair. The kitten's back was arched, and her little ears folded down as she hissed at Celia, who held her satchel as a shield.

"Meimei, don't do that," I chastised the cat. "That's rude."

"She hates everyone but Miranda," Celia reasoned. "Although, judging from the lack of bandages on your arms, Meimei likes you too."

I scooped the kitten into my arms and sat in the chair. Meimei stopped hissing, but kept one white ear cocked in Celia's direction. I buried my fingers into the cat's fur, scratching and massaging until I was rewarded with purrs. I had never had a cat before, and I could see why Meimei had brought Ma-ma such comfort and joy.

"When I was exploring the restaurant downstairs last night, I had a visitor," I said. "Melody Minnows. She was asking if I wanted to sell."

Celia rolled her eyes. "She's been sniffing around the neighborhood for years. Our businesses are on life support. The blond reaper haunts our doors. I can't really blame her for being enterprising—everyone has to make a living, right?—but these real estate people want to turn our neighborhood into office space and overpriced condos. The entire city has been gentrifying since the tech boom."

This reaffirmed what Ma-ma had written in her letter about the state of the neighborhood and what I had seen for myself since I came back. "Has anyone decided to sell?"

"Of course not!" Celia frowned. "This is our community. We're not going to be pushed out. That is our gate. Our families came here and lived here for generations. If your laolao were alive, she'd be fighting this classist eviction. If only her restaurant were still around, I don't think business would have gotten so bad." She paused and gathered herself. "I'm sorry. I shouldn't be talking about this when there are more important things to deal with. What are your plans after the funeral?"

Celia's eyes were still locked onto the cat in my arms, and her fingers were glued nervously to the handles on her purse. The street was struggling because these businesses were their lives, while I had the luxury of considering Melody's offer. My grandmother would never have sold. She would have put up a fight like they were doing now. I never knew her but I realized now she'd have wanted me to take over.

"I'm considering reopening Laolao's restaurant."

Celia, who must have noticed that the cat had dozed off, relaxed her death grip on her purse. "Is that something you want to do?"

"Yes," I replied. "I want to, but I'm nervous that I'll fail."

Celia offered me a smile of understanding. "When my parents died and left me the gift shop, I was anxious too. But running the store has given me a sense of comfort and security even though it's been fairly tough the last five years. But I won't trouble you with that. The important thing is that you want to try." She waved her hand. "I know if your laolao were alive, she'd be happy that you've chosen this path."

Celia was right. Laolao had been a great cook, and her legacy had been neglected, but now the chance to follow in her footsteps lay beneath my feet. Could I do this? I wished that Ma-ma were here to see me through this. I had so much regret for the years I lost when I should have reached out and spoken to her. I had chosen my ego over my own mother. We Chinese wore our guilt like jade: pressed against our skin, displayed with pride, and always inherited.

"Do you have the right clothes for the funeral and afterward?" Celia asked. "Black for the ceremony and white for the next one hundred days."

"I have something to wear for the funeral, but not much in terms of white to last me the hundred days. If I can, I'll wear white for a year for Ma-ma," I confessed.

Celia rose to her feet and tipped her head toward the door. "Come, let's go."

"Excuse me?"

"Turn the stove off. I'll take a rain check for the tea. I'm taking you shopping."

I blushed, taken aback at her generosity. "I can't—"

"Nonsense."

To reject her offer would cause offense and breach etiquette. "Thank you."

"Good." Celia glanced over my outfit. "Judging by your style, you love thrift shops. I know the best ones in the city."

The thrift stores Celia chose were both on Mission Street. The biggest one had two floors with the clothing racks organized by color. Celia pulled out fashionable pieces in my size like a fisherman reeling in prize bass. Despite my protests, the cart began to overflow.

She pointed to a crocheted tank dress. "This would be perfect on you and it's in excellent shape. No snags."

"This is too much." I moved to return the item to the rack, but she placed it back into the cart.

She clicked the hangers together, searching for another garment to add to the pile. "I insist. Besides, you pay for clothing by the pound here. It's not as much as you think."

"I already feel awful that you had to close your store to take me shopping."

As far as I could recall, the gift shop had never been closed during the day. Tour buses still loaded and unloaded tourists in Chinatown. If any business could survive in the neighborhood, it would be Celia's.

She stepped away from the rack, her smile faltering. "Business isn't as robust as it used to be. I shouldn't complain because the other stores are doing so much worse." Celia noticed me trying to return a sundress to the rack, and her frown deepened. "No, put it back in the cart. I'm doing this for you and for Miranda. She was always kind to me. I don't forget things like that."

Ma-ma had cultivated friendships that I didn't even know about. Things must have changed after I'd left. "If your laolao were alive, she would be happy that you might reopen the restaurant," Celia said. "The talent must run in your genes."

It was true. Ma-ma had been an excellent cook and would have excelled in any restaurant, but she hadn't had the temperament for it. Having cooked at home and worked at many kitchens abroad, I knew I was competent enough. "Yes, I can cook, but I haven't completed any formal training."

A brightness shone in the older woman's eyes and her thick lenses enhanced the effect. "That doesn't matter! I hope you can prepare food like your laolao. Hers was the best I've ever tasted, even better than Old Wu's. When I was a little girl, I would gorge on her fried tofu with chilies. I was much slimmer back then, you know."

"Was the tofu your favorite dish of hers?" I asked.

"Oh no, there's too many to count." Celia's tone softened as if she were waxing nostalgic about a lost, grand romance, rather than a recipe. "Everything she cooked was excellent. I still remember every dish that she made: beef noodle soup, braised short ribs, drunken chicken wings, deep-fried shrimp rolls . . . Your laolao cooked from her heart, and that's why her food was the best in Chinatown."

The shadow of my grandmother loomed over my future as it must have over Ma-ma in the past. She hadn't been able to live under it. In time, would I feel the same way? I still had pressing issues to tackle before I opened: financing, permits, licenses, etc. I'd need to apply for a loan or possibly mortgage the building to fund the restaurant. What if I lost everything my family had worked for?

"I hope you do it. The neighborhood will be thrilled." Celia pushed the packed cart toward the till. Not watching where she was going, she crashed against the concrete pillar. I caught her from falling, but the damage was done: one of her kitten heels buckled and tore off.

"This was a designer heel. I ate at a Michelin three-starred restaurant in Manhattan in these heels," she wailed. She hobbled to the side and picked up a pair of neon pink sandals from a nearby shelf. She put the sandals on and placed her damaged shoes by her purse.

"I'm so sorry, Celia."

"I have rotten luck. It happens." She placed her arm around my shoulders. "You have good luck, though, I can feel it. I have the firm belief that you'll accomplish what you've set out to do. My stomach tells me so. There is no one better to cook in your grandmother's kitchen than you."

I feared her faith in me was misplaced, but I welcomed it anyway.

"But the future can wait a bit longer." Celia blushed, continuing toward the cashiers. "We have the funeral to plan and these ugly pink shoes to pay for."

Yes, it was time for the formal farewell.

For the next three days, Celia and I planned the funeral. At her insistence, we invited the neighbors. Mrs. Chiu also offered to help. Because of Mrs. Chiu's reputation for honesty, Ma-ma had paid her to run her most important errands. Mrs. Chiu always smelled of musky perfume with an underlying bite of pickled scallions, a favorite topping for her morning bowl of congee. She still wielded the same heavy, cherry-colored pleather purse that I remembered: both as a weapon and as a portable storage locker. As a child, I thought of her as a busy-body gossip who had only come by because she was paid to. Obligation could never equate to friendship no matter the disguise, but I deferred to Celia.

It was a larger affair than I had expected. Everyone in the neighborhood showed up: Mr. and Mrs. Chiu, the twin Shen brothers, Celia, Miss Yu, and even Old Wu. Someone must have told him about the funeral. The incident at his restaurant emphasized our strained relationship.

"Mr. Wu, I wasn't expecting you," I said.

"I have my reasons for coming." His lips formed a thin, harsh line. "Your mother may have died alone, but she should not be interred alone."

I stemmed my rising anger. "She had me. I loved her more than anyone else in this world."

He made a hoarse sound with his throat and stepped aside.

I turned my attention to the rest of the neighbors. With each embrace, they welcomed me back and shared in my sorrow. This was more interaction than I was comfortable with. Cultivating my habit of avoidance was easier from a distance.

While I was dressed in black, everyone else wore white, the customary funerary color for non-family-members. We lit the joss sticks and sent our prayers. Mrs. Chiu arranged for a pair of Buddhist monks to conduct the funerary rites so that Ma-ma's spirit would be ushered into the afterlife. When the ceremony ended, only Celia and I stayed. All that remained was a lingering emptiness inside me.

At the crematorium, I took my place at the side of the coffin as the honored daughter and sole blood relative. The flames devoured the casket and body. When the ashes cooled, they were spilled onto a tray.

Celia watched while I used chopsticks to pick out the bones for her urn, which would be interred at the local Chinese mausoleum.

Celia's patient guidance lessened my mounting grief, yet I was still like a leaf in a river, moving chaotically through the unfamiliar ceremonies and rituals while trying to understand and absorb all the meaning behind each one.

When it came time to prepare the ancestral altar, I regained my balance. My task was to find pictures of my family. I searched the apartment, but couldn't find any of my grandmother. If my mother had still been alive, I could have asked her. If only.

Beside a vase full of pink roses and peonies I placed a framed picture of Ma-ma in her early forties, a snapshot taken with my 35 mm camera ten years ago. A chin-length bob framed her pale oval face, and a tentative smile teased the corners of her lips. I'd captured the moment right before she smiled. She had been so beautiful.

In the kitchen I made crispy scallion pancakes, fried golden, as an offering to Ma-ma's spirit. They had been her favorite. We spent so many wonderful afternoons kneading dough dotted with verdant rings of scallions. Now, the kitchen came to life with the sting of my palms slapping the dough into pancakes, the roar of the oil from the submerged golden disks, and the delicious aroma of fried flour and scallions. I split one in half to sample, the delicate layers revealing themselves as I dipped the pieces into a sauce made from soy, vinegar, and smashed garlic. Perfect. I stacked three on a plate and offered them to Ma-ma's spirit along with another prayer. We Chinese believed that the dead still ate and drank in the afterlife. This concept brought me comfort knowing that I could still feed my mother's spirit her favorite treats.

I was to pray once every seven days for the next seven weeks. I had also decided to wear white for the next year, more out of love than filial piety. There was a beauty in the rituals, a comfort to be found in the thousands of years of tradition that endured.

With the shrine complete, a genuine smile graced my lips.

Now the decision about opening the restaurant stood before me, unobstructed, like a stack of overdue bills. I needed to take a walk around the block and reorient myself. Had things really gotten as bad as Celia said? This was where I would set up shop. I had to make sure I knew what I was getting into before tethering my dreams to a sinking ship.

I bade the kitten farewell before I went outside for an afternoon stroll.

A thick layer of dust settled on the storefronts of the neighborhood, obscuring the architectural details from the twenties. In a city of grays, Chinatown once stood as a landmark of color and life: beautiful vibrant signs and extravagant chinoiserie. While as a whole this still rang true, my corner of it had become more diminished, as if the buildings on the block were now forgotten relics languishing in someone's attic. Drab, gray, and old. The weariness showed on the crumbling brick and smudged storefront glass windows. With the Dragon's Gate at the base, shops lined a hill with a narrow road between them. The parallel parking spots on one side of the street were empty. As a child, the decline was evident. Now all these years later it was even worse.

The other streets were packed with tourists strolling on the pristine sidewalks while ours remained empty. Books, teas, gifts, and traditional medicines should have drawn them to our threshold. In other parts of Chinatown, the bright signage in both English and Chinese contained a liveliness that mimicked a bouquet of lollipops. Not here. I lifted my eyes toward the store signs. The letters now appeared rubbed out by time or neglect. Everything about the neighborhood was leeched of life like a plant deprived of sunlight or a faded black-and-white photograph. Any stranger unfortunate enough to wander here would hurry through lest they, too, become infected by the malaise.

A glimmer of color attracted my eye. Melody Minnows's beautiful face greeted me from a large real estate sign, hanging over the vacant space that had been a takeout window. She was stunning in her bright pink plumage. How could this sign be the only thing on the street that still retained vibrancy?

Intricate streetlights, imitating golden dragons, still marked the way, the same beacons I had followed in the past. I remembered that sometimes a handful of tourists, cameras flashing, would make their way to the Dengs' gift shop. They would linger for a moment, murmur a few pleasantries, before returning to the empty tour bus, usually without purchasing anything. But these were ghosts of the past. Even that dwindling stream of visitors was now a dry lake bed.

Much had changed in the seven years I'd been away.

As I continued down the block, the familiar establishments drew my eye: Older Shen's bookstore, Younger Shen's herbal shop, Miss Yu's tea shop, Celia's gift shop, the Chius' convenience store, and finally, Old Wu's restaurant at the end of the road. The street was empty. The neighborhood now seemed to act as a straight thoroughfare to another destination: people merely stopped by the paifang for pictures before moving on to newer, more exciting attractions deeper within Chinatown.

This was where I was supposed to open a restaurant? The location was far from ideal. And money was definitely an issue. I had spoken to the lawyer and Mrs. Chiu about Ma-ma's finances. After the funeral expenses, the modest amount Ma-ma had left me was enough to cover upcoming permit fees, but not an update of the space nor an upgrade of the appliances.

Could I do this?

I tried giving myself a pep talk. I was twenty-eight years old, far older than Laolao had been when she arrived here all those years ago. If she could do it then, I should be able to now. The same blood pumped through my veins. But I still struggled with doubts.

The sonorous tones of the erhu, the Chinese violin, greeted me as I approached the end of the street. I closed my eyes, drawn to the song. Even the twittering birds overhead stopped. The bow across the two strings coaxed out raw emotion, a bittersweet melancholy spun from the lower register of notes.

The traditional Chinese two-stringed instrument was unusual to the Western eye. It had a long, dark spine with two spikes near the top and a round barrel at the end. One hand manipulated the bow while the other vibrated along the spine, moving up and down along the strings.

As the last note vanished into the summer air, I was released from its spell. Reaching into my purse, I showed my gratitude in the form of paper bills I tossed into the musician's empty moon cake tin.

"I never realized how much I missed your playing," I murmured. "Thank you for the song, Mr. Kuk Wah."

"You're back in town?" the older man asked.

I nodded.

Mr. Kuk Wah tugged his flat cap over his forehead and set his erhu against the brick wall. The lines around his eyes, like the roots of a banyan tree, had deepened over the years. A dark ink dragon snaked up his right forearm against a background of blooming chrysanthemums. Decades ago, after a particularly thick fog, he had appeared on this street corner to play his erhu, and ever since, like the fog, he'd come and gone as he pleased.

"Why have you returned, Xiao Niao?"

Xiao Niao was from a popular Chinese children's song and meant "tiny bird." Ma-ma and I had sung it often. I treasured Mr. Kuk Wah's term of endearment. He had played the song for me once, soon after we met. I'd sung along, reinforcing the start of our friendship.

"Ma-ma died."

He removed his hat and pressed it against his chest. Gray infiltrated his short, dark hair; he had to be in his late fifties now. "I'm sorry to hear about your mother's passing."

"Thank you. I miss her with every breath." I was surprised at how easily I could talk about my grief with him.

"Then allow me to play a happy tribute to her life." He lifted the erhu onto his lap.

The melody unfurled, dancing across the higher registers only to return to the lower notes like a flock of starlings sweeping across the twilight sky. Long interchanging notes were punctuated by staccato plucking of the strings. My heart swelled; Ma-ma would have adored this piece, a playful tune.

At the end of the song, I dived again into my purse, but the musician shook his head.

"This is a gift," he said.

A worthy tribute. My mother had loved classical music and operas. Perhaps if she had ever ventured outside, she could have met Mr. Kuk Wah and fallen in love with his erhu. In our home, listening to music wasn't a luxury so much as it was a part of life, like hanging laundry on a clothesline. Bach, Verdi, and Puccini made more of an impact on my consciousness than any modern musician ever had.

"Thank you," I said.

Mr. Kuk Wah rubbed his chin, bristling his shadow of a beard. "I hope you'll be staying even after you've settled your mother's affairs."

"Yes, I'm thinking of reopening Laolao's restaurant."

"That's very honorable of you to follow in your grandmother's footsteps."

I lowered my eyes. "I'm not sure if I can do it because there are so many obstacles to opening one. I already tried culinary school and failed spectacularly." A thread of frustration in my voice escaped without my consent. The walk around the block had reminded me how hard running my own business would be. "I shouldn't complain. I just inherited a restaurant. Everything's old but it should still be functional." Though of course I couldn't be certain because I hadn't checked yet.

"Yes, it will be difficult, but I like to think that you'll succeed." He paused, then nodded. "If this is what you want to do, then do it. It sounds like cooking feeds something in your soul like music does for me. Following your dream leads to happiness, Xiao Niao."

I clung to this scrap of hope and mulled over Mr. Kuk Wah's advice as I made my way back home.

I walked to the kitchen table and sat down. Meimei jumped on my mother's vacant seat and hopped onto the table to attack the stack of mail, batting it with her furry paws until it fell into a flat pile. While Meimei alternated her paws over the envelopes in an adorable cat version of Twister, a lilac envelope caught my eye. It bore no stamp, but my name was written in beautiful cursive on the front.

I pulled the envelope toward me. It bore the perfume of peonies and inside was a note: *Dear one, I have something for you that your mother entrusted to my care. Please come and see me at midnight. Use the alley beside the tea shop. I'll be waiting.* The note was signed by Miss Evelyn Yu.

The date given was today.

What had Ma-ma entrusted with her?

Chapter Six

My mother once told me midnight was a magical hour when the gateway to possibilities was opened. Never had I wanted to believe this more than tonight.

Miss Yu's instructions were to bypass the tea shop for the alley. I peered in the window as I walked by. Her store was small but cozy. Pastel vases presented fresh pink peonies on the windowsills while Teresa Teng sang through the speakers. My lifelong love affair with tea had begun here at a very young age. I'd had my formal introduction to rooibos, matcha, chai, maté, and pu'erh, all seducing me with their floral, fruity, earthy scents.

Lovely Miss Yu curated teas like she was a librarian scouring the world for the best books. Her diligence had kept her local customer base happy and also created a loyal following outside of the state, which must still be sustaining her. Perhaps she sold things online to offset the decline in foot traffic.

As I started down the narrow passage, a strange light pulsed at the end of it. All my life I had strolled past this alley without sparing it a thought, for it was too narrow for comfort. My shoulders brushed against the rough brick of the walls. As I walked, I became aware of the strong odor of peonies and jasmine. I inhaled deeply to draw in the lovely bouquet. The scent was from the fresh flowers of a lush garden.

The path opened into a courtyard, a tangle of peonies and jasmine framing the entrance, blooming in spectacular fashion. Silky petals brushed against my skin. The tension building in my neck and shoulders melted away as I entered a fairyland.

The rustle of the night breeze joined the familiar voice of Teresa Teng echoing from invisible speakers. Beneath my feet, a path of moss-covered stones led to a circular platform surrounded by a large, shallow pond. The night garden was bursting with a palette of muted greens, starlit ivories, and sparkling golds: the verdant lichen and waxy lily pads in the pond, the snowy white peonies and jasmine flowers, and the metallic tones of the fireflies suspended in the air, the square-holed coins lining the floor of the pond, and the special golden three-legged creatures resting on the floating fronds.

I knew these creatures from my childhood. The feng shui symbol of prosperity, Jin Chan was transformed into a golden toad for stealing the peaches of immortality. Jin Chan's three legs represented heaven, earth, and humanity. Statues of him graced every Chinese home I had ever been in, for fortune was a visitor always in demand. Ma-ma had placed one near the stairs leading to the front door.

The pond before me held eight fabled toads, each biting on a coin. If not for the subtle rise and fall of their vocal sacs, I would have thought them statues.

In the center of it all was Miss Yu. A vision in cream and soft gray cashmere, she sat at a round red lacquered table. Silver streaks like strands of starlight coursed through her dark hair. Though she was in her late forties, she could pass for late thirties or younger. The Yu family was fabled to own the elixir of youth in the form of a mythical tea blend gleaned from the Kitchen God himself. She had pinned a buttercream cashmere shawl across her shoulders with a crystal peony brooch. Underneath, she wore a dove gray tank dress with a subtle floral print. Pink jade bangles circled her wrists, tinkling when she moved.

Miss Yu smiled. "Welcome, dear one. Come, sit." She gestured to the empty seat across from her.

"I didn't know about all this." I sat down, marveling at the enchanting atmosphere around me. "It's so beautiful. What is this place?"

"It's my 'other' shop. Miranda was here once. She was my first client after I took over the duties from my mother."

Ma-ma must have visited when she was young and her agoraphobia wasn't yet an issue. It was a version of my mother I didn't know. What were her dreams then? How had she seen her future? The picture of Ma-ma communing with a younger Miss Yu made me smile.

"What did she want?" I asked.

Miss Yu held a finger to her lips. "Confidentiality is one of the cardinal rules here. You see, this is a place of divination. Clients ask a question about their future or for help in making important decisions."

I patted my empty pockets for money and was about to curse when I heard Miss Yu's giggle. She reached across the table to pat my hand.

"No, it's a gift. I don't charge for my services," she said. "And besides, this isn't why you're here."

"Yes." I remembered. "You mentioned you had something of my mother's?"

"A very important package, but we'll get to that in a minute." Miss Yu poured me a cup of tea. Judging by its fruity floral fragrance, it was tieguanyin, an apt choice. I took a sip.

Miss Yu looked at me intently. "If you could ask your grandmother any question, what would it be?"

Laolao. How could I choose a single question when I had been robbed of a lifetime with her? To distill a sea of wishes into a single drop was impossible. I wanted to know her, spend time with her, cook with her. I knew so little about her, and yet she was the bravest woman I'd never met. "If I could ask anything, it would be: How did you do it? Find the strength to leave your family, immigrate to a new country, and run a successful business out of nothing?"

Miss Yu nodded. "This is a good question to ask. Qiao was a very strong woman—as was Miranda. It's in your blood."

"Is it?" I asked. "I want to reopen Laolao's restaurant. I want to make this work, but all I see are hurdles. I don't even know if I can get the amount of money needed to start a business and complete all the legal paperwork. I don't have entrepreneurial experience. On top of that, most restaurants don't even survive their first year in business. Can I do this?" I blushed at my outpouring. I blamed grief for my recent, sudden confession.

Miss Yu reached across the table to steady my trembling hands. "Don't despair. I may have something that will help you." She reached under the table, produced a large, flat red box, and slid it toward me. "Your mother gave me this years ago for safekeeping."

I lifted the lid. A red silken scarf embroidered with golden flying sparrows lay inside. The avian pattern brought a smile to my lips. I had never seen Ma-ma wear this. It would have been perfect on her.

As I tugged the fabric loose, a book tumbled out from its embrace with a thud. Thick spined and leather bound, it was heavy in my hands. The rich chestnut cover bore no marks, no title or publisher. Upon further examination, it appeared to be handmade with great care. I opened the book and gasped. Written with an elegant brushstroke in Chinese characters was the name of my grandmother, Tan Qiao.

"Laolao," I whispered, tracing the characters with my fingertips.

I turned the cover page and discovered a recipe for noodle broth. This was familiar. Ma-ma had often cooked it when rain painted the windows or when the city covered itself in a thick duvet of fog. The rest of the pages contained recipes of every conceivable dish and ingredient. Judging by the book's thickness, there were hundreds of them.

I resisted the urge to embrace the book against my chest as though it were a child. "Can you tell me more about the restaurant?" I asked. "What was it like? What did Laolao cook?"

"The best food in Chinatown, but don't tell Old Wu." Miss Yu winked. "Your grandmother's dishes sang across the tongue. They tasted delicious, but it was more than that. It was the way her food made you feel."

This stirred my appetite to hear more. My grandmother would come alive to me through the memories of others. I smiled and gestured for Miss Yu to continue.

"Everyone ate there. It wasn't a big place, but it served the most wonderful food. She changed the menu daily, cooking whatever she found at the market that morning. Her dishes always used ordinary ingredients, but their taste was far from humble. She used her food like a delicious spider web—as a means to connect strangers. If anyone ever needed anything, she would always try to help them."

Miss Yu paused to sip her tea. "When your laolao died, we mourned her and the business we knew would die along with her, but we didn't know the neighborhood would suffer as well."

"I wish I'd had the chance to meet her," I murmured.

"You would have loved her, and she, you." Miss Yu reached across the table and patted my hand. "Your mother turned away from the family business after your laolao died. The restaurant had been very successful, but after Qiao's death, Miranda closed it down. I'm not sure if Miranda ever told you, but your grandmother was struck by a car outside of her restaurant. I think this made Miranda's agoraphobia worse. She had always been shy by nature, but the accident followed by your father's departure made her unable to leave the apartment. Miranda just didn't have the temperament to run the restaurant." She paused and her smile returned. "Your mother may have neglected the family business, but she did a wonderful job raising you on her own. I'm happy to hear that you want to reopen the restaurant and follow your laolao's path."

"This is what I've wanted ever since I was little. I wish Ma-ma were here so she could see me do it."

Miss Yu peered at me sympathetically.

Familial obligation and filial piety were powerful forces in my culture. Ma-ma had never cared for such things and had raised me to pick and choose which traditions to follow, but this wasn't something I wanted to ignore. I had my mother's blessing; right now, I should feel more confident about my choice.

"I know Laolao was successful," I said. "But will I be? I don't want to fail the memory of my grandmother. Yes, I can cook, but I'm not a professional; I flunked out of culinary school. Can I make the restaurant a success?"

Miss Yu arched her brow and the corners of her lips tugged upward. "You have asked a good question, dear one. Give me your hands." She placed my palms in hers, squeezing warmth and reassurance into them.

She closed her eyes. A rush of wind teased the leaves and stirred the blooms, releasing both fragrance and petals of varying size into the air; soaring, swirling like ethereal butterflies into the dark sky. Peonies. Jasmine. Tieguanyin. I drew the heady scent into my lungs, imprinting the memory of this moment into my consciousness.

A hush grew, swelling like a cresting wave, quieting the leaves into stillness. "The restaurant will only succeed if you rebuild the connections of what was once lost." Miss Yu spoke as if in a trance. "The businesses on the street are dying and so shall your endeavor, if you fail. Read your grandmother's book. The dishes from Qiao's wok transformed the ordinary and soothed all ailments. You must cook three recipes from the book to help three of your neighbors, as your laolao did in the past. Your success is tied to them, their businesses, and the community. You are one of them. If they fail, you will fail. If you save them, the restaurant will once again be the jewel of Chinatown, and vitality will return to the neighborhood."

A snowfall of flowers ushered in her final words, like falling stars in the night garden against a backdrop of golden fireflies. Stray petals landed on my hair and my cheeks. It tickled. A giggle escaped my throat. Miss Yu smiled and held her hands open, catching the petals in heaps to deposit into a large wooden bowl she placed on the table. I followed suit, gathering all of the fallen blossoms until there were no traces of white left anywhere.

"I will dry this and make it into tea. Stop by the shop and I'll give you a large tin." She moved the bowl to her right. "Besides that, I'm afraid I do not have any other insights to share. I am only the messenger."

Three recipes to help three neighbors. How would I know which dishes to cook—or which neighbors? I didn't know them well enough to even begin to pry into their private lives. If I was being honest, nor did I have the inclination. Where had they been when I needed them? Why should I help them now?

Miss Yu patted my hand. "I'm confident you can fulfill the prophecy and succeed." She traced one of the lines in my palm. "As I said before, the women in your family possess great strength. It's how your grandmother survived after leaving China. Strange new world, new people, new language, with nothing but her ability to cook. Qiao's food brought the community together, and in time, she was able to buy the building for your family."

I closed my eyes. My grandmother had known her path much earlier in life, but she'd had exceptional culinary skills that I was sure overshadowed my own. Miss Yu's smile calmed me. "It's not only the businesses, it's also the people that are suffering. I have the utmost confidence you will help. You have all the tools to succeed with the restaurant."

And the solution lay in Laolao's recipe book. I had to open the restaurant because this was what I was meant to do. I had found my purpose.

In the privacy of the apartment, I finally hugged the thick book to my chest. This was an heirloom—a piece of my history that I never knew existed. Laolao, the grandmother I had longed for as a lonely child, seemed more real to me now than she had ever been in my entire life. Reopening the restaurant could only bring me closer to her.

The book contained the recipes I had to cook for my neighbors. But how would I possibly be able to solve their problems?

The supple leather cover was pliant under my fingertips, the shade of cinnamon rooibos tea with a faint filigree pattern tattooed on the front. I traced it with my fingers. The more I rubbed, the more prominent the design became, transforming into ridges and valleys. The fragrance of dishes sizzled in the air: spring rolls, sweet chili prawns, steamed crabs. My stomach growled again.

The recipe book was coming alive.

Laolao.

I turned the page and read the first recipe.

Baby Oyster Omelets

Potato starch
Water
Egg
Salt
Ground black pepper
Bean sprouts
Green onions
Baby oysters

Mix the potato starch, water, egg, salt, and pepper into one bowl. Stir well until it becomes sticky. Administer the following test: take a spoonful and drip the mixture back into the bowl. The viscosity must be like honey: smooth, but not too sticky or runny.

Add the bean sprouts and chopped green onions. Stir until blended. The color of the mixture should remind you of sunshine and the green grass of summer.

Heat the oil in the wok. Using a small shallow bowl for portions, fill the bowl with the mixture, and add five to seven baby oysters per portion.

Pour it into the heated wok. Fry until the edges turn into golden lace, then flip over, wait for half a minute for the other side to cook, then serve with ketchup, hot sauce, or fish sauce.

Note:

This recipe is for the crestfallen, the unsmiling, and the ones who need sunshine in their souls. If a customer has a difficult day, this will help raise their spirits.

I served this to an unsmiling Shao, a young man who worked at the warehouses. I had never seen a person more devoid of happiness. After he tasted the dish, he confessed to me how his wife and children were still in China and he wanted to bring them over. I encouraged him to keep his hope alive for his family. He returned once a week to eat the omelets and to chat. Sixteen years later, his family sat at my counter and ate the very same meal.

I knew this recipe. Ma-ma prepared it every spring. She and I both loved oysters. The aroma of the dish rose from the pages as if the fluffy omelets were cooking nearby. I flipped through the book, unleashing scents of fragrant meals. As I scanned the lower half of each page, I realized that each recipe was like a prescription of sorts to aid people in need.

Miss Yu had mentioned that Laolao was a healer. This must be what Miss Yu was talking about. No wonder Laolao was able to help so many people in her time. All I needed was to figure out what was wrong, and these recipes would act as the remedies so I could help out the neighbors.

I dove into the book, reading, learning, and at times, laughing over Laolao's anecdotes. My grandmother had been fearless—a pioneer who'd wanted the best for others and herself. My admiration for her was tempered by the realization that Ma-ma might have found it challenging to live with such a formidable force. Despite her delicate temperament, Ma-ma had been strong and stubborn to a fault. A dragon pitted against a stone lotus.

Would I have been caught in between them if I'd grown up with both of them in my life?

In the middle of the book, there were three missing pages, evident by the ragged edges standing out as scars. What had happened here? My fingernails picked at the torn paper. The damage seemed to have been done in an act of anger, ripped out forcefully rather than carefully removed. Though the book brimmed full of recipes, I couldn't help but mourn the missing three. Why had Laolao torn out recipes from her own book?

I continued to read, hoping to find the loose pages tucked within, but in the end, there was no sign of the missing pages. I closed the book to the relief of my protesting stomach. I had eaten dinner before seeing Miss Yu, but that now seemed like a very long time ago.

Fulfilling the prophecy would not only help the neighborhood, but also perhaps help me discover more about my grandmother. I supposed that even if they hadn't been there for me, it wasn't right that the residents and their families should suffer. This street had been my home: its current state broke my heart. I had lived so long with just my mother that it was easy to forget that the family tree extended beyond us. Connections. Laolao fostered them; maybe it was what I should be working to achieve by helping the neighbors out.

In my time away, I found myself connecting to my culture wherever I traveled, but never missing the community I'd left back home. Perhaps living with my mother in isolation for so long had prevented me from forming any bonds. Ma-ma had taught me to be independent almost to a fault. But if I were to open the restaurant, I would be a part of the neighborhood now, be one of them. Maybe it was time to reconsider how I felt about this.

I pulled the recipe book close, leafing through its pages once more. I stopped when my fingers caught an edge on the end cover. The tome was hand bound with the leather stretched taut over the spine. The adhesive on the back had worn away, revealing an old photograph tucked inside. This must be why I missed it the first time I went through the book.

I had never seen this picture before. The woman in it stared back at me. Her face was masculine with a strong jaw and high cheekbones, but softened by the doe eyes that Ma-ma and I shared. A tiny mole hovered near her left eyebrow. Her direct gaze displayed an unmistakable surety of self. She was beautiful. Laolao. A sob escaped my lips. This was my grandmother, Qiao. I pressed my hand against my chest.

I should place her photo at the family shrine, but she belonged here in these pages. This was her book, her recipes, her life. With the recipe book open and her photograph in full view, I smiled at her. I could finally pair a face with her name. I wished I'd had the chance to know her.

It was late. I tucked Laolao's photograph back into her recipe book. Meimei crawled onto my lap. When I went to sleep that night, I dreamt of cooking alongside Laolao with Ma-ma hovering by the kitchen table to watch.

The next morning, I was ready to play intrepid detective. The cat followed me around the apartment like a puppy as I prepared to take a stroll outside. Last night, she had curled up around my head when I fell asleep. The apartment felt less empty due to my newfound feline companionship. I didn't know that four pounds of fluff could make such a difference. I kissed her goodbye and stepped outside.

When I had left, to say that I didn't like the neighbors would be a polite understatement. I hated them for not offering to help me and Ma-ma for so many years. I hated them for not visiting her. I hated them for treating her like a pariah because of her condition. But spending time with Celia had softened my stance a bit. Maybe it was time to move on.

Now I just had to figure out whose problems I needed to solve.

I headed for Older Shen's bookstore.

Chapter Seven

Following Chinese tradition, I would pay court to the eldest member of the neighborhood first.

Older Shen was five years older than Ma-ma. Previously, our contact had been limited to his brief, polite inquiries about my mother when I'd run in and out of his shop on errands. Now, like the mummified mammoth at the natural history museum, he seemed ancient and trapped in his own glass case of a store.

Keeping these shops in the family was tradition. The Chiu, Shen, Wu, Deng, and Yu families had lived on this street for more than a century. After the great earthquake of 1906 decimated the neighborhood, the families had rebuilt their businesses as the city did the same. They had survived the Tong Wars and outlived the diasporas, and now their roots ran underneath Grant Avenue, anchored by the Dragon's Gate, the great paifang.

Immigrants flocked to Chinatown, got their start here, prospered, and moved out after having achieved their American dream. To me, the ones who stayed should be commended for their endurance. They helped foster the influx of newcomers against the foibles of the economy.

As I reached the door, Melody Minnows emerged with a smile on her face. "Oh hi, Natalie! I was wondering if you've changed your mind. I just finished talking to Mr. Shen. We need a facelift, a jolt, to get this area going again. Can you imagine a hot yoga studio here? I have so many buyers interested. It really is the best time to sell."

Before I could reply, her phone beeped and she excused herself as she made her way toward Miss Yu's tea shop. Although I hated her motives, I couldn't fault her tenacity. If only she were working to help the businesses here instead of trying to sell each property to the highest bidder. For now, I would avoid her. I had made my decision to open the restaurant and would do whatever I could to make that happen. I just hoped the rest of the neighbors would not fall prey to her aggressive techniques in the meantime.

I returned my focus to Mr. Shen and my task at hand. "This is going to be awkward," I whispered to myself. Still, I had to persevere. I had to find out what had gone wrong in the neighborhood before I could open the restaurant. Had the neighbors simply given up? I'd assumed that they stayed because they either wanted to help the incoming immigrants or weren't successful enough to move away to the suburbs. Aside from the obvious financial ones, what other problems did they have? They were strangers to me, as I had become a stranger to them. *Listen to their problems and then cook for them,* I said to myself. Laolao's recipes would provide the solutions, but I must determine the neighbors' dilemmas on my own.

A set of bells tinkled as I pushed the glass door open. The blast of the air conditioner set off rows of goose bumps on my skin. The bookstore was three times larger than Laolao's restaurant. Every available wall was covered with bookcases, but most of them were empty. I remembered when magazines, newspapers, journals, and classic novels like *Romance of the Three Kingdoms* crammed every shelf. Now, every periodical was dated from months or years ago. Some of the overhead fluorescent lights were dead, and the remaining ones flickered in an erratic pattern. What had happened here?

Mr. Fai Shen, the older brother, was perched atop a worn bar stool. As I approached, the scent of pistachios and candied ginger overpowered the more subtle smells of paper and dust. Shen's stained fingers pried shells open, pinching the green nutmeat as he pored over his daily newspaper. Scraggly whiskers graced his upper lip, and a brown bubble of a mole sprouted near his left nostril.

He chewed on the pistachios, setting aside the shavings in a pile while pushing the shells into floral patterns. Today's display was chrysanthemums in a basket.

"Mr. Shen?" I asked.

He dropped his pistachio shell and blinked rapidly a few times. Finally, he squinted at me, smiling. "Hello there, young lady. What can I do for you?"

"I wanted to thank you for attending Ma-ma's funeral," I began. "How have you been? How is business?"

Older Shen mustered a weak smile. "I'm doing okay. As for business, you don't have to worry yourself about that. We are managing fine."

Denial to save face. It was a tactic I knew too well. I opened my mouth to protest, but that avenue of argument would be unfruitful or, at worst, cause offense. I decided to take a different course. "I wanted to let you know that I'm staying and working toward reopening the restaurant."

"Oh, that's nice of you to follow your laolao's path." He paused and scratched his temple. "That's a hard endeavor. A restaurant is a difficult business to run, and most don't survive within their first year."

"I have to try. I really want this."

Older Shen's eyes grew wide. "I hope you know what you're doing."

I couldn't answer him with the truth that I was terrified of failing. My failure at culinary school haunted my every step. Three heartbeats of awkward silence followed until I shattered it. "Have you read any new, exciting books lately?"

"People don't want to buy books anymore, or if they do, they don't want to buy them from me. The tourists seem to be passing by instead of lingering. It wasn't always like this. In the old days when your laolao had her restaurant open, the street was so full that we had festivals. I wish . . ." His voice trailed off, leaving me leaning over the counter.

"What do you wish for?"

He shook his head. "I shouldn't burden you with my problems. It's not right."

The Chinese custom of swallowing one's misery was keeping me from what I wanted—a detailed description of what ailed him so I could figure out which recipe to use. If only I could reach across the counter and shake his confession loose.

The phone rang on the counter. Older Shen held up his finger, excusing himself. I ducked into one of the empty book aisles. Picking up an old copy of *Reader's Digest*, I flipped through the pages while I eavesdropped.

"Hello?"

"I told you to sign off on the advertisements. Why haven't you done it yet?" The booming voice across the line left no doubt as to who was calling. It was Older Shen's twin brother, Guang, the owner of the herbal shop across the street. His voice was so loud he may as well have been on speakerphone. The twins were the last in a prosperous family, descended from wealthy merchants of Shanghai.

Older Shen sighed. "I can't afford it, Guang. You know business hasn't been——"

"We will waste this opportunity if you don't sign off," the disembodied voice on the phone thundered back. "The paperwork is due tomorrow."

The fluorescent lights overhead began to fizzle out, one by one. If it weren't for the sunlight streaming through the windows, the store would have been shuttered in darkness. Tiny crackles of electricity emanated from the receiver in Older Shen's hand.

"I can't justify the costs——"

A bright spark of energy leaped from the receiver, forming a glowing chain before wrapping itself like a shackle around Older Shen's forearm. He pulled at his forearm, trying to dislodge the intruding force. The voice on the other end boomed. "If you don't spend money, you're not going to get anyone into your store. Advertising is the way to go."

"I need to put money into some improvements. The store needs updating. It's been years since I've kept up with the bookselling trends and what customers want. I can't sell what people don't want to buy. Independent bookstores must make the buying experience more exciting to survive."

"You're wasting your money. People should know you exist first before you rearrange your inventory."

"And what about what Ms. Minnows offered? Don't you think——"

"Sign the ad contract, you old fool! I'll pick it up later this afternoon. Don't even think about talking to her. We are not selling!" An audible click followed, and the luminous chain vanished just as suddenly as it had appeared. The lights overhead returned to their normal, gently flickering state.

I peeked around the corner. Older Shen stared at the receiver, his knuckles white from his tight grip. His hand shook as his stare bored a hole into space. I had seen this before in myself. This was impotence. It was in the rage I sometimes felt toward my absent father. Older Shen must feel it now, but toward his brother.

Yet as if nothing had happened, he set the phone down and waved me over. I placed the magazine back onto the shelf and returned to the counter.

"Please let me know when the restaurant opens," he said with a lopsided smile. Bits of red hid in the crevices of his yellowed teeth, remnants of the candied ginger he favored. He grabbed a fistful of White Rabbit candies from under the counter and placed them before me.

These Chinese candies had been a staple of my childhood. Encased in edible paper, they were creamy and sugary, and melted in my mouth. The white rabbit design on the wrapper never failed to make me smile. Many rainy days had been brightened up by a visit to Older Shen's bookstore.

How had I forgotten this? I must have buried these memories like a child hiding toys in a sandbox.

Now they came rushing back. I remembered that Shen had snuck *Lao Fu Zi* comics in for me with Ma-ma's magazines. I'd been grateful for the levity they brought in the days Ma-ma suffered from her depressive spells. The slapstick gags and encounters with ghosts provided endless entertainment. I loved them so much that I brought my copies along with me wherever I went.

What other kindnesses had I suppressed memories of? The narrative of the neighbors' apathy was something I had clung to for so long. Now a few traitorous memories were beginning to unravel it. First

Celia, now Shen. Could it be that they were not, and had never been, as uncaring as I had believed?

"I will." I returned his smile and shoved the candies into the pockets of my shorts. "Thank you."

I left the scent of books, papers, and pistachios behind to return to the street. Now I knew Shen's problem. He needed courage: to come out of his shell, stand up to his younger brother, convince himself of his own vision for the business, and fight for his bookstore. There was a Dungeness crab recipe for bravery in Laolao's recipe book. Yes! This must be what Miss Yu was talking about. Maybe I *could* help him. Hope swelled inside me.

One down, two to go. I hoped the other two issues would be as easy to uncover as this one.

Across the way was my next destination: the herbal shop owned by Younger Shen, the one who had just been bellowing at his brother.

I paused before the door to Younger Shen's shop, inhaling from my diaphragm. I sucked in as much oxygen as possible before stepping inside, but the brew of strong odors still assaulted my nostrils. In this store, the shelves were covered with large glass jars containing every known Chinese treatment for ailments ranging from flatulence to erectile dysfunction. Expensive items such as shark fins were kept behind the counters.

Another dormant recollection surfaced as I strolled through the narrow aisles. As a child, I was fascinated by the hairy ginseng and had called them golden fairies because their roots looked like limbs. Younger Shen had once given me a small ginseng root as a gift. I'd brought it home and begged Ma-ma to help me make clothes for my fairy.

Memories kept coming the longer I walked these streets, beginning to tear away at the animosity I long held for these people who I thought had shunned my mother. I supposed it was far easier to be angry at others for the isolation I'd felt than to place the blame on Ma-ma.

"Little one!" Younger Shen called out from the back of the store, waving to me from the counter. His crooked smile matched his bright eyes. He was as wide as his older twin was narrow. The rumor was that he had stolen almost all of his brother's chi in the womb, leaving only specks for his older sibling.

The radio behind him blared his favorite—country music. Randy Travis crooned "On the Other Hand" while Younger Shen tapped his fingers against the counter to the melody. In his pink plaid dress shirt and purple corduroy trousers, he was as visually loud as the odors around him were strong. If Older Shen needed courage, perhaps his brother needed subtlety.

"I'm sorry about what happened to your mother," he bellowed at me over the music.

"Thank you," I said, raising my voice to reply. "I miss her so much."

Our words fizzled beneath the blare of music like fireworks disintegrating in the night sky. Anyone else would lower the volume, but this was Younger Shen. A dull pounding crept into my temples.

"Are you planning on staying?"

"Yes, I am working to reopen the restaurant downstairs."

"The what?"

"The restaurant!"

"I hope you can cook like your grandmother. Come by and let me know when you open."

"How are you doing? How is business?"

"Fine. Everything is fine!" He launched into an impromptu karaoke session. I didn't think it was possible, but he was louder than the speakers. It was surprising he hadn't gone completely deaf from years of this.

I tried to banish the urge to climb the counters behind him so I could shut the stereo off. "Do you have advice on running a business, Mr. Shen?"

"Yes! You need to turn a profit. If you don't turn a profit, you fail," he yelled as his reply.

And water was wet. His answer was perhaps a deflection since his own business didn't seem to be thriving. I tried once more, hoping to gain any kind of opening by using what I had learned from eavesdropping on the brothers' argument. "Any tips on how to invest in advertising?"

"Yes, icing on the cake is a good idea if you're baking. You should also use sprinkles."

"No, advertising!"

"No icing?"

I blew out my lips. "Can we speak outside?"

"I can't leave the store." He shook his head.

"How about—"

Two customers came through the doors, diverting Younger Shen's attention. I nodded, waving goodbye. My ears rang as I escaped the herbal shop to the tune of Reba McEntire's "Sweet Dreams." My trip to the herbal store had been a complete failure, and I didn't have the energy or the hearing capacity to make another attempt.

Sucking a deep breath of fresh air into my lungs, I turned my head toward the Chius' convenience store. The slightly uphill street was empty and gray in the morning light. High-rises from the next block cast a shadow over the mismatched shops of the neighborhood. I had always liked how the unique architectural style of every building reminded me of an eclectic collection of books. The contrast gave it character.

A palpable silence flooded my ears, as if I'd been submerged in water. The failure of the businesses here permeated the air. No wonder no one lingered.

I hurried to my next destination in an effort to shake off the unsettling feeling.

The convenience store was crammed uncomfortably full of merchandise. When I was younger, I'd often imagined I was entering a house of cards, and I'd feared that if the couple added one more thing to any shelf, the entire place would surely collapse in on itself.

Mr. Chiu sat behind the counter, fixated on two screens: the grainy CCTV security monitor, and another television playing a kung fu film starring Donnie Yen.

"Hello, Natalie," Mr. Chiu said, half turning away from his screens as I approached the counter. "How are you doing?"

"I'm good. I wanted to thank you for being there for me at the funeral."

"No problem, no problem," he replied, returning his attention to the kung fu movie.

I cracked a weak smile. This conversation might end up being similar to the one I'd had with Younger Shen. There must be something that would tear the older man's attention from the screens and get him to open up.

"Mr. Chiu?" I asked. "I was wondering, could I—"

The bell at the door jingled. I moved aside to make way for the incoming customer by hiding behind the narrower aisle.

"Wayne!" A sharp voice, one I recognized.

Mr. Chiu tore his eyes from his film and stared up at his wife. "What's wrong, dear?"

"What are these extra charges?" Mrs. Chiu held up a folded sheet of paper. "You know we can't afford it right now."

I blushed. The Chius had always been one of the most solid couples in Chinatown. They had five children, and their business was a fixture in the neighborhood. Mr. Chiu still manned the store while Mrs. Chiu had a second job as an independent consultant for the multilevel marketing item du jour, which in the past had ranged from containers to scent dispensers to beauty and diet regimens. But now their relationship seemed to be faltering, if the anger in Mrs. Chiu's voice was any indication.

The cracks in this neighborhood were also hidden behind closed doors, bolstered by pride and old-world stoicism. They were suffering, but would never ask for help.

I shouldn't be here, but leaving now would out me as an eavesdropper.

"Why would you do this? We can't afford to close the store for a weekend to go mess around in Lake Tahoe. Have you forgotten how old you are? Really, Wayne."

"Bernard offered to watch the store for the weekend."

"Our son has a family of his own. It's selfish of you to ask him to do this," Mrs. Chiu huffed.

"I haven't spent time alone with you in so long. Anita, please. It's only for three days. You've been working so much—"

"I've been working because we need the money. If it weren't for my jobs, we'd have lost the business years ago. I'm doing this because you wanted to stay here." Her shoulders sank and her voice softened. "I appreciate the gesture, but you should have asked me first. If you want to know what I want, then see if you can get a refund. I'll be home late again tonight. Don't wait up, you'll need your rest for your shift tomorrow."

She turned and left.

Mr. Chiu held up his hand as if it could have stopped his wife from leaving. He sighed and lowered his head. My heart ached for him. He loved his wife so much. Their marriage was suffering because the neighborhood was dying.

The Chius were the perfect candidates for the second recipe— they needed a love potion of some sort. As for their financial problems, if the prophecy were true, and the restaurant were to open and succeed, there was a chance the neighborhood could be saved. Prosperity could spread once it had been established. A little hope went a long way to furthering a purpose.

"Natalie, you can come out now," Mr. Chiu called out from his booth. "I'm sorry you had to see that."

I stepped out from the side aisle. He was no longer staring at his screens. Instead, he gazed at the door—miles away, following his wife wherever she had gone. I knew how he felt because I'd pined this way for my mother during our separation. It hardened my resolve to help the Chius as much as I could before it was too late.

"My family ran this store for decades. I didn't want it to stop with me. My children don't want to run it, and I refuse to be the one abandoning my family's legacy. Why can't I have both my wife and the store? It worked so well before. Now, my wife and that agent want me to sell. You know, we were happy . . ." Mr. Chiu averted his eyes.

I gathered my courage and approached the counter. "I have a dish for you and your wife that I'll bring by soon. You were so kind to me during my mother's funeral. It's the least I can do."

He nodded and waved goodbye.

I had three people to cook for and two problems to solve. I could no longer deny that I genuinely wanted to assist them. These weren't strangers I could dismiss. I realized this must have been how Laolao felt about her neighbors and her community. I still had to find the third person, but it wouldn't hold me back from cooking for the people I had already found.

Tomorrow morning, I would cook in Laolao's kitchen and prepare her dishes. Time to shake the cobwebs off and test my culinary skills.

Chapter Eight

Nothing made me happier than the act of cooking. My happiest memories were of spending time in the kitchen with Ma-ma as we prepared our meals. The best cooks doubled as magicians, uplifting moods and conjuring memories through the medium of food.

Cooking had always been a source of personal joy, but now it had an added purpose: it would be the key to achieving my dream of running a restaurant of my own. Ma-ma had loved me with the same fierceness that Laolao had possessed for the restaurant. I now understood she had feared I would be caged by my dreams and that she thought she was protecting me. If given a choice, I'd want both a restaurant *and* a family to call my own. The closest I had come to having my own family was a failed engagement to a wonderful man in Manila, which fell apart because of my inability to commit.

This was my paradox in love: to want something so badly, but to also be afraid of being tied down by it. I couldn't allow this to cross over and hinder me in my mission to open the restaurant.

This restaurant must succeed.

But before I could cook Laolao's recipes for the neighbors, I needed to practice. I had seen a dumpling recipe in the book that I wanted to try.

I moved the Victrola downstairs to keep me company, and Bizet's *Carmen* echoed through the restaurant. The ruined statue remained on the counter, but now it was flanked with pots of orchids borrowed from the windowsill upstairs. A small wooden bowl was set before it as an offering, filled with various hard candies.

Earlier, I had removed the last of the plywood from the windows, the planks crackling against the steel of the crowbar as I revealed what had been lost in the last thirty years. The now-clean picture windows showcased the dying grayness of the neighborhood. I glanced around and realized the monochromatic palette had spread to the interior of the restaurant. The inside windowsill took on the gray tinge. I brushed my fingertips across the surface and they came away with silvery pigment, but without the sheen; as if I had painted it yesterday.

The gleaming windows served as a reminder of my final goal: to see the sparkle return to the place, inside and out. As the "Habanera," my favorite piece in the opera, wound down, I found my attention wandering to the few people hurrying by. Had it been so long ago that tourists lingered? What had happened to this place to cause the decline?

According to Ma-ma's lawyer, whom I had spoken with on the phone earlier that morning, everything was in place if I wanted to operate the restaurant. He pointed me to resources for the permits and licenses I needed, and he also disclosed an extra stipend that Ma-ma had set aside in the will. The extra cash would help pad the emergency fund and pay for a new fridge, as I had discovered the current one was shot.

I'd ordered a cheap replacement early this morning from an online clearance sale and scheduled for it to be delivered in the afternoon. I unlocked the door and stepped outside to take a look at the restaurant from a stranger's perspective. I sighed. The sign above was faded beyond recognition, but for now, it would have to do. I headed back inside.

The finishing touch this place needed was the smell of good food. It was time to cook.

Fried Dumplings

Dough:

- Flour
- Salt
- Sugar
- Water

Filling:

- Water chestnuts
- Bamboo shoots
- Ginger
- Garlic
- Green onions
- Minced pork
- Brown eggs

For the dough, combine the flour, salt, and a pinch of sugar in a large bowl with the water. Knead, cover the bowl, and let the dough rest for thirty minutes.

Mince the water chestnuts, bamboo shoots, ginger, garlic, and green onions before incorporating them into the minced pork. Add the eggs. Set aside.

When the dough is ready, roll it out and cut palm-size circles for the dumplings. Spoon in the filling and fold the edges as you would when making a paper fan. The crispness of the edges will be amazing when fried.

Deep-fry until golden.

Yields 50 dumplings.

Note:

These dumplings should inspire happiness, for this is a recipe I learned from my mother. Her dumplings always brought me such joy. I saw them as bundles of sunshine.

Serve this to those who need a smile. This dish is great for any occasion as it is popular with the young and the old.

I placed a bouquet of green onions, ginger, and garlic on the counter beside bunches of water chestnuts and bamboo shoots. A packet of butcher-paper-wrapped minced pork huddled with a carton of large brown eggs.

With the Victrola now playing *Aida*, I combined the dry ingredients, kneading them together. The mixture warmed in my hands as I worked it, and I added more flour to achieve the right consistency.

When the dough was ready, I laid it in a covered aluminum bowl to rest. I washed my hands before tackling the filling, mincing golden ginger and green onions with Laolao's still-sharp knife. My fingertips unfolded papery shells of garlic, releasing the aromatic cloves within. I used Laolao's knife again to transform them into tiny cubes before depositing them in with the ginger and onions. I had chosen bamboo shoots and water chestnuts for their crispy texture, and I diced them and tossed them into the growing pile as well.

Finally, I unwrapped the ground pork and threw it into the bowl, incorporating all of the diced ingredients along with a dash of pepper, which was my addition. Opening the carton, I reached for two brown eggs, cracking them against the rim of the bowl. The sunny yolks dripped down followed by the clear bridal train of the whites. I stirred everything with a large wooden spoon, mixing, pulling, and blending the filling into a marbled masterpiece.

I rolled the dough out onto the flour-dusted counter, where I used a circular template for the dumplings, adding a spoonful of filling in the middle, and closing each one with accordion folds.

Making dumplings had been a weekly Sunday affair with Ma-ma. We'd wash down the kitchen table and I'd be tasked with the choice of which record to play. Sometimes I'd gone by the artwork on the covers or I'd ask my mother about a song and which opera it came from by humming it. Dumplings could not come into existence without the aid of arias and orchestras.

Now the finished dumplings populated the large metal tray. I poured refined peanut oil into the wok, turning up the heat on the gas stove. The blue flames licked the darkened bottom of the wok.

While waiting for the temperature to rise, I conducted an imaginary orchestra with long wooden chopsticks. I dipped one into the oil and watched for the signs; telltale bubbles around the submerged shaft meant the temperature was perfect.

The first sacrificial dumpling was tossed into the wok. The oil danced, enveloping the pale dumpling in a cloak of bubbles. Soon, it floated upward, a golden buoy in an amber sea, before I whisked it away with my chopsticks.

I set the dumpling on layers of paper towels to soak up the excess oil. I waited as long as I possibly could for it to cool before giving in to temptation, biting into the golden, crisp dumpling and the steaming filling inside. The crunch from the wrapper created a satisfying explosion in my eardrums. It was perfect.

Now assured of their quality, I tumbled half a dozen dumplings into the oil. The batch yielded fifty, just as the recipe indicated. I had more than enough left over for an offering for Ma-ma and some to share with Celia too.

I picked up Laolao's photograph and placed it on top of the closed recipe book. "I'm cooking in your kitchen with your recipe," I said to her. "I wish I could watch you cook. You must have been a wizard in the kitchen. I could have learned so much from you, about cooking, business, life. If only you were still here."

I returned her picture to its place inside the recipe book before arranging half of the dumplings on a covered catering platter I'd found on the high shelves in the kitchen. I placed the rest of them on three plates on a round tray to carry upstairs to the apartment. After depositing two plates into the fridge, I headed for the family shrine with the last one. The final plate with eight dumplings was set before Ma-ma's photograph. I bowed and sent silent prayers to my mother's spirit. Then I spoke and hoped that somewhere my mother could hear me. It was something like a prayer.

"I miss you and think about you all the time. I've decided to open the restaurant. I am so happy that you gave me your blessing after all, Ma-ma. It's what I've wanted for a very long time. Miss Yu said that in order for the restaurant to be successful, I have to cook for three people. I'm helping the Chius and Older Shen. As for the last person, I don't know yet.

"I didn't know how bad things have gotten. The neighbors really are in trouble. I will help them, Ma-ma, not only because it's what the prophecy says, but because it's the right thing to do. This neighborhood will be saved.

"I love you, Ma-ma. Always."

I returned to the restaurant's kitchen to prepare two extra dipping sauces to accompany the dish. Because I knew I would be delivering some of the dumplings to Celia soon, I left the front door open so I didn't have to struggle with it later when I'd be carrying the food. Humming "O patria mio," I took out the covered tray from the fridge, careful not to jostle the contents inside.

"Excuse me," a deep voice called from the entrance. "Are you open?"

I almost dropped the tray. A stranger stood at the doorway. Judging by his leather messenger bag, lanyard, and hipster glasses, he had come from Silicon Valley. There was something adorably askew about him: odd locks stuck out from the gelled ink black mass of his hair, smudges graced the corners of his glasses, a missing button winked from the top of his shirt, and mismatched socks appeared between the bottoms of his pant legs and his shoes. Anyone would find him appealing, but for me, his glasses tipped the scales. Even the most beautiful man alive was much more attractive to me bespectacled. He was irresistible.

"I might be, but I don't have Wi-Fi," I replied. These IT types always wanted that.

"I came for the dumplings. I've been following the smell from Mission Street."

"You walked all the way from there?"

"They smelled really good." He glanced up at the chalkboard. "Are you Qiao then? Of Qiao's Cafe?"

On a lark, I had written my grandmother's name there this morning. "No, that was my grandmother."

"Please tell me you still have some dumplings left. I'm dying to try them."

Delivering the dumplings to Celia could wait a little longer. My first unofficial customer was here. His ID card, with matching picture, read Daniel Lee.

Daniel took a seat at the counter, slinging his messenger bag onto the stool beside him. An irresistible aroma of roasted coffee, dark chocolate, and a hint of spearmint clung to him. Though we were around the same age, there was something old about him, as if he had a secret arcane hobby such as stamp collecting.

"Do you work nearby?" I asked.

"At a small start-up on Mission Street. Health-care based." White earbuds peeked from his collar as he leaned forward to inhale the dumplings I placed before him.

I resisted the urge to lean my elbows on the counter and observe him like a zoo animal. He was transfixed by the dumplings, examining each one as if it were a jewel, and sniffing, monopolizing the aroma for himself. He licked his lips.

Eating was a selfish act, and sometimes one requiring privacy. True consumption was carnal.

My skin flushed, broiling like a sizzling strip loin on the grill. As the flames licked higher, my blood felt hotter than the Egyptian sun.

I fanned myself before reaching inside the fridge under the counter for a can of soda. As I hastily guzzled the cool beverage, some of the clear liquid dripped down my chin and onto the neckline of my white cotton tank dress.

Daniel's eyes, however, were directed at his plate of rapidly disappearing dumplings, and so he didn't notice my mess. If I hadn't known his occupation, I would have thought he was a professional competitive eater.

"That was delicious," he declared, patting his flat belly.

The squeaky-clean platter proved his veracity. "I suppose it must have been. You don't have a girlfriend cooking for you at home?" My question was brazen, but at least if there was someone else in his life, I would know now, and the sting from it would be more fleeting.

"No, I don't, and this is better than anything I've eaten in ages. This must be the first time I've been in Chinatown since I was in college." He grinned. "Cheap and greasy food was the motto back then, but this . . . It's transcendent. You have a gift. I can't wait to see what else you cook."

I couldn't help but grin at the revelation that he was single.

Daniel tilted his head and stared at the goddess statue, examining her from every angle.

His scrutiny made me self-conscious, as though he were critically examining my flaws instead of the statue's. "I mean to repair her, but with the preparation for the restaurant, there hasn't been time."

"This kind of deterioration is more than oxidation," he said. "But even though she's in pretty bad shape, I think she can recover from this."

"The damage is pretty extensive."

"Yes, but there is always hope. Underneath all this is something beautiful. It just needs time and patience to come out."

Our gazes met.

One of his gadgets beeped. Then another and another, like a string of Christmas lights coming to life. He smiled and pressed a button, shutting everything off. "I was stuck trying to fix the bug in this code for a week, and now I think I finally know what I need to do to resolve it. This is a good day." He pulled out a fifty-dollar bill from his wallet and placed it on the counter. "Thank you for the meal. Please keep the change."

Daniel Lee waved goodbye and vanished down the street, humming an unfamiliar jazz tune.

The paper portrait of Ulysses S. Grant stared back at me from the counter. I picked up the fifty and placed it into the empty till of the cash register. The close of the drawer followed the satisfying ring of the sale. Daniel's enthusiastic response had just elevated my confidence in my cooking abilities. This was what it would be like to run my own restaurant. Satisfaction warmed me from within.

He ate all the dumplings. Celia would have to wait until I made another fresh batch.

I blushed, remembering my heated reaction to Daniel. What had happened to me? It must have been him or the dumplings. Watching him eat had been akin to pornography, and I was never the amorous type.

In high school, I'd dreamed about traveling and seeing the world when the other girls mooned over boys. My first kiss had been clumsy. Winston Law was aiming for my lips and missed, slobbering all over my chin instead. Eleven-year-old Winston paved the way for a long string of mediocre companions: *boyfriends* would have been too generous a term.

So I'd learned to live without romance. Love was like getting the unwanted gift of an elephant I could never afford to feed or house. Besides, it always ended in tragedy: my father had abandoned my mother, and the heroine or hero—or both—died in all the operas Ma-ma and I had listened to. No, love was a virus I never wanted to catch. It always ended badly, and even when it did happen, I ran away from the boyfriend and the situation by adding another stamp to my passport.

I thought I might have escaped my commitment allergy with Emilio in Manila, but that had ended too. We had been engaged, but I'd chosen to run away from my own wedding. I abandoned him before he had the chance to do it to me. A year later, thinking of him opened wounds I had thought were healed.

But I dared not linger on my own problems when I had others to help.

Chapter Nine

Opening Laolao's book, I flipped through the pages in search of a recipe for Older Shen. The anecdotes helped guide me to one that boosted courage. I reread the recipe for Older Shen and headed to the market. The crabs, because of their freshness, needed to be picked up and cooked on the same day. The preparation ritual was one I had practiced when I was younger and learned from my mother.

Back home, I freed the two feisty crabs from a paper bag. I placed them in a plastic tray of ice, slowing down their metabolism before the cleaning. Using a worn toothbrush, I scrubbed any sand and algae from their hard shells while avoiding the pinch of their claws.

Steamed Dungeness Crabs

Cooking oil
Ginger
Dungeness crabs

    Chicken broth
    Salt
    Shaoxing wine
    Sesame oil
    Green onion or a leek

Add the cooking oil to a large pot to stir-fry the slices of ginger. Place the cleaned crabs in the pot along with the chicken broth. Add salt according to taste.

Simmer for ten minutes. Add the wine, stir. Wait for the shells to turn bright red-orange. After two minutes, add the sesame oil. Garnish with chopped green onions and then serve.

Note:

Crabs are precious and have a natural armor like the warriors of old. They are the perfect ambassadors for courage.

I serve this to new immigrants coming into the area. They need as much bravery as they can muster to navigate this country.

Following my grandmother's recipe, I poured Shaoxing rice wine into the great stainless-steel pot over the steamed crabs. For eight minutes, I watched their shells change from tawny brown to brilliant red before adding the last ingredient: sesame oil.

Older Shen's prescription for courage was ready. I picked up the phone and dialed the number for the bookstore.

Given the rules of Chinese etiquette, the odds of my invitation being declined were low. As I expected, Older Shen accepted my offer to come dine at the restaurant. I wondered how Laolao's recipes worked.

There was nothing in the book about how soon the food would take effect or what I was to expect.

He would be here soon. I fished the crabs from the pot and placed them in a clay bowl. Blooming with tendrils of steam, the shells glistened red-orange. I placed the lid on top to trap the heat within, bringing the dish to the counter for my guest right on time, for Older Shen was tapping on the door. A smile tugged at my lips. He was dressed in a dated tweed suit complete with elbow patches. His shy smile complemented his combed gray hair and clean-shaven face.

I opened the door. "Welcome."

"I haven't been here in years." He scanned his surroundings before turning to the scarred goddess with a frown. "She's not what I remembered. She was beautiful when Qiao was here."

I followed his gaze. So my suspicion was correct: the goddess had been lovely once. I still hoped she would be again.

Shen's nose twitched as he sniffed the air. "Crab? Oh, I love crab."

I guided him to the counter where I had set his plate. He perched atop the stool and unfurled the napkin I'd provided, tucking it into the front of his collared shirt. His brown eyes widened when I lifted the lid off the pot.

The release of steam created a sigh in the air, acting as the prayer before a meal, the ceremonial ribbon cutting before the devouring. Eating crab was a leisurely pursuit. The sweet treasure of crabmeat could only be unlocked by a deft grip or the aid of a steel seafood cracker.

I offered the coveted heavy female crab to my guest. He smiled and brandished his cracker, shattering the shell in strategic spots. He attacked with purpose: disassembling, dissecting to get to the jeweled fat and eggs inside.

While Older Shen ate, I proceeded with my own crab, prying the carapace open by pulling on its apron. The juices dripped down my fingers as I attacked the meat in the body first. My favorite parts were the legs because of how little effort they took compared to the claw and the minute chambers of the body. I sucked the meat from the hollow legs, careful to avoid the plasticky cartilage. The sweetness of the crab complemented the spicy, tangy dipping sauce I'd provided. Flecks of green onion and yellow disks of chili pepper seeds floated in the red wine vinegar. That recipe was also in Laolao's book, but it pleased me that I'd already known one of her recipes by heart.

Older Shen wiped his mouth, pulling his shoulders back, straightening his spine as if he were being pulled upward by an invisible string. The faded threads of his tweed jacket shifted, vibrating until the color saturated, blooming into a bold palette. The sweeping change traveled onto his skin, leaching away the pallor, tempering the grays in his hair, adding a spark in his faraway eyes. Chi gathered around him. Tiny, almost invisible motes of energy clung to his presence like garlands of Christmas lights.

Was all this from Laolao's food? This was incredible. I couldn't believe it was working.

"Mr. Shen?" I asked. "Are you all right?"

"I . . ." He cleared his throat. His reedy voice deepened, growing louder. "I feel great. Better than I have in my life. New batteries."

"New batteries?"

"I have always thought I was given a damaged set of batteries when I was born. It felt like a limitation I couldn't overcome. Right now, though, I feel happy, energized, like I could conquer the world. But this is strange . . . It will take time to get used to." He stood and bowed. "Thank you for the meal and more."

"You're welcome," I said, watching him leave. A surge of excitement flowed through my body. It worked! There was no longer any doubt of the efficacy of Laolao's recipes. Older Shen changed because of the dish—I had seen it for myself. The recipes exceeded my expectations; I could only hope they helped as much as I needed them to. If they did, I could meet my goal of opening the restaurant and saving the rest of the neighborhood. Just in case, I made a mental note to check in on Older Shen in a few days.

I turned to Laolao's photograph propped against her recipe book and murmured my thanks.

My phone's screen flashed with a text from Celia, reminding me of our lunch date in a few minutes. I grabbed my purse and headed out.

Success tasted better than a plump char siu bao right out of the steamer.

I stepped outside and twirled with arms outstretched, eyes to the sky as a cluster of blue scrub jays flew overhead, following my movements. The vibrant parade of blue acted as a contrast to the bleakness around me. In my moments of joy, I always had an entourage of birds trailing above me like an avian bridal train made of feathers and sky instead of pearls and lace. The birds found me no matter where I was in the world.

Tormented by the creatures she couldn't reach, Meimei batted against the windows of the apartment. I laughed and waved at her. The cat ignored me, her focus trained on the elusive prey on the other side of the glass.

Laolao's recipe had worked for Older Shen. I hoped that when I cooked the chicken wings, the Chius would also benefit from some magical meddling. All I had left to do was find the last person in need, and I would fulfill the conditions for opening the restaurant.

Rushing to Celia's gift shop, I pushed the door open and found her clucking over the shelves, righting merchandise, and rearranging a row of smiling ceramic pandas. She hummed "My Favorite Things" from *The Sound of Music*, sashaying her wide hips to the melody.

Long-dormant memories of her resurfaced. The longer I stayed here, the more I remembered what I had so easily discarded when I left home. Celia ate well and it showed, but she was a connoisseur, not a cook herself. It was no secret that her culinary attempts had resulted in emergency visits from the fire department. She would be the ideal customer for the restaurant I was trying to reopen.

The strand of pearls around Celia's neck paired beautifully with her bright yellow peplum dress. She squinted through her tortoiseshell glasses as she tried to fix the last figurine's pose to match the others. Her high voice broke out in a shrill vibrato as she sang.

She swung out her arm in a sweeping gesture and sent a row of smiling ceramic dragons crashing to the floor. "Oh no!" she wailed in a singsong voice as she assessed the damage.

I spied the broom behind the counter and fetched it along with the dustpan.

Celia bent down to collect the big pieces. "I don't know what's wrong with me," she said. "I'm snakebitten. Although, I should count myself blessed that a real snake hasn't bitten me yet."

"I'm sorry, Celia." I deposited the fragments into the trash and returned the broom and dustpan behind the counter.

"My klutziness isn't your fault." She waved her hand and sighed. "Let's move on to happier things. What's happening with the restaurant?"

I grinned. "I saw Miss Yu. She told me I needed to help three people so I can open the restaurant. I've already helped Older Shen."

"Oh, that is excellent news indeed!" Celia smothered me with her generous bosom. "We can celebrate during lunch. This is great progress."

I could barely nod, for I was lost in the scent of lilac talcum powder and Chanel No. 5. I politely extracted myself and took a quick step back as insurance against being ensnared once more.

"The clothes look great." She gestured to the ivory romper I was wearing. "You look good in white. You have the figure for it."

"You're too kind."

"Miranda always had a trim figure and so did your laolao. It's in your blood. And what's in my blood . . ."

"Is style," I declared. It was true. Celia possessed an impeccable, arresting sense of style that could be featured in any sartorial publication.

A soft, rosy blush spread across Celia's cheeks. "An exchange of mutual compliments is the best way to start our lunch. You can tell me all about your victories, and I'll fill you in on the latest gossip."

Flipping the Open sign on the door to Closed, she must have noticed my guilty expression. "It's a slow period now anyway. The morning rush, however little it is, is done, and the rest of the day is dead. You're doing me a favor by breaking the monotony. Besides, this is the most exciting date I've been on in years. And don't even think about offering to pay for lunch. I'm covering it because I invited you."

I was disarmed by her kindness and her generosity. Celia Deng had never been anything but sweet to me, and she had nothing to gain from doing so. She was another example that proved the neighbors weren't as toxic as I'd wanted them to be.

How much had I missed being away, and what had I overlooked while I was here? Did I not see because I'd refused to?

We chose a sushi bar two blocks over. Celia ordered an assortment of rolls and a basket of tempura vegetables and shrimp. In between bites, and sips of matcha tea, I brought her up to date and regaled her with the tale of my victory with Older Shen.

"So you have to help the Chius and then you're done?" she asked.

"No, I still have to find one other person to help."

"The Chius are a mess." Celia fanned herself with the drink menu. "They've been hit the worst by financial problems, and it's sucked the love out of their marriage. I'm glad you're helping them."

"Other than the meal for Fai, have you tried out any more recipes?" She wiped the corners of her mouth.

"I cooked dumplings and meant to save some for you, but I had an unexpected customer."

"Ha! People come from miles around for good food. I can take a rain check on those dumplings. Some of your laolao's cooking skills must have passed on to you. Miranda had it, too, but she never cultivated it. I know because I've tasted her dishes."

"This must have been after I left."

Celia shook her head. "I used to visit when you were in school. Miranda would cook a little something to snack on, and it was always delicious."

I was comforted by the fact that although I hadn't known much about it, the two women had been friends, and not just through necessity.

"Was she depressed when she was growing up?" I asked.

"Miranda wore her sadness like her natural hair color. It was a part of her for as long as I can remember. It's not like she wasn't capable of happiness, she just felt sorrow more keenly than the other emotions. She was my closest friend. Even though she was older than me, it didn't matter."

"What about her agoraphobia?"

"When she was younger, she still went outside. Everything got worse after your grandmother died. Your laolao's accidental death hit her hard. She was never at ease going out of the house, and then your father . . ." Celia sighed. "It's like she believed that going outside would place her in physical danger."

"Did she ever try to get help?"

"As far as I know, Miranda never saw anyone to treat her condition. I think it was a source of tension between her and your grandmother. Your laolao didn't know how to deal with her depression and anxiety. My parents tried to convince her to get help for Miranda, but Qiao didn't understand. Mental illness isn't treated as well as a case of arthritis in our culture."

If I hadn't already liked Celia before, I'd like her even more now. It gave me great comfort that someone else saw my mother as a person, and not as a cursed eccentric.

"I wish I could have done more for her," I confessed.

Celia reached across the table and patted my hand. "Oh, darling, we all do. At least you're doing something for her now."

"You may have tasted her food, but you've never tasted my cooking. I'll need to make something for you soon so you can see for yourself."

Celia smiled. "I think great cooking is in your blood. Your restaurant will be wonderful and it will help the neighborhood so much. Some people pray to Jesus, Allah, or Buddha, but I worship sublime cuisine. It has been there for me all my life. Food comforts, heals, and is the only lover I will ever take." The last line was delivered with a wink.

I stifled a giggle. "But you haven't found your true love yet. I don't think you should settle."

"It's not settling. My future boyfriend will know soon enough that food is my husband and he's the mistress."

We both erupted in laughter.

And so I found an ally in the most unexpected of places.

It dawned on me suddenly that the last person I needed to help was, of course, Celia.

After my lunch date with Celia, I visited the market again. I emerged from the floral shop with armfuls of lavender peonies and violet hyacinths. The flowers were for Ma-ma and Guanyin. It might have been a trick of the light, but the statue of the goddess seemed less melancholy this morning, though the pits and craters still scarred her. One day, I vowed, I would see her restored to her original beauty.

The sonorous notes of "Celeste Aida" greeted me as I came out of the store. Mr. Kuk Wah, his head moving in unison with his bow, sat at the curb playing his erhu. If the soul could exist outside the body, his would be his instrument.

For five minutes, the world stood still. Nothing existed for me but the voice of that erhu.

I swayed to the music like seagrass, undulating to the shifting notes. Hope stirred within me, surging with the melody, uplifting me like no other force in this world could. I was my mother's child, a true melophile through and through. Too soon, it ended.

"Thank you, Mr. Kuk Wah," I murmured.

He set aside his instrument and smiled. Tiny lines wrinkled around his dark eyes. As was his custom, the musician wore a palette of grays and blacks, dressing in the same monochromes found in the cement sidewalk underneath him. "I'm glad you've decided to stay. Is the restaurant open yet?"

"Not quite. I need to do a few things first."

He arched his brow. "Conditions imposed by the city?"

"No, not that." I paused then corrected myself with a laugh. "It may sound silly, but a mystic told me I needed to help three people first so the restaurant can succeed."

"Mystics are meant to be heeded, even more so than regulations and rules—not that you should disregard the latter. If you need to help three people, perhaps you can help me. Did I tell you I was married once?" He pulled off his cap and held it against his chest. The dragon tattoos on his arms shifted, coiling against his skin, their bright scales glinting in the sunlight. "I loved her, but did she really love me? Even after all these years, I am uncertain. If only love was a physical quantity that could be measured and weighed so that one could be sure of his lover's affections." He lifted his eyes to meet mine. "I know what you're going to ask. What happened? Well, we quarreled and parted ways. I've tried for years, but she won't talk to me anymore. Can you help me? I need advice."

Since I was on a roll, helping out another neighbor, especially one I considered a friend, seemed an easy decision. I smiled and bowed. "Mr. Kuk Wah, will you do me the honor of having tea at my grandmother's restaurant?"

"I would love to," he replied.

After running upstairs to refill the vases of the family shrine, I opened the door to the restaurant for the musician. Walking inside a cloud of the peonies' and hyacinths' perfume, I replaced the flowers in the vases for the goddess, discarding the old. As promised, I served the musician a pot of tea.

"You are making reparations to Guanyin," the older man commented after sipping his jasmine tea. "I wonder how long it will take for her to forgive."

I adjusted the flowers. "All I want is to see her smile again."

The musician studied the statue, counting all the scars as if taking a census. He hummed an unfamiliar tune, which repeated every four bars as his two fingers tapped on the counter. When he found a pair of forks nearby, his feet resumed the beat as he clashed the tines against each other. The melody echoed in the small space until he ended it with a flourish.

"What were you playing?" I asked.

"Something I made up for my wife. I call it the 'Love Trap.' I set a snare for her and she fell in. She was happy for a while, but somehow, she escaped and is forever lost to me."

I laughed and shook my head. "I apologize. It's not your sorrow that I am amused by but your logic. When I was in Italy, I worked at a cafe in Udine. Every morning, a regal woman came in asking for a cappuccino while she read the morning paper. The diamond rings sparkled on her fingers as she held the cup to her lips. She told me once that she had been married five times and the only reason was because men assumed wooing is a onetime effort. If she had been wooed during her marriages, perhaps she wouldn't have been as wealthy, but she would have been happier. It makes me think: could you woo your wife now?"

"I'm not so sure. Wooing is a skill I haven't practiced in years."

"Then hone it like playing the strings of your erhu. It must be like riding a bicycle."

"More like fumbling for a flashlight in the dark."

I laughed before tossing the pile of old flowers into the trash. "She loved you once, enough to marry you. Surely that means something."

"Perhaps." A shadow traveled across his face and his dark eyes grew distant. The tattooed dragons on his forearms constricted, tightening around his skin, scales shimmering under the pendant lamp like burnished metal. "But love can fade over time the way a beautiful note vanishes in the air after being played."

"Then keep playing. Play until you ensnare her heart again."

"But will it work?"

"You won't know until you try."

He leaned over the counter and rested his chin on his hands. "How did you get to be so knowledgeable about relationships?"

I laughed. "I'm not. I'm an impostor who only gives good advice to others."

Mr. Kuk Wah would be horrified if he knew about the wreckage of the relationship I had left behind in the Pacific. I had broken a man's heart and run away from the consequences. Emilio would forgive me sooner than I would ever forgive myself.

"Where did you go just now, Xiao Niao?"

The musician's question snapped me back to the present. I blinked and tucked the painful memory away, burying it under the sand so the waves could wash all the traces away.

"I'm sorry, Mr. Kuk Wah. You have my full attention again."

He lowered his eyes and cleared his throat. "So I'm supposed to woo my wife?"

"Yes, just like I'm supposed to woo my future customers with my food." I tipped my head toward the Victrola in the corner with the wooden box of records beside it. "Perhaps you can find some musical inspiration."

Mr. Kuk Wah smiled as he walked over to the antique player. He treated the introduction with quiet formality, as if he were on a first date with an elegant woman. First, he lifted the lid, admiring the turntable and whispering something inaudible into it. He traced the ornate swing arm of the turntable before lifting it to accommodate the incoming vinyl. After his silent homage, he crouched down to leaf through the records, humming a cheerful tune.

I disappeared into the kitchen with lightness in my steps to refill the pot of tea. The joy the musician felt for my beloved record player was infectious. Minutes later, he had chosen *La traviata*. I grinned at his romantic choice.

Tomorrow, I would cook the chicken wings and help the Chius solve their own love dilemma.

Chapter Ten

The recipe dictated that the chicken be marinated in the morning and served in the afternoon or evening of the same day.

Drunken Chicken Wings

Garlic
Five-spice powder
Peppercorns
Chilies
Paprika
Chicken wings
Shaoxing wine

Smash the garlic cloves before adding them to a bowl with the rest of the spices. Massage the seasonings into the chicken wings before adding to the wine.

Cover.

Marinate for three hours to encourage new love and six hours to rekindle a love gone sour. Do not marinate for longer than eight hours.

Finish by deep-frying.

Note:

Love and inebriation produce the same effects: bouts of joy and impaired decision making. I am approached often by lovers to help solve their problems. I try my best, knowing that meddling in the affairs of the heart can lead to interesting situations.

I combined garlic, five-spice, black peppercorns, Thai chilies, and paprika in a large bowl for the seasoning. I tumbled two pounds of chicken wings out of their brown paper wrapping and into the waiting bowl, where I kneaded the pungent mixture into them, squeezing the spices into the meat like an experienced massage therapist. Another bowl full of Shaoxing rice wine awaited the wings as the next step after their rigorous massage. They soaked and relaxed, basking in the pool of wine to become drunken like their name. I set them aside to marinate in the fridge.

I called up the Chius to invite them for a snack. Mr. Chiu promised to come by at two with his wife. As I thought of the couple, my mind wandered to another dormant subject with painful memories: my father. If Mr. Kuk Wah was determined to fix his marriage, why didn't my father want to save his? Why had he left us?

I'd watched Ma-ma raising me alone and wondered if things would have been different if my father were around. Perhaps if he had been there, Ma-ma would not have had all those dark spells or the hours she'd spent miles away in her mind while her eyes remained hollow and empty. I'd been so helpless when Ma-ma suffered those debilitating episodes. I'd done what I could by running to the restaurant to pay for food, even when I was so young I could barely reach the counter, but I couldn't talk to her about things the way another adult—a partner—could have.

If my father had been there, maybe Ma-ma's demons wouldn't have controlled her. He could have saved my mother's life when I wasn't there.

Perhaps, I mused, I had transferred my potent wrath for my father onto the neighbors. It was easier to have active targets than a missing one.

Yes, life could have been different, but hoping for these possibilities was akin to catching sunlight in a butterfly net. Like my father, my mother would never return. I had no choice but to turn my eyes to the future. Mr. Kuk Wah could still change his fortunes, and, with my help, so could the rest of the neighbors.

I heated up the oil in the wok and waited until it reached temperature.

What magical results would Laolao's drunken chicken wings bring?

The side dish for the drunken chicken wings was a pickled slaw. This was my recipe and something I had picked up from my travels in Vietnam. I julienned carrots and daikon radish, dancing my knife across the wooden block, tapping until the vegetables turned into perfect matchsticks. I added ribbons of napa cabbage and romaine lettuce before drizzling a light dressing of white vinegar and sugar on top. I tossed the medley until the sweet tanginess enveloped all the contents.

Once the slaw was done, I checked the wok with its refined peanut oil. When it was heated, I tossed the wings into the liquid depths, sending the oil roaring with their entrance. I scooped them out with my golden net only moments later.

After tasting the first portion and deeming it perfect, I tossed more of the wings into the wok to have them emerge crispy and fried to perfection. Soon, the two-pound batch of drunken chicken wings rested on a rack. I divided the portion with a pair of stainless tongs for each of the couple's plates, arranging them alongside a generous heap of colorful slaw.

The Chius needed help. I couldn't bear watching their marriage break down. As much as I didn't want to care for them, I couldn't deny that I was starting to see the neighbors as individuals instead of a faceless mob. I wasn't the misanthrope that I'd thought myself to be; I didn't have that luxury now that my fate was tied to theirs.

The bell at the front door of the restaurant signaled the arrival of the Chius. I washed my hands and popped out of the kitchen to welcome them. Mr. Chiu stood a step behind his wife with a wistful expression on his face. Mrs. Chiu busied herself with examining the statue of the goddess.

"I remember a time when Guanyin was radiant," she said in a hushed tone. To my surprise and to his, she turned to her husband. "Do you remember, Wayne?"

He cleared his throat. "Of course. We had our first date here and she was on the counter. How could I forget?"

She turned to me, brushing his comment aside. "I can't stay for long. I have appointments this afternoon. It was kind of you to invite us for a snack."

I gestured to the stools by the counter. "Please, have a seat. I will bring you the food shortly."

Returning to the kitchen, I added the finishing touches to their plates with an ear cocked toward the dining area. Eavesdropping was a social transgression, but since I was already meddling in their lives, it felt like a minor offense—although, lately, I'd been a repeat offender.

"Anita . . ."

"Don't. I came here for her, not you. She just lost her mother and you're only thinking of yourself," Mrs. Chiu hissed. "You're always thinking only about yourself."

"I'm thinking about *us*. I can't stop thinking about us." The tone of his voice shifted from a plea to a question, one a lawyer might ask in front of a jury. "Our son told me that you still keep your wedding ring on when you visit him. Why do you keep it on when you've told me—"

"Because I haven't decided yet."

"Then there's hope."

I didn't hear an answer from Mrs. Chiu, so I took the silence as my cue to bring out the food and a fresh pot of tieguanyin tea. I'd arranged the crispy chicken wings on a bed of romaine hearts to showcase the contrasting colors of golds and greens. Every chef was an artist at heart. The key to the most successful dish was to first seduce the eyes and the nose, for if the dish failed in this, no one would want to take the next step of tasting it.

"I hope you like chicken wings," I declared, emerging from the kitchen.

Mr. and Mrs. Chiu both stared at the plate in awe. Mr. Chiu wiped his hands with a napkin before picking up a drumette with his fingers. Mrs. Chiu picked up her fork and stabbed her wing, avoiding the dilemma of messy fingers.

A loud, satisfying, crunching sound emerged as they ate. As I watched, fractures ran along the surface of their skin, reminding me of shattered porcelain. The cracks deepened as they ate. Once they were finished, tiny streams of glittering gold filled the cracks: mending, repairing what was broken, and transforming it into something far more beautiful. It was similar to a piece of kintsukuroi I'd picked up in Kyoto, repaired pottery that had been mended with gold.

The Chius turned to each other. Their eyes met and their hands reached for each other, fingers and palms touching. Mrs. Chiu reached for her husband's cheek with her free hand. "Wayne, I'm so sorry. I really do love you." She sounded almost surprised to remember.

He leaned over and kissed her. "Let's get out of here."

A girlish giggle escaped Mrs. Chiu's lips.

The couple walked out in a half embrace, side by side.

As they exited the restaurant, the glass door swung open. Dressed in a plum frock, Celia panted, bracing herself against the opened door. Her round face was flushed and her perm askew. She caught her breath before shrieking, "Where are the chicken wings?"

I swallowed before confessing, "I'm so sorry. I only made enough for the Chius."

Celia staggered to the counter and sobbed. "No! I smelled them and came as quickly as I could. I almost threw my ankle out running over so I could get here before anyone else." She banged her fists against the counter. "But I'm too late." She sighed.

Oh no, the wings were her favorite. If I had known, I would have set some aside for her. A twinge of guilt stabbed me. Celia sighed and sniffed. The ghost of the chicken hung in the air. She inhaled the lingering aroma, excavating the layers like an olfactory archaeologist.

Her bottom lip trembled. I reached for Celia's shaking shoulder and squeezed. "It's all right, I can always make you more."

"You can?" She lifted her head. "It's been decades since I last ate those chicken wings. I thought I would never see or eat them again. Yet this morning, I smelled them in the air. I thought I was having a stroke.

But the aroma grew stronger and when I saw the Chius come out of the restaurant, I knew it must be true. If the smell is any indication, you have re-created your laolao's dish perfectly. I didn't think it would affect me this way, but your grandmother's food was incredible."

It must have been. My grandmother's book was magic after all. It wasn't necessarily in the ingredients or the techniques, for I'd been cooking a few of these dishes for years without the startling results I'd recently witnessed. Instead, there seemed to be something tangible happening underneath the gastronomic chemical reactions. Those who'd required sustenance had received delicious food. Those who had needed more, Laolao's recipes had healed.

I patted her hand. "I promise I'll cook for you soon. I've been helping the neighbors, but I never asked you if you needed any help. Just say the word, Celia, and I'll do what I can to help you."

"No, I don't need anything." She lowered her eyes and shook her head. "You should focus on helping the others."

"How about dinner? At your place. I'll deliver it tonight, unless you have plans of course."

She grinned. "It's a date!"

After I walked Celia back to her store, I returned upstairs to the apartment to do some much-needed reading. Although Celia had requested the chicken wings, I wasn't sure if they would be beneficial for her given the effects I'd seen with the Chius.

I had to find a new recipe and prepare a dish for Celia for tonight. Meimei assumed her position on my belly while I flipped through Laolao's recipe book.

How could I help my friend? I'd asked her if she needed anything, and of course, she directed me to help someone else. I was more determined now to find something in the book for her. She didn't need a love potion or more courage. I admired Celia for who she was: kind, generous, funny, stylish, and unapologetic in the way she devoured life. I could tell by the lack of tourists in the area that her business had suffered, but there was no easy cure for that in my grandmother's book, nor did I expect one to be there.

Luck. I remembered Celia's rash of misfortune with the shoe and the smashed figurines. She'd mentioned it herself yesterday. A little good karma couldn't hurt, and it would be subtle enough to give her a boost. After all of the kindness she had given me, this was warranted.

There must be something that imbued luck in these pages. The recipes ran the gamut of vegetarian, fish, chicken, beef, pork, noodles, soups, stews, and desserts. They also spanned cuisines from Cantonese, Sichuan, Shanghainese, and even Taiwanese. My grandmother must have expanded her repertoire. The care and poetry of each recipe was accentuated by its simple instructions and colorful anecdotes.

This book had traveled across the ocean of time—a priceless family heirloom smuggled out of China when Laolao had immigrated to San Francisco. Though it had been too long since it had last seen the light of day, I now knew I wanted to make certain my family's legacy lived on. My mother chose not to uphold it, but I wasn't Ma-ma.

The kitten pushed her head against my hand. I had forgotten to keep petting her. I resumed my massage and was rewarded with purrs that sent vibrations across my skin. I'd never known the cure to loneliness lay in feline companionship.

I returned my focus to the pages and found the right recipe for Celia: Laolao's famous noodle soup. Carrying the book with me, I headed downstairs to the restaurant and double-checked the fridge and pantry for the ingredients. I had everything I needed. It was time to cook.

Noodle Soup

Beef, pork, and chicken bones
Ginger
Star anise
Peppercorns
Onion
Carrots
Dried mushrooms
Fifteen spices [redacted]
Water

Boil all of the ingredients in a large stockpot to distill their properties. Luck takes time to brew. Boil for a minimum of three hours. Take care to skim the surface with a spoon to rid the broth of rising impurities.

Note:

This flavorful broth can be served on its own or with fresh, handmade noodles.

Cook this for those who need an extra boost. Caution, this is not meant to change one's fate. This broth is to unlock possibilities: to choose the right course of action, instead of the wrong one. Luck can sometimes be interpreted as making the right choices at the right times.

I cooked this for a hardworking entrepreneur with many failed ventures. He was worried about his declining finances

and the ability to feed his family. The broth managed to
clarify his mind, and in time, he changed his own luck. This
isn't meant to be a cure-all but a push in the right direction.

My grandmother must have been up to her armpits in her neighbors' entanglements. Meddling in other people's affairs was akin to painting with lemurs—there was a certain level of patience and courage involved. I wondered if all of her recipes worked the way she had intended. They must have to have earned her such a legendary reputation.

I chopped the ginger root and dropped the slices into the boiling pot as the rising steam bloomed upward, flowering like a cloud. As instructed by the book, I added the list of fifteen spices and ingredients with the precision of a scientist. This was one of my grandmother's most treasured and complex recipes. Ma-ma had tried to replicate this many times, but according to her, nothing had ever compared to the flavor profile of this soup. I fanned the aroma toward my twitching nose as the broth changed, unifying the ingredients into an intoxicating combination. I dipped my spoon into the pot for a taste and closed my eyes, enjoying all the flavors. Even knowing the components and preparation method, the result was nothing short of extraordinary.

The taste reminded me of one of the rare stories my mother had told me about Laolao. It was said that my grandmother's famous bowl of noodles had cured a visiting monarch from Europe of her homesickness on a cool February afternoon. The foreign queen, staying in the presidential suite of the upscale St. Francis Hotel, had requested that a bowl of them be delivered every morning for the duration of her stay.

I never understood why Ma-ma had decided to share a piece of my grandmother that day. At the time, I'd been so grateful for the gift that I'd never questioned the motive behind it, but now, I believe it was one of the rare times Ma-ma had showed me that she missed my grandmother. Despite their differences, their complicated relationship must have been based on love after all.

With the broth simmering, my attention turned to making the noodles from scratch. There were no shortcuts in my family's cooking. Without fresh noodles, a beautiful broth was wasted, and without a sublime broth, fresh noodles failed to shine.

I kneaded the flour with my hands, working, pushing, molding, shaping; aiming for the right consistency where the mixture would lose its stickiness. As the dough rested, I covered it with a damp cloth. It needed to be rolled, then sliced with a sharp, dry knife. Once the strands were cut, I untangled them, allowing them to fall into neat, fist-size piles perfect for single servings. The golden masses reminded me of the hanks of yarn my mother had used to crochet the afghans that were still in the apartment. I laid the bundles to rest in a large metal bowl, sealed it with industrial-strength plastic wrap, and tested the tautness as if it were a drum before I tucked it inside the fridge. The noodles would be ready for throwing into a boiling pot right before serving at Celia's place.

I exhaled and leaned against the counter. The aroma from the broth alone soothed me. I was walking on my grandmother's path, bringing a sense of fulfillment I yearned for in the turbulence of the present.

I prepared a smaller pot of water for the noodles right beside the large pot of simmering broth. The low rumble of the boil faded against the backdrop of *The Magic Flute*. Listening to music without the pops and crackles of well-worn vinyl was akin to experiencing the African savanna through a zoo exhibit. Authenticity in its splendor always carried flaws. The breeze swept in, carrying with it the intoxicating aromas from the kitchen and my hopes of success.

Celia was the last person I needed to help. After this, I could bury myself in the process of filling out all the paperwork to reopen the restaurant. I could have opened one before, but it would have been very difficult without the financial means to do so, and it had never felt right. Perhaps because it was that I'd never found the ideal place that enabled me to continue pursuing my dream. Maybe I had been waiting for Ma-ma's blessing, which had never come until now.

Like most inhabitants of the neighborhood, the shopkeepers lived above their stores. It was an arrangement of convenience and necessity. In the past, these apartments had been like the bunkhouses of bachelors, journeymen who'd searched for Gold Mountain and then worked on the Central Pacific Railroad. The lone immigrants cramped into spare spaces like puzzle pieces until they brought their families over from China, and then their lodgings became even more cramped, transforming rooms into rabbit warrens with entire families sleeping in the same bed. The luxury of personal space that my family had enjoyed was as rare as our lineage: one daughter in each generation with no siblings to speak of.

At dusk, Grant Avenue was quiet under the glow of the green dragon street lanterns. Armed with a stockpot and a sealed container of the fresh, uncooked noodles, I ventured into the night. The upstairs windows above the gift shop were open, allowing yellow incandescent light to bathe the sidewalk below.

I squinted up at the orange polka-dot curtains fluttering in the night breeze. "Those Canaan Days" from *Joseph and the Amazing Technicolor Dreamcoat* blared from the stereo. Celia must have smelled her dinner as it cooked. The older woman leaned out the open window. Large rollers festooned her dark hair, weighing it down like too many summer apples on a tree. A thick cream collar trimmed the carnation pink housecoat covering her shoulders. She wore no makeup, but the same tortoiseshell frames perched on the bridge of her nose.

"I hope my dinner is ready," she declared.

A minute later, the door to the apartment swung open. Celia helped me carry dinner upstairs. I had never been in Celia's apartment, but its layout was similar to mine: two bedrooms, one bathroom, and a modest kitchen combined with living room. The decor was cheerful and very much a reflection of her personality: pale walls and furniture were accented with bursts of color in pillows, accessories, and posters of every successful Broadway show imaginable. Playbills in heavy plastic jackets populated bookshelves along with various souvenirs: a carved and painted lion from *The Lion King*, a glass slipper from Rodgers and Hammerstein's *Cinderella*, a sequined purse from *Cats*, a rainbow woven basket from *Joseph and the Amazing Technicolor Dreamcoat*, and a porcelain mask from *The Phantom of the Opera*.

Everyone in Chinatown knew Celia closed her gift shop two weeks a year. One week she spent in London's West End, and the other on Broadway in New York City. I'd heard from Ma-ma that what occurred during those trips was a musical and epicurean bacchanal. Front-row seats to shows where every sequin and sprinkle of glitter was within reach. Expensive wines paired with five-course meals at tables booked six months in advance, including a rare seat or two at chefs' tables in the intimacy of the kitchen. Was Celia still able to go on these trips, or were times too tight?

"I'll need to use your stove to heat up the broth and cook the noodles," I said.

Celia directed me to her tidy kitchen. It was immaculate from obsolescence. I placed the broth on the stove and searched the cupboards for a small pot in which to cook the noodles. Every door I opened contained a variety of wines, snacks, magazines, even shoes.

"I think it's at the top over there." She pointed to the farthest cupboard from my position. "As you can see, I'm not the best cook. I'll burn the neighborhood down if given the chance."

I found a small pot that suited my needs and gave it a quick rinse in the sink. "I can always teach you if you're interested."

She displayed her perfect manicure with an impish grin. "No, thank you. My hands are only meant for dialing takeout. But I can watch. I always love watching other people cook without the fire department being called."

Celia set the table and brought two bowls for the soup to the counter beside me.

I scooped the noodles from the boiling water, pausing to watch them wriggling in the air, like fish battling against being parted from the sea. I submerged the noodles by ladling the fragrant broth into the bowls, covering them until they relaxed under the golden surface. I arranged chopped mushrooms and some steamed bok choy as a garnish to add more color and texture. Lastly, I sprinkled tiny rings of spring onions over the soup with my fingertips: flecks of green suspended in gold.

"It smells so good and just like your laolao's." She closed her eyes, sniffed, and hovered her face over her bowl. "It's as if I'm tasting it again for the first time."

Food possessed the power to evoke memories. I associated every dish with a moment of my life. Nothing transported me faster and more vividly. The sweetness of mango pudding brought me back to sitting on the sofa with Ma-ma as she braided my hair before school, admiring her handiwork as she'd hummed. She always waited for me after class with a pot of jasmine tea and a plate of fruit crème cookies. In between bites, I would tell her about my day.

I took a sip of the broth as I watched Celia eat. After seeing what had happened to Older Shen and the Chius, I wasn't sure what to expect.

She wound her chopsticks around the noodles, creating a tornado, spinning them as if she were wielding a fork. Celia took a bite of the bundle, then sipped the broth. Tendrils of steam rose from her skin, changing into red and gold banners unfurling above her. Once she had finished, the banners disintegrated into mini bursts of fireworks. She was so enraptured by the food she failed to notice.

Celia smiled like a child who'd just decided between two different types of ice cream. She suddenly exuded confidence. This was the definition of luck from Laolao's prescription.

"It's funny," Celia said. "I feel much clearer about things. Like I can think straight for the first time in a while. That reminds me, I saw a very handsome man come into the restaurant. I didn't know you already had a boyfriend, at least not one in the area."

"He's a developer working at a company on Mission Street." Heat rushed to my cheeks. "And he's not my boyfriend. I don't even know if I'll see him again."

She rested her chin on her hands. "Oh, he's coming back. He'd be coming back regardless because of the food."

I laughed. "You make it sound like I deliberately set a trap."

"It's not a crime to want to have everything: love, money, success. Judging by the blush on your cheeks, you like this one."

I did, though it was too soon to tell. He was like the first page of an intriguing book I had just started. If only the fear of mucking it all up didn't loom over my head like a beach umbrella.

"New love is supposed to be exciting. You look like you're about to get a colonoscopy." Celia reached across the table to pat my hand. "Did you have a bad relationship before this?"

"No," I confessed. "I was the one who did the damage. I left my fiancé at the altar."

Celia sat up. "No, you didn't!"

I trusted her enough to bare the ugliness of my romantic history. "I did. It wasn't exactly at the altar, but two weeks before the wedding. His name was Emilio. I met him and his family while I was living in Manila."

"He was Filipino then? Not Chinese?"

I nodded.

"What was he like?"

"He was handsome, very sweet, and definitely too good for me," I said with a sigh. "Ma-ma would have approved of him if she'd had the chance to meet him. He was an English professor at one of the city's universities. We dated for six months before he proposed. At the time, I thought it was my ever after."

"What happened?"

I closed my eyes. Words spilled out of me quickly as if the speed would lessen the pain. "I couldn't go through with it. I was terrified he would wake up one day and see who I really am, and leave me. I left him before he could leave me."

Celia sighed. She got up and embraced me. "I'm sorry," she murmured against my shoulder. "You deserve love. It's hard for you to see now, but I'm going to do my best to convince you to believe it. We women have to stick together." She poked my arm. "This man sounds promising. I hope it works out."

"I don't know. It's too soon to tell." I blushed.

"And the restaurant will be wonderful when you open! I know you're worried but it will all be fine."

"Did I tell you I flunked out of culinary school? When I moved out, I'd saved enough money for my first year and I couldn't make it. I don't have the right qualifications. That matters, right?"

"What matters most is that you'll be cooking and people will fall in love with your food as they did with your laolao's. Remember that you've helped Fai, Wayne, and Anita. Evelyn's prophecies are never wrong."

I should have corrected Celia. She had declined my offer, but I did it anyway. I should have revealed that she was the last one I'd decided to help, but I feared the possibility that she would be upset and our newfound friendship would be broken. Instead, I chose silence and hoped I would not regret it later.

"You can have it all," Celia said. "You just need to believe that you can."

Chapter Eleven

The next morning I awoke with a lightness of spirit. The birds outside my window trilled with an infectious song. My happiness reverberated with every note while Meimei clucked at the unseen birds. Today, I would start tackling the paperwork for the restaurant.

After a hot shower, I tied my hair into my customary ponytail and stepped into a white cotton tank dress, one of the many pieces Celia had bought for me at the thrift store. I was still adhering to the Chinese mourning tradition by forsaking all bright colors.

Before I sank into the mire of bureaucracy, I picked up Meimei and settled her on my lap. My fingers found her furry, tufted ears. "I'm glad you're with me."

She turned her head and nuzzled my hand.

"I miss her too. I hope I can make her proud."

The cat mewed.

"Oh, Ma-ma, I wish you were here."

As I fed sheets of paper into the printer, the thought of my father crept into my mind. Wherever he was, he probably didn't know Mama had died. I never truly accepted that he chose to leave us. I didn't want to know why he left. I didn't doubt Ma-ma's love for him or question her unworthy choice in a husband—after all, I was its by-product. But what worried me was the fear that I'd inherited her flawed ability to choose a mate. I failed Emilio. Would I do the same to Daniel if I dared pursue anything with him?

I shook my head. I had to stop thinking this way. Failure wasn't an option, not in love and not for the restaurant.

I printed out the business license form and placed it with the others: federal employer identification, legal building permit, seller's permit, food handler's permit, sign permit, health operational permit. I even printed out forms for a music license and an alcoholic beverage license—maybe I could make them fit into the budget. The folder had become bloated like an overstuffed dumpling.

I kissed the top of the cat's head before I made my way downstairs to fill out the paperwork. I could have done it upstairs at the kitchen table but I had an ulterior motive: I wanted to lay another "trap" for a certain someone.

I decided to make Laolao's dumpling recipe again because I already had the ingredients. The scent of Laolao's food must have acted like culinary pheromones to lure Daniel here. Had he arrived before or after I'd fried them? I couldn't remember. How had he smelled my cooking from so far away? There was a tap against the door. Celia stood at the doorway. She appeared refreshed, her dark curls crisper than ever and her tortoiseshell glasses glinting in the sunlight. She wore a lime green frock with a print of tiny red cherries accented by a starburst citrine brooch.

I went to the door to meet her.

"Last night was fun," she said. "Thank you for confiding in me." A deep blush spread across her cheeks. "I hope you know that you can trust me."

"Of course." I smiled. "I consider you a friend."

"Good!" She sniffed the air. "Are you cooking something right now?"

"Not yet, but I will be."

"I can't wait to smell it. The best part of your laolao's cooking— other than eating it—was the way it filled the neighborhood with such delicious scents." Celia checked over her shoulder as the dragon hiss of a tour bus's air brakes signaled the oncoming stampede of tourists. "My luck has turned! It's the tour group that Old Wu promised yesterday. Oh, I really needed this! I'll be back later." She waved goodbye and sprinted down the street to open her gift shop, an adorable human streak of lime green and cherry red.

It was working! Laolao's recipe had turned Celia's luck. I couldn't wait to check in on the rest of the neighbors later. The restaurant's success hinged on helping them, and although my motives hadn't been altruistic in the beginning, I now found myself wanting to engage with the people who lived nearby. Cooking for them cut away some of the veils of formality. After all, I'd been privy to their heartaches, and they knew I had lost Ma-ma. Exposure had banished the years of unfamiliarity.

I heated the oil in the wok, and waited for it to get to the right temperature before tossing in a dumpling. It sank below the bubbling surface only to rise in golden splendor when done. I fished it out and waited. Science gauged the speeds of light and sound, but what about aroma?

I ran to the front door and propped it open.

Would it work again this time?

Should I fry more dumplings?

Should I fan the wok while cooking?

I stared at my phone to check the time.

Two minutes had passed since I fried the dumpling. Soon, two had turned to five.

The idea that he could have been a food-induced hallucination took root, merely a romantic dream borne from the whispers of my heart.

Seven minutes.

He wasn't coming.

I should be concentrating on cooking for the neighbors anyway instead of chasing an irresistible illusion.

Why did he have to be so handsome?

Just then, the bell above the door jingled.

Daniel came into the restaurant with a wonderful smile. As he made his way to the counter, I battled the rising nervousness and giddiness inside me.

Armed with his familiar leather messenger bag and a blinking assortment of gadgets, he perched upon his designated stool. Behind his horn-rimmed glasses, his eyes closed as he inhaled, drawing as much of the delicious air into his lungs as he could, his rib cage expanding like a hot-air balloon. His navy tee had some sort of programming code on it, obscured by his striped overshirt.

"You do know I'm not officially open, right?"

"Then I'm coming in to get a sneak peek before everyone else. There's nothing wrong with that, is there?"

I smiled. "A cook always likes to hear when someone likes her food."

"Speaking of which, I'd love more of those addictive dumplings, please. As many as you can serve. I've had dumplings before, but nothing like these. They're different. Very googol."

I didn't understand why he compared the dumplings to a search engine, but I nodded my head anyway and pointed to the kitchen. "I'll be back with the food."

I dropped three batches of dumplings into the wok, wanting to serve Daniel the freshest fare possible. As they cooked, I pulled out a large melamine platter and a pair of chopsticks from the shelves.

The restaurant's serving ware was worn but still functional and, at this point, even if I wanted to update the collection, I couldn't afford to. Besides, my grandmother had used these very bowls. If I replaced them, I would lose that connection with her.

I looked over at Daniel. His pupils were dilated. The corners of his mouth turned up, wolfish, grinning, but not at me—at the full tray I was carrying. A trickle of sweat traveled from my hairline and down to my brow, setting off a slow burn under my skin. The dials on my internal stove clicked as my temperature climbed, flaring, pulsing, unfurling like a bushfire. His lust for the food had once again become mine. His passion was my aphrodisiac.

After unloading the platter, I didn't dare linger, lest I combust while I watched him eat.

In the kitchen, hissing steam rolled off my skin as I downed glass after glass of ice water. The galley was once again enveloped in a thick fog, as thick as the foam of a Florentine cappuccino. Slowly my temperature returned to normal, but my heart still galloped in my chest. What was it about Daniel that affected me so?

Ma-ma had never warned me about this, although she'd had a warning pertaining to everything else. We had never had the talk about the birds and the bees because she was too busy talking about demons. I guess they were more important than sex education.

The public school system taught me everything I needed to know physiologically, but we had never learned nuances such as romance.

And coming from a broken home, I'd had no romantic role models to follow. The best part of any relationship was the beginning: the potential, the attraction, when the enjoyment of each other was the only focus. But the longer a relationship dragged, the more exposed I was to the ugliness of my flaws.

I'd been afraid that Emilio would realize I was unworthy of his love. I'd left him before he could leave me.

And so I always ran.

Because, in the end, I was most afraid I would end up like Ma-ma. Trapped in the ghost of a relationship if not an apartment.

Daniel didn't even know my name. It wasn't as if we'd shared intimate conversations. I served him food and he ate it. I knew nothing about him save for his incredible appetite and the information on his lanyard, yet I liked him enough to tell Celia about him.

I needed to know more, but I was afraid to speak to him and burst this bubble, the fragment of hope that this could turn out differently than the wreckage of my past dalliances. Infatuation from a distance was safer than engaging and discovering that it wasn't meant to be. I told myself to be brave, but I still wasn't sure I could do this.

I peeked through the doorway. As anticipated, Daniel was finished with his meal. Three clean bowls were stacked on top of the empty platter. His long fingers tapped an unfamiliar up-tempo rhythm on the counter. The way he splayed his fingers suggested he was quite adept at the piano. The lanyard hanging from his neck bobbed with the movement.

"You play the piano?"

He pulled the earbuds out. "For as long as I can remember. Didn't your parents also force you to take lessons? It's the Chinese way after all."

"Nope."

"Maybe you had a violin under your chin instead?"

"My mother missed the music lessons memo. I never took piano, though I do admit, I'm curious about what I missed out on."

"Most people will tell you horror stories about how it was like prison because they'd be stuck on that bench until their sentence was done. For me, though, it wasn't torture because I love music." There was a spark of mischief in his brown eyes. "What kind of lessons did your mother put you through?"

The visual of a pint-size Daniel playing the piano danced in my head. I'd never had many friends growing up, but I felt as if Daniel could have been one. He must have been adorable and quite serious about the task at hand, just as I'd been when listening to my mother as she instructed me how to properly use a knife. When I was growing up, Ma-ma was leery of strangers coming into the house and never liked the idea of my leaving for an hour or two for lessons that I would have to travel outside of our neighborhood to get to. Instead, I found my way inside the kitchen, learning about the power of spices, how to fillet a fish, and the art of dim sum.

"She taught me how to cook," I replied. "Everything I know I learned from her and from working in other chefs' kitchens."

"She must have been an amazing chef. Those culinary lessons you got are priceless. So this means she ran the restaurant before you? I don't remember this place being open last year or the year before that."

"No, it was closed for a long time. My grandmother was the one who was in charge, but that was decades ago. When my mother had me, I guess she decided to focus on her family and abandoned it."

Daniel opened his wallet, revealing crisp bills.

"You're paying too much. I'm starting to crack down on the handouts."

"It's not a handout." He placed a one-hundred-dollar bill on the counter. "This includes the tip."

I slid the bill back across the counter. "I'm not even open yet. It's too much."

"The food was good." He pushed the bill back.

Before I could countermove, he placed his hand over mine. The warmth of his touch sent blood rushing to my cheeks. He squeezed before letting go.

"I know what I like." Daniel's brows narrowed. A hardness entered into his features, and it caught me by surprise. "I love your food and if you continue to cook, I'll keep following its aroma every morning. Your dumplings are exciting—there isn't anything in the city that compares to them. It's only a matter of time before the foodie intelligentsia get a whiff of this place. We'll see then how much you'll charge to turn people away at the door."

My mother had once compared compliments to birds: if you don't chase after them, they come on their own. "Thank you," I repeated. "You seem to have grander dreams about my restaurant than I do. I need to cook you something different sometime so you can see the range of my skills."

He tapped the hundred-dollar bill on the counter and winked. "That would be great. Good old American capitalism is your friend. So, uh . . . are you seeing anyone?"

I bit my lower lip. "No. I just moved back because my mother passed away."

"Oh. I'm sorry to hear that." He lowered his head. "It must be why you're always wearing white. I should have known."

He'd noticed what I wore? "Thank you. I miss her every day."

We stared at each other and he smiled. It was a simple gesture, so earnest in its essence that I couldn't help but return it. His dark eyes were molten underneath the thick glasses, the shade hovering between dark and milk chocolate.

I stared, losing myself in the fond memories of chocolates in their paper shells at Christmas, in the surprise and discovery of the filling inside, the strong, earthy scent of cacao, and the taste of the trinity— the over-the-top sweetness of the white chocolate, the smooth finish of milk, and the bitterness of the dark.

Daniel stared back at me, but at last, he looked away. "I think I need one more day."

"One more day?"

"To get the courage to ask you out. I'll be back tomorrow."

With those last words, Daniel slipped his earbuds in, retrieved his messenger bag, and hummed a lively jazz tune as he walked out the door.

Tomorrow couldn't come soon enough.

Yes, I was smitten.

And what would I cook for him tomorrow? Something interesting and new. My initial fascination had transformed into something I didn't want to identify. The attraction was strengthened even further by his passion for my dishes. He believed in me, and since I had lost my greatest champion in Ma-ma, I couldn't find a stronger aphrodisiac in the world. Tomorrow, I resolved to say yes and see where this would lead.

In the meantime, I needed to follow up with Older Shen and the Chius. If their situation was anything like what had happened with Celia, I should be in for a delightful surprise.

Chapter Twelve

Two days had passed since I cooked for Older Shen and the Chius. I hoped it wouldn't be too obvious to spy on them now. I headed out of the restaurant's kitchen, grabbing my purse on the way.

Right in front of the convenience store, Mr. and Mrs. Chiu were tangled together like two horny teenagers in a closet. From this angle, I couldn't tell where one ended and the other began. They weren't even coming up for air. Every few seconds, the missus kept trying and failing to launch her legs around her husband's waist. When Mr. Chiu's wandering hands traveled to cup his wife's buttocks to assist her, I decided it was time to duck back inside. I covered my mouth to smother a giggle.

The only difference between the Chius and the drawings in the *Kama Sutra* was that the former was clothed. Despite the secondhand embarrassment, I was grinning.

It had worked!

The gastronomical chemistry of Laolao's recipes that had once helped her community was now helping the neighbors through my hands. All of those people had come to the restaurant once, seeking aid and comfort, and Laolao had been able to help them. Here was the incontrovertible proof that I had helped. The last time I saw the Chius, they'd been arguing, and the passion seemed burnt out of their marriage. This was certainly an improvement.

Of course, I hadn't checked on Older Shen yet, but if Celia's luck changing and the Chius' romantic rekindling were any indication, the recipes were working. I was much closer to opening the restaurant and ensuring its success.

I still had to file the paperwork and look into whether the building needed to be inspected. After I addressed the technicalities, I should plan the grand opening, and it would only be fitting if it was marked by a huge feast with multiple courses. I wanted to invite all the neighbors and Daniel. But first I needed to see how Shen was doing, to make sure I truly had helped all three.

My phone buzzed in my purse. I fished it out and discovered a text from Celia.

Guang popped out of his herbal store and helped me pry Anita and Wayne apart so they wouldn't be arrested for indecent exposure. Did you see them?

I grinned and typed back.

Yes. What are you doing for dinner? I want to cook you something that's different from last night. I need your help with an idea I'm planning for the restaurant.

Celia wrote:

It's a date. Drop by after the shop closes at six. I have news. We have much to talk about.

I hoped her news involved more good fortune.

My happiness, unadulterated, rose above the clouds of my grief like the sun emerging after a thunderstorm. It was a perfect day. I only wished Ma-ma were here with me. She could have at least gotten a scandalous giggle watching the Chius' peep show from the window. Oh, how I missed her.

I headed back out to drop by Older Shen's bookstore. There was a sign on the door saying, "Closed for repairs." I peeked inside. He was perched on a ladder, fixing one of the cracked ceiling tiles. Drop cloths covered the bookshelves while boxes of new fluorescent tubes littered the floor.

I tapped the glass and waved.

He waved back, gesturing for me to come inside.

The floor was a land mine of loose parts, discarded cardboard, Bubble Wrap, and assorted tools. I tiptoed around a box of ceiling tiles to get a closer look. The strong smell of fresh paint dominated the space. A calming turquoise hue supplanted the eggshell on the walls. Three plastic-covered club chairs and an area rug had replaced the unused bookcases—a reading corner.

The bookstore was undergoing a renaissance.

"Mr. Shen, how are you?"

"Great. Do you like the new wall color?" He set down his screwdriver. "Maybe I should go bolder with teal or scarlet."

"No, no. This is perfect. Very soothing and conducive to reading."

Older Shen adjusted his collar. "I want to have local authors come in. Get more kids and families in here. That reminds me—the children's section needs to expand too."

The revitalization had also affected his wardrobe. He wore a sharp, peacock blue jacket with a black silk shirt over dark denim jeans.

"I love the changes you're making. It will be great for business," I said.

"I hope so," he replied. "I love books. The business is much tougher now than it was when my grandfather ran the store. I'm going to adapt and not let it die out."

I smiled.

I had helped him find his voice. *This* was the Older Shen who'd been hidden underneath the candied ginger and pistachio shells for all these years. He had found his courage, his boldness. Perhaps I really had fulfilled all of the conditions and could move ahead with my plans. Then the neighborhood, including my restaurant, would be saved from the real estate vultures who wanted to gentrify it.

The neighbors could have left at any time if they had wanted to, but roots ran deep. Because they'd stayed, their situations had grown more dire. If I had been in their shoes, I guiltily realized, I would have sold and run. "Why did you stay?"

"My family had always been here. My parents and their parents were a part of the business association. They taught us how important it is to be a part of the community. Guang and I are the only ones left: our cousins have all moved out to the suburbs to expand their families."

"I thought you were like Celia, that you liked running the store."

"I did. I'm starting to remember why I chose the bookstore in the first place." Shen picked up his screwdriver again. "Oh, I've also started doing something I've always wanted to do for years."

"What is it?"

"Ballroom dancing," he said, smiling.

The thought of Older Shen practicing the Viennese waltz or Argentine tango made me happy. With its romanticism, passion, and nobility, it was a pursuit worthy of him. I hoped I would get a chance to watch him in full regalia, twirling a partner in a frothy confection of sequins and silk.

"That's wonderful, Mr. Shen."

He blushed. "Are you ready to open the restaurant?"

"Not yet, but I'm working toward it."

"Good, because a new restaurant will do wonders for the neighborhood—especially if the chef is a Tan. You cook as well as your grandmother did."

Older Shen's compliment touched me. Warmth flooded my cheeks, and my vision clouded with unshed tears.

"Really?" I whispered.

He nodded. "It's in your blood."

It was. I was a Tan woman. My grandmother and my mother were strong. Their strength was mine.

With evening approaching, I grabbed my purse and headed to the market again for fresh fish. Celia was expecting a wonderful dinner, and I knew exactly what to cook for her. I picked out a fat red snapper whose crystalline scales rivaled the trendiest pieces in the jewelry district in SoMa. As I walked home, I heard the underlying sound of the erhu embedded in the soundscape of the busy intersection. I checked in the usual places, but Mr. Kuk Wah was nowhere to be found. I wanted to look for him, but I knew if I lingered too long, Celia's special dinner would suffer.

I returned upstairs to cook, bypassing the restaurant; perhaps because this was my own dish and not Laolao's. I was preparing inihaw isda, a recipe I had first tasted in Manila over an open fire pit.

My fingers caught the deep nick in the lower corners of the wooden cutting block. It was made by Ma-ma's cleaver when she'd sliced a stubborn piece of beef tendon. Though my mother was gone from this world, it gave me comfort that her presence lingered in every spice and utensil.

I reached for the two beefsteak tomatoes in the grocery bag. The shade of their skins bore a hint of orange, indicating the firmness of the juicy flesh within. My sharp blade sliced into the fruit: dripping, sticky, dotted with the jeweled seeds inside. I cut the flesh into tiny cubes as the scent of sunshine and vines filled the air. I transferred the tomatoes to a ceramic bowl before rinsing the board and knife clean.

Using the flat side of the blade, I smashed three cloves of garlic. The fragrant aroma teased my nostrils as I rolled a fat red onion onto the board. The papery amaranthine skin crinkled under my fingertips.

According to Ma-ma, the red onion contained too much chi, the reason it caused so many tears. She compared the red onion to Younger Shen—rich in color and bold in flavor. I never questioned her logic, for no other onion induced the same reaction.

I popped a strip of peppermint gum into my mouth. When I was very young, my mother had prepared a hot and spicy tofu dish that included a red onion. As always, I had stood by the counter, watching, waiting to steal a morsel. The instant her knife cut into the red onion, it was like a pipe burst within me, unleashing a torrent of tears. My mother picked me up by the armpits and carried me to the claw-foot tub in case my tears overflowed while she phoned and asked Mrs. Chiu to run a quick errand. Ma-ma returned to the bathroom with packs of peppermint gum from the Chius' convenience store. Whether it was the novelty of the chewing gum or the powers of my mother's secret knowledge, my tears soon stopped flowing.

I dispatched the onions into a neat pile of translucent half crescents as the artificial mint flavor coated my tongue. The next ingredient involved the bouquet of coriander resting at the edge of the counter.

I pulled a generous clump from the bunch and plucked the leaves from their stalks in my culinary version of he loves me/he loves me not.

I lifted the bowl to my nose and sniffed. This needed more garlic. I rechecked the ratio of ingredients and peeled three more garlic gloves. Tossing the components together, I set them aside and turned my attention to the fish.

First, I placed the cleaned snapper on a bed of aluminum foil sprinkled with sea salt and olive oil. I then stuffed the tomatoes, garlic, onions, and coriander into the belly of the fish before sewing it shut. The first time I'd tasted this, the snapper was skewered and turned over open flames. To accompany it, I'd drunk the sweet juice from young coconuts cut with machetes, taken off the very trees above us. Now that I was back to apartment living, I had to modify the recipe and grill the fish in a closed packet. The texture of the skin wouldn't be as crisp, but the flesh would be even more tender. If I had thought Celia preferred the crisp texture, I would have fried it with the stuffing mixture served on the side.

The fish was ready to be baked. I prepared sinanag, Filipino garlic fried rice, to accompany the fish: jasmine rice, smashed garlic cloves, sea salt, and a sprinkle of vegetable oil. Knowing Celia, she would love her apartment to be the theater for the meal—provided I could convince her to remove the stack of magazines currently in her oven.

"I come bearing gifts," I announced as Celia opened her front door for me.

She cooed over the mysterious foil packet resting in the baking pan. "Dinner cooked by someone else is the best kind of courtesy a guest can give."

We settled into the couch, waiting for the oven to heat up. Celia poured us both a glass of sparkling Italian blood orange sodas. She might not be able to cook, but her stock of beverages was impressive.

"You'd think the extraction process would have been easy today." Celia wrapped her arms around her middle and giggled. "But Anita had a death grip on Wayne's neck. Guang had to pull them apart. I have to say, though, I heard they were like this as teens. It was common to see them making out in odd places, and I believe your laolao even had to separate them at one point. I'm happy for them. I don't think they've spent much time with each other in the last decade."

I laughed. I couldn't help but be pleased with the results of my efforts. I had to tell Celia about the true nature of the recipes. "I did it," I declared in a loud whisper. "I did this."

Celia's eyes widened behind her glasses. Her mauve painted lips formed an O. "How?"

"Laolao's recipe book." I reached into my tote bag and produced my grandmother's book. "She has hundreds of recipes in here. When Miss Yu gave me the prophecy, she also gave me this from Ma-ma."

Celia gawked. She made a vague gesture that looked like a hybrid of the sign of the cross and Madonna's "Vogue" dance moves. "It's real. I always suspected your grandmother had a book because I caught her writing something down in the kitchen a few times."

"Do you want to read it?" I asked.

"No, no." She blushed. "It's a family heirloom. I feel honored enough that you trusted me to show me."

Celia had proven herself my only friend—one I had desperately needed since I lost Ma-ma. I'd never had many friends, even before I left home. Ma-ma had taught me that she and I were enough, and while we lived together, we had been. But in the last seven years on my own, I had learned that loneliness wasn't the best companion.

The scars from my father's abandonment had shaped me into

a paradox, someone who didn't want to be alone but still shut people out.

My mother had physically isolated herself from the world, and I'd done the same in my travels. I often wondered how much daughters emulated their mothers with or without their conscious control. Had I inherited Ma-ma's habit of human quarantine like I had inherited the shape of her face? I realized now that trust could be liberating, especially when placed with people like Celia who treated it with care. I had thought I was completely alone when I lost Ma-ma, but I wasn't. I had Celia. For a brief moment, I contemplated telling her about my meddling. There was still a secret between us. Although it worried me to keep something from her, I told myself that some good deeds were better left unsaid.

"Of course I trust you." I tucked the book away, my fingertips lingering over the embossed leather cover. "You mentioned you had news?"

"I think I have a solution for increasing business for the shop and the neighborhood."

I clapped my hands. "That's excellent! Tell me everything."

"This morning's tour bus was a blessing. I wondered what would happen if I could get regular traffic coming to my shop, so I started talking to the driver and the tour guide. They said they stopped here because of a specific request: probably from Old Wu's nephew. Apparently, he had to call in favors because over the years, our neighborhood has lost its appeal. For the last decade, the buses would drop off people at the paifang, then move them deeper into Chinatown, never stopping in front of the store like it did yesterday. Sure, we were lucky if we had a few stop by, but it wasn't enough."

"Why didn't you all do this earlier? Asking the buses to stop by?"

"We did. They weren't interested, and over the years, the local ones stopped taking our calls. Maybe the problem is that we didn't think big enough. This had me digging into out-of-town tour opera-tors. I think I have a solid plan that might save us all. If Old Wu's nephew can do this, so can I. I'll book the tour groups myself. I swear my luck has been on fire lately," she said.

"Luck is all about making the right choices. You're making your own good fortune," I remarked, feeling a pang of guilt for not telling her what I'd done.

Celia's smile brightened her lovely face. "I saw Daniel walk by. Do you have news too?"

"He said he'll ask me out tomorrow."

"Tomorrow? Why not today?"

"I don't know, but I'm nervous, so I'm okay with the delay," I confessed. "I like him a lot."

"He's adorable. And if I was younger—"

The oven dinged, leaving us laughing at the timely interruption.

Despite my warnings that it would take another forty-five min-utes, Celia parked a chair before the oven to stare into the window, watching the foil packet for any micro-reaction. As the fragrance of the fish diffused in the air, she moved closer, sniffing with the tenacity of a bloodhound.

"Snapper?" she asked.

I nodded.

When the timer rang out, Celia jumped to her feet, clearing out of the way so I could open the oven door. I pulled the pan out and placed it on the stovetop. The foil packet sighed as I pulled it open, hissing as it yielded its bounty. Clouds of steam puffed upward, releasing the tantalizing aroma into the air. The fish's reddish skin had a beautiful overlapping pattern that looked as if it had been painted by some way-ward mermaid. My sharp scissors snipped the stitches in its belly, spilling the filling onto the plate.

I scooped us both two helpings of the garlic fried rice and portioned the desirable parts of the fish, the head and the belly, for Celia, while I took the tail.

The piece of fish on my fork bore the sign of perfect execution: moist, milky translucence, and a silky texture that sprang to the touch. Infused with the fragrant stuffing, the tender fish melted in my mouth, dissolving in a mélange of delicious flavors—the trio of boldness from the coriander, garlic, and red onion tempered by the sweet tanginess of the tomatoes.

Success.

"Oh, this is divine," Celia purred. "I haven't had many Filipino dishes before. You'll have to remedy that."

"Thank you." I sighed. "I can't believe I'm getting ready to open the restaurant." Or that by doing so, I was putting down roots.

"This is for all of you," I said. "And for Ma-ma and Laolao."

"I am glad you stayed. Now you realize that you're one of us and we take care of one another." Celia patted the empty spot beside her on the couch.

After we finished eating, I loaded the dishwasher, turned it on, and returned to the living room to take my seat beside her. "I'm glad Ma-ma had your friendship when I was gone."

She squeezed my hand and sighed. "I think it's time I tell you what happened after you left home. The day you hopped on a plane, Anita told us that Miranda quarreled with you and that you'd left. We knew she was alone so we all helped. Fai came by once a week to drop off new books and magazines for her. Guang took over buying her groceries. Evelyn delivered teas and stopped in for frequent visits while I'd come over to watch K-dramas with her."

I hadn't known any of this. My face must have betrayed my distress because Celia squeezed my hand.

"She made us promise not to tell you. Your mother didn't want you to feel guilty and come home. Miranda loved you too much. Even though you had parted on ill terms, she didn't doubt that you'd come back eventually. She understood that you had to leave to pursue your dream, and she respected that."

Ma-ma, you weren't alone. They loved you. I smiled. My brilliant mother, who couldn't go outside, had brought the neighborhood inside instead.

Then a question escaped from me, something I had been keeping to myself for so long that it had eaten a hole in my heart and poisoned me. "Where were you all when I was younger? When Ma-ma couldn't get out of the house and I was left to pick up the pieces . . ."

"Oh, Natalie . . ." Celia embraced me. "I'm so sorry. We should have done more. We wanted to, but Miranda insisted that we leave you two alone. She didn't want our help. In hindsight, we should have been more adamant. Miranda was very angry back then because of your grandmother's death and your father's disappearance. She didn't want anyone's help. She shut us out for years."

A sob escaped, shaking my shoulders. After all this time, I thought they'd shunned us, yet it was Ma-ma who was responsible.

"I think when you left, she finally realized that we did care about her, and she let us in. Are you all right?" Celia asked.

I wiped the stray tears from my eyes. "Yes. It makes me happy knowing Ma-ma was in such good hands."

"We loved her. Miranda might have kept herself physically isolated, but she was never alone." Then Celia's eyes, through her tortoiseshell glasses, grew distant. "We should have done more. We should have insisted on helping, if only for your sake." Her elegant brows furrowed as if asking a silent question.

"What's wrong?" I asked.

"I still don't know why Miranda stepped outside the day she died.

It was so unlike her. I can't stop wondering what happened." She blushed. "I'm sorry. I shouldn't have brought it up."

I had wondered the same thing when I arrived. But to investigate further would only bring heartache, for there was no answer as to why Ma-ma had left the apartment. I had to come to terms with this.

"It doesn't matter now because we can't change the past; we can only alter the future." I cleared my throat and mustered a smile. "So, the restaurant . . ."

Celia brightened. "I am so happy you're doing this."

"I am not sure if the building needs to be inspected. I've done some research and filled out a ton of forms. I imagine there will be issues bringing the restaurant to code since it's so old."

"I wish I could help you, but I don't know much about the restaurant business," Celia confessed. "We can ask Old Wu. He's part of the business association. I can arrange the meeting if you want. It will have to be at his restaurant because he's so busy. You can make a good impression if you do this because of how traditional he is. He'll appreciate what you're doing and how good it would be for the neighborhood."

I wanted to say no, but, if I did, I would waste an important resource. I had no idea what I was about to do, and I needed help. After the explosive homecoming Old Wu had greeted me with, my reluctance in asking for his aid was natural. But I shouldn't turn any potential help away. "Yes, please," I said. "The worst he can do is say no."

Celia smiled. "He'll say yes. He knows the problems in the neighborhood. He'll want to help. For years, the business association has tried to reinvigorate our corner of Chinatown and fight off gentrification, but nothing's worked. Your restaurant might be the key to it all."

Her belief in my abilities mirrored Daniel's. I didn't understand the source of their confidence.

"Why do you believe in me so much?"

"Because this is what you're meant to do," she replied. "You cook like your grandmother, which means you cook from your heart. Your food is so delicious because of how much care and joy you put into it. Don't even think about dismissing the compliment. I'm an authority on eating food, and I know what I'm talking about."

Seeing how I looked in her eyes made me want to believe in that reflection. If only Ma-ma had told me something similar. I could have stayed home, gone to culinary school, and opened the restaurant with her blessing, staying close the whole time.

"I'm not arguing," I said.

She wasn't the only one who'd said they believed in me; so did the people Ma-ma tasked me to help, her neighbors. My neighbors too.

After coming home from Celia's, I settled in to do some late-night research. Armed with a cup of oolong, I sat on the sofa with the laptop on the coffee table. The cat jumped onto the table and moved to the side of the screen, tracking the cursor, batting it with her paws, wondering why she couldn't hold it down. "Do you think you can fill out the paperwork for me?" I asked her.

She meowed and stuck her little pink tongue out.

"Not even for catnip? I can get you one of those fish things stuffed with it. I hear cats find it very exciting."

I picked her up. The cat crawled out of my arms and climbed onto my chest. She placed a paw against my lips.

"All right, no catnip. Dumplings then?"

She purred.

"You have the same taste as Daniel, little one."

Meimei tilted her head toward the printer. I sighed. "Let's get back to work."

I sorted the forms I would be mailing out from those I needed to submit in person. I rechecked my to-do list to make sure I hadn't missed anything. I had: the neighborhood notification for the planning department in the city. I didn't think much of it when I first read it since I doubted my neighbors would object. But now a fearsome thought entered my mind: Old Wu, although his restaurant didn't face Grant Avenue, could still be classified as a neighbor. He could provide the opposition I dreaded when applying. Celia was planning to ask him to help me, but I feared instead he would only stand in my way.

To banish bad thoughts about the old man, I immersed myself in the joys of research by checking out the websites of the restaurants in the area. I opened a notebook and began taking notes about pricing, common menu items, and hours of operation, and started a running tab of ideas of how to set myself apart from the competition.

I went to bed with Meimei asleep on my belly. The dreams I had that night were of the restaurant and Daniel. He had said he was coming back tomorrow to ask me out. What should I cook for him?

Chapter Thirteen

In the morning, it came to me. I went down to the restaurant and cooked youtiao, my favorite treat. It wasn't one of Laolao's recipes, but a dish Ma-ma had served that never failed to bring me sprinkles of happiness. There was much to celebrate: Older Shen's revitalization efforts for his bookstore, the Chius' marriage, Celia's upturn of luck, and my being closer to my goal, even though the nagging fear of Old Wu still weighed heavily on my mind.

Hot oil bubbled in the wok as the pale, thin strips of dough took their plunge. My chopsticks snapped into action. I rolled the dough, spinning, turning the pieces so each side cooked evenly. Soon, the raw beige gave way to golden sunbursts, with each ray tipped in crisp light brown. They floated to the surface like wayward pool noodles only to be rescued by my intrepid chopsticks.

I heaped three onto a plate to bring upstairs to the family shrine.

I delivered the youtiao and sent a quick prayer to Ma-ma. Back downstairs in the restaurant, I resisted the urge to sit by the window until Daniel arrived, and distracted myself by leafing through my grandmother's recipe book. I didn't want to appear desperate despite the fact that I would be horribly disappointed if he didn't show up.

Yesterday, I was afraid he wouldn't come too.

How long would it be until he arrived?

I busied myself by arranging and rearranging the fritters on a platter. Keeping an eye on the time on my phone, I managed to create seven different patterns with the long donut sticks with my trembling hands. Anticipation battled dread in the arena of my stomach.

Finally, the tiny bell at the door rang. I peeked into the dining room to see that Daniel had walked in. I exhaled a long sigh of relief. He wore his telltale earbuds and the wide strap of his messenger bag over one shoulder. My heartbeat accelerated like a hummingbird seeking the nectar of a flower.

"I haven't had youtiao in a long time. That's what I smell, isn't it?" He grinned.

I returned to the kitchen to gather the donut sticks, piling them onto a large oval plate. I poured him a glass of cold soybean milk to go along with the snack. I wanted to join him, but out of shyness I followed my usual protocol: unload the food on the counter, return to the kitchen to avoid gawking at him eating, and then come back to collect payment. However, despite my good intentions, I accidentally caught a glimpse of his first ecstatic bite. Heat blossomed from my neck and my collarbones, exposed above the white crocheted tank dress I was wearing. I reached into the fridge for the pitcher of ice water, downing it in a few gulps as the usual billows of steam rolled off my skin, puffing upward as if from the stack of a small locomotive. How could I go on a date with him without suffering a battery of embarrassing side effects?

Pursuing a romance with Daniel presented more challenges than I'd previously imagined. My former boyfriends had never elicited anything more than a slight wobble in the stomach, replicated easily by eating questionable street fare. Even with Emilio, my longest relationship, I had never reacted this way. But I found myself nearly combusting as I watched Daniel eat—almost as if I were watching pornography. What was it about him that made me feel this way? What if he kissed me? Would I burst into flames?

Maybe this time, I wouldn't ruin my own relationship. This fear had caused me to run in the past, but I didn't want to flee from Daniel. I wanted to find out what happened next.

Yes, I was still scared. But I wanted to risk it.

Daniel was finishing up as I walked back into the dining room.

Was he leaving already? Had he forgotten about the date?

"Come on." He held out his hand.

"What?"

Daniel tilted his head toward the door. "Let's go for a walk."

I placed my hand in his. I was afraid the contact would result in an incendiary mishap, but nothing out of the ordinary happened. He had a warm, firm grip, banishing the memories of all the clammy, sweaty hands I had held in the past.

We walked underneath the Dragon's Gate and headed west along Bush Street.

"Where are we going?" I asked.

His brilliant smile showcased either perfect genes or an excellent orthodontist. "I want to take you to the heart."

He meant the heart in Union Square. In 2004, a heart sculpture had been displayed there to raise money for San Francisco General Hospital. It began with one and multiplied into many around the square and the city. It was one of the things I'd missed while away from home but kept up with online. Seeing a different artist paint multiple hearts every year brought me joy because I saw these sculptures as stand-ins for a real, physical heart—that the beauty within the rib cage could manifest in such riotous colors. I hadn't seen them yet this year. How did Daniel know I cared so much about this place?

Summer in San Francisco was comfortable compared to other places I had been. August in most countries above the equator was punishing, leaving residents in a viscous state between solid and liquid. But here, the breeze teased the trees, rustling the green leaves and stirring the birds.

A pair of goldfinches trilled overhead, following us, hopping from windowsill to windowsill, until they flew away, ushering in a couple of mourning doves. The carousel of birds continued, species after species, trailing behind as we neared Union Square.

"Do you see the birds?" I tugged on Daniel's hand. "Look at the blackbirds over there. They're coming in pairs."

Perched on top of the awning of a nearby bistro, blackbirds with ruby red paint strokes on their wings chirped merrily.

Daniel tilted his head and studied them. "I've never seen this happen before. It's like a fairy tale, isn't it? Perhaps a great omen for what's to come?" He resumed humming an unfamiliar song, one he'd begun the moment we crossed the Dragon's Gate.

"What is that tune? I don't think I know it."

He tilted his head. "I'm not sure."

"Whatever it is, it's nice." I tipped my head toward the birds. "It seems like we've attracted an audience."

Daniel smiled as we made our way into the square and toward the heart sculpture. He never walked ahead of me. Instead, he matched my steps, walking along at my side, often glancing down to make sure I was still there, as if our linked hands weren't proof enough.

"When I was a kid, I carried this stuffed animal around everywhere with me. I can't remember what kind it was because even in pictures it was tattered beyond recognition." He tilted his head toward the birds. "My father kept throwing it into the washing machine to wash away whatever adventures I had with it that day. My mother mended it until she got tired of it and taught me how to do it myself with a thread and needle. She called it surgery practice."

A grin spread across my face. "What did you call your little friend, and what sort of adventures did you have?"

"Birdie. To be fair, I stuck to a theme. I named my toy dog Doggie and my plastic pig Piggie. As for the adventures, they're classified, but I *can* tell you that they involved a lot of traipsing in the mud, dirt, and sand."

"You had toys and I had books. I loved my comics. My favorite is *Lao Fu Zi.*"

He returned my smile. "Ah yes, the old man and his band of misfit friends. My father loved them too—he kept them on the coffee table."

"I always wondered why the main character seemed to fall in love with ghost women."

"Ghost women have their allure. I see it." The heat of Daniel's gaze settled on me.

I blushed. "You do know I'm not a ghost."

"Oh, I know," he said. "You're real, all right."

We stopped at one of the hearts in the square. The current version was made to appear like frosted glass. I walked toward it and reached out to touch the smooth surface. Iridescent pigments swirled underneath the fiberglass. Stunning.

"It reminds me of the ocean," Daniel said. "What you see inside of a seashell."

I nodded. "It's lovely. I wish I had found something like this on a sandy beach somewhere. Can you imagine such a treasure?"

"I can." He was staring at me, holding me in his eyes.

A silence rolled in and blanketed the city, blotting out the chatter of strangers, the drone of traffic, the tinkling of leaves, and even the sound of my own breath and heartbeat. The instant of clarity before the exhale.

He took my other hand in his, pulling me closer, and leaned in for a kiss.

I had feared when his lips brushed against mine that I would catch fire from the fever burning under my skin. Instead, a slow hiss escaped as steam released into the air from our heat. My heart sang, fluttering in my chest in joy. *This* was what I had been missing. If I could kiss him forever, it would still not be long enough. In that moment, he was everything I wanted and needed.

And so we kissed behind a veil of our own making. The fog rolled off our skin and into the city.

After the kiss, I could no longer trust my senses. My internal compass spun, whizzing, only pausing to point in his general direction. The kiss, the fog, the bliss. Daniel made me believe that I didn't have to be alone.

We stopped at the paifang to say our goodbyes. His army of gadgets chimed and buzzed. He needed to go back to work, but he lingered for a moment longer, his shy smile tugging at his lips. "I'm leaving for a tech conference tomorrow, but I'll be back in a few days."

"What do you do exactly?" I asked.

"I'm the senior VP of software engineering at the company. It's a hybrid of coding work and managing people under me. The title is lofty." He laughed. "When I get back, how about having our first date?"

"This wasn't our first date?"

He shook his head. "I'll need the extra days to plan. How about noon on Thursday, and I'll drive us there."

I said yes.

Chapter Fourteen

Celia was tidying up her shelves when I arrived to tell her about my walk. When the final bridge figurine was turned the right way, she turned toward me. Her perfume of gardenia and lilac hung in the air. She wore a yellow frock also patterned with gardenias.

"Are these new?" I asked. "That means the tour group bought a ton of stuff."

"They did," she replied. "But I need plenty more busloads before I can start seeing profits again. The sooner you open the restaurant, the better—we need every tourist draw we can get."

I took a deep breath and exhaled. "The neighborhood notification is really worrying me. Everything could fall apart before I can even start."

"But we all want you to open. You're not going to get any opposition."

"I'm concerned about Old Wu," I said, finally giving voice to my fear.

He was the only person who might block me from reopening, and he had enough clout to do it. Old Wu would be my competitor, and he'd never disguised his distaste for me. I didn't have the financial means to fight him or the courage to do so. And yet Celia wanted to arrange a meeting with him. How could I face someone who could only see me for all my failures?

Celia scrunched her nose. "Technically, he's part of the neighborhood, but he wouldn't do that. He knows how bad it is for us, and blocking you would hurt the chances of reviving our businesses. He's going to help you, not hurt you."

"I hope you're right." I tried to be optimistic but I was still concerned.

"If he doesn't, I'll stand by you and so will the others. You'll see," Celia said. "Oh, I saw you take a walk with a very handsome young man earlier. How are things progressing with Daniel? Well, I hope."

"I think so. We're going on a date on Thursday when he comes back from his conference."

Celia giggled and clapped her hands. "Excellent! I told you that you can have it all. Ah, and after the romantic drought you've suffered. Oh, that reminds me! I have news!"

"What is it?"

"I have a meeting with one of the tour companies later. I'm following up on my hunch. I know it'll pay off."

I pushed the fear of Old Wu interfering with the restaurant away for a moment to soak in Celia's revelation. She seemed to have found her stride. She was definitely excited about her newest venture. And with the increased traffic, the rest of the neighbors would benefit as well.

After saying goodbye to Celia, I headed back to the restaurant. I remembered the kiss I'd shared with Daniel. Our date was in a few days. I couldn't be happier as far as our relationship was concerned. Things were trending upward, imbuing me with hope and elation, yet part of me still worried I would ruin it all somehow.

Mr. Kuk Wah stood across the street with his prized erhu in tow. The colorful tattoos on his arms contrasted beautifully with the palette of muted grays of his wardrobe. The street musician's smile illuminated his entire being, so much so that I couldn't help smiling in return.

I let him into the restaurant.

"My wife is talking to me again, and I have you to thank," he declared, following me inside.

"I helped you?"

"Yes. She's talking to me now. It's been years since we last spoke."

"That's excellent news!" I clapped my hands.

Mr. Kuk Wah tucked his erhu under the counter and took a seat.

"So, tell me everything." I leaned across the counter with my chin resting on my hands.

"My wife is very superstitious. She tends to believe in curses, and that's probably why she hasn't spoken to me. She thought I was cursed somehow, but something has changed recently. I don't know what, but all of a sudden she answered my calls. She spoke to me and remembered she loved me."

My heart swelled, expanding in my rib cage as I listened to Mr. Kuk Wah's story of love resurrected. My advice helped him. This was how Laolao's recipes were intended—to heal, to repair relationships, and bring people back together.

"Now I want to help you. I want to repay the debt. Is there anything you need help with?" he asked.

"Yes, yes, there is," I confessed. "I'm afraid I'll self-sabotage this wonderful thing with someone special."

He took off his flat cap and placed it on the counter.

"Is it possible that the past can repeat itself?" I asked. "I have a date with Daniel. I'm thrilled, but also afraid of committing past sins. Once I caused a great deal of pain to a good man, and now it's almost like I don't feel worthy of this new relationship."

"Everyone is worthy and deserving of love. Look at me! My wife is talking to me again, and I thought I had screwed up my marriage a long time ago. You've proven there is always hope for redemption." He asked, "What happened?"

"I was afraid and I left Emilio at the altar. I can never forgive myself for the pain I caused him," I replied. "What if I'm not meant to be in love because I hurt the one I'm supposed to care about?"

"I sincerely doubt that." Mr. Kuk Wah stroked the stubble along his jaw. "I'd like to think you have learned from your mistakes. We all do. That's the only good outcome from making mistakes, isn't it?"

"Is it fair that I ruined Emilio's life, yet I get a second chance at happiness with Daniel?"

"It's not mutually exclusive. I understand that we Chinese love misery and self-flagellation, but we also should seek every scrap of joy we can get. Allow me to put it this way: would you want Daniel to suffer because of this Emilio?"

I snorted. "Of course not."

"Then go on your date. You will solve their problems afterward," he advised. "Have some happiness for yourself. Go on your date, Xiao Niao."

"I will." I was nervous, but I would try. It seemed to be the time for new beginnings.

"If you need further advice, I will ask my wife. She has always been wiser than I will ever be. She'll think of something."

I smiled. "I'm glad she's talking to you again."

Mr. Kuk Wah was right. My opportunity to alter the course of my romantic life was in a few days, and I needed to make the most of it.

Chapter Fifteen

I left my dark hair down in thick waves and chose a strapless, bohemian maxidress. It was a feminine piece Celia had picked out. If I ever needed to go shopping again, I'd ask her to come with me. Her eye for fashion was unparalleled. I finished the outfit with a pair of plain gold earrings, matching bangles, and gladiator sandals.

The cat loved the bangles and the sound they made as they shifted on my arm.

I refilled her food and water bowls before heading downstairs to the restaurant to wait for Daniel.

He arrived five minutes before noon. My heart jumped when I saw the smile on his face. Daniel carried a bouquet of powder pink peonies. His outfit today was a crisp, long-sleeved plaid shirt over a solid white tee and dark jeans. If his clothes were ever drying on the line, it would be a dream to bury my face in the fabric, inhaling his intoxicating scent of chocolate, spearmint, and coffee.

I opened the door.

"Hi." His dark eyes drank me in. "These are for you." He handed me the bouquet.

"Thank you." I lowered my face into the soft petals. "How did you know I love these?" I placed the flowers in an empty vase I found in the restaurant's kitchen before grabbing my purse from the counter.

"I was torn between these or hydrangeas. I wanted something big, lots of petals: what a cloud would look like in flower form. You can imagine how the florist reacted when I described it." His sheepish grin caused me to smile.

"Why clouds?" I asked.

"Because you belong in the sky among the stars."

My feet floated off the ground as we walked outside. There was an earnestness about him that seemed to stem from the conviction with which he approached life. Daniel seemed to have a steady compass, one I both envied and admired.

"Where are we going?" I asked, locking up.

"To an art gallery. My friend has an exhibit, and judging by the way you loved the flowers, I hope you'll enjoy it."

An art gallery. Ma-ma mentioned once that her first date with my father had been in the same setting after I told her our fourth-grade class had a field trip to the art museum. It had started there and ended in the destruction of my parents' marriage. A sense of foreboding tugged at me, but I brushed it away. I needed to trust the man who held my hand and whose eyes gazed at me with such care.

He drove us to our destination in the Marina District. Pockets of blue from the bay were reflected in the windows of the small building. Inside, there were swatches of sheer white fabric concealing the view of the exhibition sign, which read: "Petals: An exhibition by Swapna Mehta."

Daniel held the door open for me as we headed inside. The interior was cooler than I had expected. Daniel removed his overshirt and settled it on my shoulders. I was enveloped by the warmth from his body heat and comforting scent.

"You forgot, didn't you?" A petite, Indian American woman with a dazzling smile walked over and gave Daniel a playful smack on the arm. "I told you on the phone to make sure she brings a sweater."

He smiled and introduced me. "Swapna, this is Natalie. Natalie, this is Swapna, the artist herself."

Swapna extended her hand. Her dark eyes sparkled. She wore a long, aqua knit sweater over white culottes. Very artsy and lovely. "Pleasure to meet you. Daniel said the nicest things about you."

I couldn't stop the fountain of glee from bubbling inside me. He had been thinking of me as much as I had of him. I shook her hand. "Nice to meet you as well."

"The exhibit is pretty straightforward. You'll understand soon why we have to keep it cold in here." She waved to someone by the entrance. "I'm sorry, I have to go. I hope you two enjoy yourselves."

Daniel and I entered the first room. I gasped. On the largest wall, pressed between circular sheets of glass, were petals of every color imaginable forming a mandala. The explosion of colors complemented the complexity of the arrangement. The air was filled with the heady smell of a full, floral garden.

"It's so beautiful," I said.

Daniel walked alongside me. "Swapna knows what she's doing. She went to the Rhode Island School of Design before moving here. She did this all herself. It took months of planning. Like you, she's found her true calling. It's amazing to see when that happens."

"Running a restaurant is a lot more complicated than I thought." I pulled my attention away from the mandala. "I feel like the odds are already stacked against me, but I think I have it under control. It would have been helpful if I had finished culinary school."

"You can cook. Everything else, you can learn. Sure, papers, degrees, or certificates are great, but it's not the only way to get things done. A few of my friends don't have computer science degrees, yet they run very successful tech corporations."

We walked to the next room. This installation was a floor rug made of petals. Alternating colors of purples and golds formed the main border while the field was an ombré sea of blues and fuchsias. A center medallion was composed of gold and scarlet tulips. The design reminded me of Islamic mosaics I'd seen in pictures of the Alhambra in Spain. Swapna's palette was intensely vibrant.

The weight of my confession pressed against my better judgment. I shouldn't have burdened Daniel with my worries. "I'm a horrible first date for dumping my problems on you. Please, just ignore what I said."

"I want you to succeed in your restaurant. Of course, I'll help." His dark eyes bored into mine. "You care about this, so I care about this. It's that simple."

The third room showcased a rain shower. Blue hydrangea petals were suspended from the ceiling via invisible fishing lines, like raindrops. There must have been thousands of them, and the effect was breathtaking. The sound of a gentle rain shower filtered through the stereo system. Magical.

"This is one of the most beautiful dates I've ever been on," I said. "I never imagined flowers could be transformed this way."

"Now you know why I had such a hard time finding the right experience for you. Three of those floral raindrops, I am responsible for. I had to learn how to sew on the fly. Swapna had me prove my friendship via needlework."

We held hands and walked into the final room. Inside was a snow white wedding gown made of gardenia and rose petals. The twelve-foot-long train bisected the room, reminiscent of the central aisle of a church. The silhouette of the dress was the same shape I would have worn if I had married Emilio that day. Guilt punched me in the gut.

"Are you all right?" Daniel asked.

He must have noticed the change in my expression. I could have chosen to keep my mouth shut and remain silent, but I didn't.

"It looks like the wedding dress I had. I was engaged once, but I never made it down the aisle." I stopped. I never even had the chance to tell Ma-ma about it. At the time, I planned to tell her, and if I had gone through with it, we would have had a ceremony at the apartment for my mother's sake. But the wedding never happened, and my guilt for keeping it from her disappeared along with a future I once envisioned. Had I made a mistake again in disclosing too much to Daniel too soon? Once revealed, the truth expanded, free of its cage. Trying to coax it back in was as futile as trying to shove toothpaste back into the tube.

"Can you tell me what happened?" he asked.

"I wasn't ready. I should have told him how I felt before everything was set. If I could do it all over again, we'd take the relationship slower. I didn't want to hurt him, but I did."

"It's in the past. You're here now, and I for one am glad you didn't get married. Things have a way of working out. A few months ago, I thought I'd be living in Seattle. I got a job offer there and was thinking of accepting it, but I didn't. If I had, I wouldn't have met you."

"There's something refreshing about living your life without regrets, isn't there?" I asked.

"I agree. I never want to say the words 'if only.' It would mean that I'd missed out on something very important to me."

He meant me. I was the important thing. Was this how Ma-ma

had felt? Accepting love and feeling worthy of it? My mother knew she'd found her mate almost instantly. It had taken me a few more meetings, but I was coming to a similar conclusion. I could only hope that I didn't screw this up somehow by running away.

After the art gallery, we headed in search of Daniel's favorite food truck. He'd promised me the best cabeza tacos I'd ever taste. We grabbed two orders and two sodas before finding a picnic table near the water. The tacos were juicy and heavy on the cilantro, which I loved.

He leaned over and wiped a spot of sauce near my chin. "Good?"

"Very good," I replied. "You know that I'm an only child. How about you?"

"One older sister. Alana lives in St. Paul with her wife, Helen. She's a physiotherapist with her own clinic. They have two boys, Matty and Tim. I try to see them as much as I can. My parents moved to Minnesota to be closer to their grandkids. My sister tells me that I get custody of our parents when I have kids."

I laughed. He sounded like he was quite close to his family despite their being thousands of miles away. Ma-ma would have loved him. "Do you want to have kids eventually?"

"I'd be happy with one or five. You?"

"I want a daughter. Anything more will be a blessing."

He smiled. "A mini version of you would be adorable."

I could get lost in his eyes and his words, the way sincerity rang through each look and compliment. I felt spoiled, like a child with carte blanche in a sweet shop. It was a foreign and exhilarating sensation.

"Why are you being so wonderful to me?" I asked him.

"Because you're worth waiting for."

Daniel leaned across the table. His handsome face hovered inches from mine. The air around us popped with bubbles, evanescent, floating like miniature balloons. The same kind that were populating the soda bottle by his hand.

I inched closer. The instant my lips touched his, the bubbles hovering in the air exploded into minuscule fireworks. The sound of fizzing erupted around us, waves and waves rising from the cool glass, bursting into stars. Bliss.

We walked along the waterfront and counted the boats in the marina.

I didn't want the date to be over. I yearned to know more about this wonderful man who held my hand and my heart. "Why don't I come over and cook you dinner?"

He smiled. "We'll have to hit the grocery store beforehand. My fridge is pretty empty unless you count the random condiments and bottles of iced tea."

"You can't cook?" I feigned shock by pressing a hand to my chest.

"Mac and cheese. Out of the box. And possibly ramen. Even then, it's touch and go."

"Let's go get supplies then. Prepare to be dazzled."

He smiled at me. "I already am."

After a trip to the nearest Asian supermarket, we headed for his condo. Daniel owned a two bedroom near Valencia Street in the Mission District close to his work. It was one of those narrow builds that had more levels than square footage. No wonder Daniel kept in great shape; he walked to work every day in addition to climbing stairs.

The clean and tidy spaces showed a minimalist aesthetic. Framed vintage sci-fi movie posters and the modern light fixtures added pockets of color. I lingered and studied the family pictures hanging against the wall by the staircases. The order of the shots was chronological, with the most recent ones taken at a family vacation in Hawaii. Daniel, his sister, her wife, their two kids, and his parents all sported sun-kissed smiles by the beach.

"I love that you're close to your family." I straightened one of the frames by tipping the bottom right corner down.

"I don't know what I'd do without them. We all still take trips together every winter." He set down a bag of groceries to point to a picture of his parents. "They've been married for thirty-three years. When my friends' parents were divorcing, mine stayed united. I asked my dad about it, and he told me that it's because he and Mom are a team. It explains why the childish tactic of asking the other one for a different answer never worked."

"I wish my parents were like yours." Envy coated my words the way powdered sugar clung to a beignet. "I loved my mother, but I never knew my father. He left us before I was born."

"I'm sorry," Daniel said.

"He made his choice. He's out there in the world living his own life without a thought about what he left behind. I don't know anything about him, not even his name, because Ma-ma never talked about him."

"Your mother was a very strong woman. I wish I had had a chance to meet her."

And with those words, the brief shadow of my father's abandonment vanished in my mind. I smiled. "I think she would have liked you."

"Maybe you'll get to meet mine one day."

The kitchen and dining area were on the second level. Daniel's kitchen was empty of nutritional food, but like Celia's cupboards, it was packed with snacks: roasted seaweed, potato chips, candy, cookies, chocolates, and sugared cereals.

I washed my hands at the sink. "Your nephews must love it when they come over."

"Both my sister and mother are horrified at my diet. They're very grateful I have a good income to make up for my deficiencies in the kitchen."

He pointed me toward the cupboards that housed beautiful, pristine cookware: a set of pots, pans, even a roaster. I brought out a small pot and a wok. "These are aspirational, aren't they?"

"My mother insisted." Daniel leaned against the counter. "I may have used the skillet once or twice in my attempt to cook eggs."

"Since you're here, you might as well help me cook. Maybe you'll learn something."

Like I had at Celia's, I'd be cooking one of my own dishes, as the magical side effects were from Laolao's recipes, not mine. At the supermarket, I decided to make classic comfort food: mapo tofu and fried eggplant with garlic sauce. The former was my idea and the latter Daniel's request.

Daniel might not appreciate most of what his mother had bought him, but I was thankful for her generosity. The prospect of making a decent meal without proper tools and equipment was daunting.

After demonstrating how, I tasked him with chopping the eggplants. His dark brows furrowed as he approached the assignment with care. By the time he finished, I'd already started stir-frying the ground pork and chilies for the mapo tofu. We worked side by side, Daniel listening intently as I explained what I was doing. His thoughtful questions reflected his consumption of foodie documentaries, books, and articles.

"I've always been fascinated by the lack of measurements. It seems to be the common sign of a true chef." He took out two large bowls and two plates from the upper cupboards. "My parents shared cooking duties. They made decent meals, but it was always from someone else's recipes."

I dipped a spoon into the spicy mapo tofu and blew across it to cool it down. "Here, taste."

He hurried over to my side. "This is my favorite part."

I slid the spoon through his parted lips. He let out a honeyed *mmm*. "Good?"

"Not as good as the chef herself."

Daniel slid his arms around my waist before lowering his head to kiss me.

The bite of the red chilies from the sauce lingered on his lips. He tasted like everything I always wanted and needed. While I drowned in his kisses, a glowing warmth radiated from our skin, sending tiny bursts outward like a Fourth of July sparkler.

If this was love, let me disintegrate into a thousand beams of light in the night sky.

After the early dinner, I returned to the apartment humming the tune the birds had sung as Daniel and I walked in the park. I dropped off my purse and picked up the cat, holding her against me in a joyful dance.

"I really like him, Meimei," I whispered to the purring ball of fur against my neck. "He's wonderful. I know you'll like him, too, when you finally meet him."

The cat kept purring.

"I'll figure out a date. It'll be soon, I promise."

A sharp argument drew my attention to the street below. I moved toward the windows.

The Chius.

Chapter Sixteen

Out on the street, I heard them before I saw them.

The Chius stood arguing outside of their store. Miniature fire-crackers popped in the air. I ducked out of view but couldn't help wincing from the explosions.

Mr. Chiu placed his hands on his hips. "Come home, Anita. This is ridiculous. You can't keep staying out of the house because we're quarreling."

"You don't love me enough." Mrs. Chiu wagged her finger at her husband. "I have sacrificed so much for you because I love you. You say you love me more, then show me!"

"How can I show you if you won't come home?"

"What have you given up?" She reached out to her husband and tugged on his sleeve. "I always set aside my needs to accommodate yours. When was the last time I visited my family in Buffalo?"

He pulled his arm away. "You never asked. I thought you—"

"Do I have to ask, Wayne? I haven't seen them in over five years. You know they can't come to visit me because it's too expensive. I missed my nephew's graduation from law school, my niece's wedding, and my sister . . . When she was sick, I couldn't go to her side." She sobbed. "If you loved me as much as you claim to, you would put me first every once in a while."

"How can you question my love for you? How can you doubt our marriage?" Mr. Chiu covered his eyes. "This isn't a matter of checks and balances. You don't quantify love."

"Easy to say when you're not the one always at a deficit. I'm the one with the shortfall. Me. And this is why I'm not coming home." Mrs. Chiu balled her fists and walked away, leaving her husband alone to collect himself.

Fine lines formed under Mr. Chiu's loafers. They spread out in tiny cracks, chipping away at the smooth surface of the sidewalk. The fractures branched out in a spiderweb formation, a miniature earthquake without the seismic vibrations, carving out the hardened concrete as if it were made of candy glass. The lines stretched onto another block of sidewalk, then another, until it reached the road and stopped.

Mr. Chiu retreated into his store.

The scars on the sidewalk lingered, an ugliness marring what was once something smooth and whole. What was happening with Laolao's recipe? It was supposed to help my neighbors. I had followed the recipe to the letter. I had seen it work.

Celia had been fine. Were the Chius the outliers? What about Older Shen? Why was this happening? I thought the recipes worked. I wondered whether Miss Yu had placed her confidence in the wrong person.

Miss Yu. She would be the perfect person to help me.

I rushed to the tea shop and yanked on the door handle. It rattled, but didn't budge. Locked. A handwritten sign was taped to the glass: "Out for the day." I leaned against the locked door and sighed. The grayness of the neighborhood was spreading, enveloping everything with a nothingness. I rubbed my eyes, but the blur lingered, rubbing out the details: the mortar between the bricks, the art deco architectural features, even the dragons on the lampposts. They were vanishing.

We were vanishing.

I ran toward Older Shen's bookstore to check on him.

The bookstore was empty. The recent bustle of repairs had stopped: no sign of tools or paint cans anywhere. New recessed lighting installed in the ceiling illuminated bare shelving while the walls sported a deeper, richer hue of turquoise than I had seen last. The store was perfect except for the alarming lack of books. Paperbacks, journals, magazines, newspapers, even community newsletters had disappeared.

Older Shen stood beside the counter. He toyed with his phone, swiping and clicking as if wielding a remote control for a nonexistent flat-screen. A heavy cast wrapped around his left calf, and a pair of crutches was under his arms.

"Mr. Shen, what happened?" I asked.

He glanced up and pointed at the cast. "Hello, Natalie. Ah, you mean this?"

I nodded. My stomach wobbled as blood rushed to my cheeks. Had I caused this like I had the Chius' separation?

"Renovations. Recessed lighting adds more value than the fluorescent lighting." He set his phone aside. "I also changed the color of the wall. It needed to be bolder. Much more appealing, don't you think?"

"Yes, your customers will love this."

He leaned over, holding a hand beside his mouth, and mock whispered, "It's not for the customers."

My stomach lurched, pitching forward as if I were on a roller coaster, heading for a precipitous descent. "Who is it for?"

"Prospective buyers! I've been checking over the listings for commercial buildings. The prices have gone up, and I could sell this place for a lot more than I ever hoped for. Ms. Minnows has been very helpful. I can retire in style and travel the world like I've always wanted to do."

Melody Minnows. It was as I feared. If Older Shen sold the business, his store would be the foothold for those who wanted to gentrify us, converting the building to office space or overpriced condos. Once one business owner sold, more would follow until this neighborhood died. The community derived its strength from being whole. Like the Dragon's Gate, Older Shen and the others were intrinsic to this street.

"Mr. Shen, you can't listen to Ms. Minnows. She may not have your best interests or the community's interest in mind," I said.

Older Shen looked around. "For years, I've been tethered to this place. Perhaps it's time to move on, to try something new, and see what else is out there." He nodded. "Change can be good, right?"

"Sometimes, but I think you're making a mistake. You said you wanted to improve your business, and the changes you've proposed will make it better. Besides, don't you want to be here to see the results of your efforts?"

His brow furrowed. "It's easier to sell. Why struggle when there is a better way? There is no pride in eking out a living. Longevity isn't admirable if it's a result of mediocrity. Haven't we all been the same way? The neighborhood has been struggling for decades. It was never the same once your laolao died and the restaurant closed. The tourists dried up. Why stay if it means financial ruin and misery?"

"I still have hope that things are meant to turn out better. Isn't it more commendable to fight than give up?"

"Perhaps, but it's time to start thinking about myself and not what everyone else thinks is best for me. I can walk away a rich man, and after years of hard work, I deserve it. It's wiser to know when to walk away."

His words burrowed into my being. Walking away was my modus operandi.

I understood what it was like to need freedom. I would be a hypocrite to argue, so I kept my silence.

"I'm sorry I've upset you," he said. "Sometimes, there are things you just can't prevent from happening: natural disasters, death, economic downturns. You do what you need to do to survive and adapt. Ms. Minnows says the sale will increase all of our property values. A business is a tricky thing, as you will see soon enough when you run the restaurant."

How could I tell him that his decision to sell his bookstore on Ms. Minnows's advice had shattered my dreams of opening? How selfish was I that I only wanted him to stay for all the wrong reasons when he should have the right to choose what was best for himself?

Had I helped the neighbors with the solution that I'd wanted for them instead of what they actually needed?

All I knew for sure was that now I had failed both the Chius and him, three of the people I had chosen to help. This wasn't what I had intended. "I—"

Ms. Minnows entered in a pink version of her power suit. She greeted Older Shen with a pair of air kisses on the cheek. "Oh, Fai, you did a really good job finishing up the space. And I have excellent news. Three start-up firms contacted me with interest. We may even have a bidding war. And if you can get your brother to sell, we can add more to the pot." She turned to me. "Or you, Ms. Tan. The more properties I sell on this street, the bigger the price tag and appeal for these companies. We can call it an innovation park!"

I leveled a glare at her, one Ma-ma had often used when she

suspected I was lying. "Right. Because a tech campus is what the pai-fang represents. Nothing says Chinatown like a bunch of overpriced condos and office space."

"It's going to infuse money back into the neighborhood. Do you prefer that the buildings die and be demolished? At least this way, it will be better off."

"They'll never demolish the paifang."

"Well . . . the gate would stay. It's a landmark after all," she responded with a robotic smile. "Your people will have the rest of Chinatown."

"Yes, *my people* will always have Chinatown. We haven't quite been driven out yet." I turned to Older Shen and tipped my head. "Please consider my words, Mr. Shen. This doesn't feel right. There must be another way."

I made my way out of the bookstore without looking back.

As I walked away, I realized I couldn't do anything about Older Shen selling, nor was it my place to tell him not to. I wished he could find someone better to sell to. Ms. Minnows was right about the sky-rocketing real estate market in San Francisco: Older Shen would have offers for the building in no time, but if he sold, what would prevent the rest of the neighbors from doing the same?

Older Shen had broken his leg. Mrs. Chiu had moved out with the threat of divorce. Had Laolao ever failed this way? She had helped so many people in her time with no disastrous results, at least none that I'd heard of.

Did Laolao's recipes have staying power because her roots to the community were deeper than mine? Would my attempts at her recipes always fail or be temporary at best? Ma-ma had told me once that I would never cook as well as Laolao. Why had I thought I could do this?

I realized suddenly that I'd toyed with people's lives for my own personal gain. Asking Older Shen to stay because I needed to open the restaurant would be wrong. Worse, it was the same as asking the Chius to save their marriage; not for themselves, but for me. My intentions were good, but my motivations had not been so pure or altruistic.

My doubts billowed as dark as the clouds overhead. An ominous rumble echoed in the distance, the briefest of warnings before the rain descended. Fat droplets pelted my hair, soaking my white sundress and leather sandals. Unrelenting droplets heaved from the sky, soaking everything in sight, the gutters, the newly formed cracks in the sidewalk, painting everything in tones of gray.

I ran home through the downpour.

Laolao's recipes were backfiring, and I had to find out why.

Chapter Seventeen

Meimei greeted me at the door and meowed to be picked up. I had gotten used to carrying her, and it seemed she preferred this mode of transportation to walking. She purred in my arms: soothing, rolling vibrations that traveled under my skin and mimicked the thunder outside. Even after only a short time, I loved her and I couldn't think of my life without her. She must have given Ma-ma so much comfort and love.

I carried Meimei to the sofa and held her up so we were eye to eye. "What are we going to do about the neighbors? Everything is falling apart and I'm responsible for all of it. I have to help them."

The cat mewed.

"Because . . ." I sighed. "It's the right thing to do and they're good people."

The cat mewed once more, her musical voice ending on a high note as if she were asking a question.

"They aren't strangers anymore. They helped Ma-ma while I was gone and stood by me at her funeral. They're supporting me with the restaurant. They're my neighbors and I care about them."

I read over my grandmother's book feverishly, unable to find any disclaimers. I had followed the instructions to the letter and had seen the immediate results. Those who'd eaten the food had remarked that I'd nailed Laolao's recipes. What had I done wrong? Was I not a good enough cook?

My fingers lingered on the ragged edges in the book. When reading through the recipes the first time, I had noticed the three missing pages and wondered what they contained. Could the damage be related to the disasters I'd caused? I didn't know, and I felt a stab of pain as I realized I couldn't ask Ma-ma and Laolao about it—they were gone.

No matter how many times I checked, there were no clear answers in the book, no recipe to undo what I had done. But if I didn't find the solution soon, I feared it meant impending doom for Celia. What would happen to her because of my ineptitude?

I spent half an hour peering through the apartment windows, stalking Celia's gift shop, indecisive. She had mentioned conducting meetings with tour operators. Would she be safe? Someone was arguing outside.

Again.

My stomach clenched, as did my jaw. I moved to the windows to investigate. The squabble grew louder until I could make out the words.

"No, you can't do this to me!"

Celia.

"I am not obligated to refund your fees." The stranger in a faded tee and jeans crossed his arms over his chest. "It's in the contract."

"That's five thousand I can't afford to lose," Celia pleaded. "This is a scam. You can't do this."

"And what are you going to do about it?" He raised his arms in the air and made a rude gesture before walking away.

Celia's shoulders undulated, bobbing up and down in tandem with each sob. She dashed to her building and slammed the door.

And just like that, my last good deed fell apart. My heart ached for Celia. Something was definitely going wrong with my versions of Laolao's recipes. The initial effects were exactly as described in the book, but the conclusions were going sour. Somehow, the magic was being corrupted and I had no idea why. I might not have bargained for the aftershocks, but I was the one using the recipes.

I'd done this.

I needed to claim responsibility no matter the consequences. Celia would be blaming herself right now, and that wasn't fair or right.

Grabbing my purse, I headed to Celia's, armed with the truth and the acceptance of the censure that would come along with it.

When I arrived, Celia was in the midst of drowning her sorrows in a pile of barbecued pork buns. Judging by the number of crumpled papers, she was working on bun number four. I joined her at the kitchen table. "Help yourself," she sniffled. Celia's high standards had demanded one dozen of the best pork buns in Chinatown as comfort food. I picked up a bun, squeezing it with my fingers and watching it spring back against my palm. I bit into the soft, steamed bread, the sweet, saucy filling of minced pork belly dripping onto my tongue. I devoured the rest of the bun and soon another, and another. The palm-size buns vanished into my stomach but failed to assuage the uneasiness in it.

She sniffed. "Is it horrible that I thought I'd get ahead even if it was only for a little while? I was doing so well. The tour operator promised me more than he was able to deliver. I should have gone with the others with better reputations, but I gambled. I was too greedy. He was probably right. I'm old and foolish."

"You're not." I swallowed. "It's my fault. All of it."

Celia set her half-eaten bun down. "It's not like you pushed me into signing a sketchy contract."

The truth was a tricky creature. It was lauded and respected, yet heartbreak, sorrow, and betrayal were among its followers. I had to tell Celia about my meddling now.

"I used Laolao's recipes to give you extra luck," I confessed. "I'm sorry that it turned out so horribly. I know you never asked me to. I thought I was helping you."

Celia's face was a kaleidoscope of emotions, shifting from realization to embarrassment to rage. Hands balled into fists at her side, her flushed visage contorted into a grimace.

Anger was unpredictable: the length of the wick and the force of the explosion varied per person. Ma-ma's wick had been forged in camphor and bitterness. Coiled for months, it waited for its timed detonation every year in the middle of June when she slammed cupboard doors and stomped until the floorboards creaked. I'd never asked why, for it was obvious. I knew my mother and I had directed our anger at the same target—my absentee father. June was the month he had left her.

Ma-ma had once said that you never truly knew a person until you'd seen them angry.

"I trusted you!" Celia's voice was a low hiss, like a mother chastising her misbehaving child in public. "I said I didn't want you to help me. We spoke about your recipes. You manipulated and used me. How many times could you have told me but chose to remain silent?"

I didn't answer. Nothing I could say would lessen her pain.

"I thought we were friends, but all this time, I was nothing but a pawn in your quest to open your restaurant. Like the others! You don't care about us. You're just like Melody Minnows!"

A fiery glow surrounded Celia, Bunsen blue at the core and orange at the edges. I squinted at the light. I fumbled for the right words, but all that escaped was an apology. "I'm sorry, Celia. I wasn't using you. Our friendship matters to me. It's the truth, but it doesn't make it better."

"I never asked for this. All I gave you was kindness, and this was how you repaid me." She paused to sniffle. "You should have told me the truth. I deserved that much."

Her shoulders drooped like the limp bunches of coriander on the last day at the market. "Get out," she whispered.

The cat roused me the next morning by licking my cheek, the roughness of her tongue jarring me awake even though I had no intention of getting up. As the wrecker of lives, I didn't want to face the damage I had wrought.

I moved to the living room, where my grandmother's book rested on the coffee table. Pulling it toward me, my fingers sought the place where three pages had been ripped out of the book. What important information was in these missing pages? Could it contain the solution I was looking for?

I'd found nothing else in Laolao's book, so I closed it.

I wished Ma-ma were here. She might know the answer. If only there were a connection to heaven, I would wait under the stars for a signal and the opportunity to communicate with my mother once more. Perhaps she could tell me how to fix the mess I'd made of the neighbors' lives:

The Chius were headed for divorce.

Older Shen had a broken leg and was selling the business he loved so it could be turned into an overpriced condo.

Celia hated me and was worse off financially than before.

Fulfilling the prophecy seemed impossible. Save the neighborhood? I'd only ensured its destruction.

"Can I even fix this?" I asked the cat. "I've failed them all and myself."

Meimei butted my side while emitting a series of loud meows.

"There isn't a solution in the recipe book. We checked, remember? There is no fix-all recipe. Maybe I should choose a different approach? There has to be something that will combat what I've cooked."

Meimei jumped off my lap and hopped onto the coffee table. She batted Laolao's book with her paw.

"No, I already looked there," I told her.

She meowed back, continuing to tap the thick book.

"I've gone through it many times. Laolao doesn't have any solutions in there."

Meimei sat up. Her ice blue eyes focused on me, and her paw tapped the cover again. I couldn't help but laugh. This tiny little creature was adamant.

"Fine." I picked up the book and opened it. She batted the pages, her paws turning them back and forth until she found one she decided to sit on.

"You do know this is an important book. It's also very old, so we have to be careful." I shooed her off the pages.

"Are you telling me I should cook to get out of this?"

The cat tilted her head.

"Cooking got me into this, so cooking should get me out of it?"

I could see the logic. "But what would be different this time? Maybe it was my fault. I was so busy looking for cures that I didn't look for any warnings."

Perhaps I had been searching for the wrong information. I should be looking for guidance on *how* to use the recipes, not what remedies they provided.

Startling the cat, I began skimming ahead, flipping through the pages in rapid succession, searching for instructions. I came across the word *harmony* and three recipes referring to one another. According to Laolao, these had to be cooked in unison. This was it!

I yanked a notepad from the counter and jotted down the required ingredients. I could prepare a feast for the neighbors that would bring about harmony to eradicate the discord I'd sown. It would only make sense that the way to fix all this would be to use this triplet of recipes the way my grandmother advised. Simple. I was so busy trying to find a way to reverse what I'd wrought that I hadn't considered a different approach. Maybe this could work! All I could do was try. Sharing a meal always brought strangers and family together.

I could fix this mess.

I picked up the cat and twirled her around the room. I kissed her little face as I danced. She stoically accepted my joy at finding the solution. I performed one more shimmy before getting down to work.

In three days, I would hold a dinner and invite all of them. They wouldn't be able to turn down the invitation because the dinner would be held in my mother's memory.

I had no guilt for invoking my mother's name. Nothing else would coax my fractured neighbors to come together. The three new recipes would counter the three dishes that had failed, I told myself. They had to work.

By the afternoon of the dinner, all of my neighbors had confirmed their attendance—even Celia, to my surprise. I wanted to think that if she could talk, Meimei would praise my ingenuity and agree that my plan would work.

Laolao's recipe book lay on the counter among garlands of fresh vegetables and meats wrapped in butcher paper. Stainless-steel pots gleamed from a recent scrubbing while my grandmother's wok, with its darkened patina, sat on the stove's burner. Wagner's "Ride of the Valkyries" played on the Victrola.

It was time to cook.

Spring Rolls

Carrots

Green beans

Garlic

Shrimp

Pork tenderloin

Fish sauce

Salt

Pepper

Bean sprouts

Green leaf lettuce

Pre-made spring roll wrappers

Coriander

Hot sauce

Crushed peanuts

Sauce:

Apple cider vinegar

Sugar

Soy sauce
Water
Chili flakes
Garlic
Cornstarch

Julienne the carrots and green beans. Mince the garlic. Butterfly the shrimp, and slice the pork tenderloin into tiny strips.

Heat the wok and stir-fry the pork and shrimp with a sprinkle of fish sauce and garlic. Set aside.

Stir-fry the carrots and green beans with a dash of salt and pepper for four to five minutes to ensure they retain their crunch. Lastly, stir-fry the bean sprouts for two minutes.

Toss the filling together, mixing the vegetables with the meat.

For the sauce, mix the apple cider vinegar, sugar, and soy sauce in a bowl. The ratios depend on your taste as well as the portion of the filling. Boil the water and add the ingredients, all the while stirring to dissolve the sugar. Once the mixture is boiling, add the chili flakes and the rest of the minced garlic along with the cornstarch to thicken the sauce. Always add more garlic than you need because there can never be too much of it. Keep stirring to avoid clumps from forming, and once it has thickened and is the proper viscosity, it is ready.

Place a lettuce leaf on the wrapper. Stuff the leafy canoe with the filling and top with a generous helping of the sauce. Add coriander leaves, hot sauce, and the crushed peanuts as a garnish before wrapping everything up.

Note:

Time is the key to these spring rolls.

This is a meal designed to entice conversation and build connections, for it involves active participation: kinship. Communication is important to bridge any chasms or mend any feuds. This is one of the three dishes that promote harmony.

Each person makes their own spring rolls, and in the process, ingredients are passed around and shared. As much time is spent in preparation of this dish, more time is taken in its consumption.

It is perfect welcome fare for newcomers.

The spring rolls needed the most preparation time, so I tackled them first. My sharp knife minced the onions and garlic, and julienned the carrots and green beans, transforming them into colorful edible confetti. I set aside the garlic and deposited the rest into a hot wok. The vegetables sizzled on impact, dancing in the heat as I stirred, mixing greens, oranges, yellows in a culinary palette. The vegetables would add crunch when added to the seasoned, minced pork.

Watercress Soup

Leftover soup stock, or new stock made from water and
   chicken neck bones
Ginger
Fresh watercress

Sesame oil

Green onions

Salt

Boil water with the chicken neck bones and two slices of ginger. As the water bubbles, scoop out the impurities rising to the surface in the form of floating clouds. If you have leftover soup stock, skip this step.

When the stock has been purified, drop the bundles of fresh watercress into the boiling pot along with a few drops of sesame oil. Boil until the watercress rises to the surface.

Serve in bowls garnished with minced green onions. Add salt according to taste.

The soup evokes the feeling of wading into a river: the warmth of a summer's day, the softness of moss on polished stones.

Note:

The balance achieved in this soup brings a lightness of being. The soup brings clarity to clouded minds.

Serve this to the indecisive. It will bring them comfort when their decisions become clearer.

This is the second of three dishes that promote harmony.

At my side, the boiling water bubbled. The base of the watercress soup was a broth made of chicken neck bones. I unwrapped the chicken bones from the brown paper and they tumbled into the pot along with a few slices of ginger. The subtlety of the broth and its main ingredient, watercress, promoted healing.

Clear Soda Shrimp

Ginger

Salt

Pepper

Clear soda

Black tiger shrimp

Sesame oil

Cilantro

Water

Sauce:

Soy sauce

Vinegar

Garlic

Chilies

Cut two slices of ginger. Pound them flat and toss them into the pot with the salt, pepper, and clear soda. When the stock is boiling, add the shrimp. Keep stirring. Watch for the color to change from glossy, striped gray to blush pink, and then you know it is cooked and ready. The shells must appear glossy and smooth. If the shrimp shells become wrinkled and inseparable from the meat inside, they are overcooked and will be rubbery in texture. Undressing a shrimp should be an easy task if it is cooked perfectly.

Pour the pot's contents into a strainer, separating the

shrimp from the stock. Add a sprinkle of sesame oil to the shrimp and sprigs of cilantro for plating.

Serve with a sauce made from soy sauce, vinegar, smashed garlic cloves, and chilies.

Note:

The first time I drank clear soda, I marveled at its properties. It was like drinking liquid sugar, and I knew it would pair well with the natural sweetness of shrimp.

Serve this to those needing respite and peace. There are those who desperately need a sense of calm because they are facing difficulty in their lives. The sweetness of the dish will temper and soothe the soul.

This dish is meant for those seeking serenity. This is the third dish that promotes harmony.

The gray shells of the shrimp gleamed like smooth pebbles in a stream. Ten minutes before the guests arrived, I would submerge them into a hot bath of clear soda accented with slices of ginger. I watched and waited, checking for when the shells turned coral. The soda enhanced the natural sweetness of the shrimp. This dish would be the last to be cooked because of its short cooking time.

I also prepared a batch of scented jasmine rice. Every Chinese meal was accompanied by the requisite rice or noodle staple. Since I'd given such care in the three special dishes, plain white rice would serve as a subtle accent.

I smiled at the photograph of my grandmother. "Thank you, Laolao, for your recipes and your wisdom. I hope this works and I make you proud."

The dinner would soon be ready and the guests were due to arrive.

Chapter Eighteen

I knew my neighbors would come to the dinner at the restaurant because etiquette and duty guaranteed their attendance, but I was concerned about the possibility of another disaster happening. Ever since I had decided to hold the dinner, I had refused to entertain any negative thoughts, but I found them encroaching now. Ma-ma had once said, "No matter how much you try to direct fate, eventually, she finds a way to do what she wants." Tonight, I hoped fate would be on my side.

Older Shen was the first guest to arrive.

I opened the door. "Welcome."

Dressed in a powder blue velour tuxedo and splashed in expensive aftershave, he hobbled inside on his crutches. He'd brought a bouquet of drooping pink chrysanthemums. "These are for you. Congratulations! The food smells wonderful."

I accepted the flowers, murmured my thanks, and helped him to his seat. The scarlet carnation on his lapel clashed with his outfit. My invitation hadn't indicated a dress code, but I appreciated that he was taking the event so seriously.

"That is an interesting outfit, Mr. Shen."

"Thank you." He winced and stared at his leg.

"Are you all right?"

"The leg is worse than before. Recovery isn't going as well as I hoped, I'm afraid."

"I'm so sorry, Mr. Shen."

"It's all right. The accident was my fault. I should have been more careful."

A twinge of guilt hit me.

Miss Yu made her appearance next. She was resplendent in a pastel palette of roses and lavender. A rose sheath dress with embroidered matching flowers was completed with a crocheted lavender shawl. The familiar perfume of peonies lingered in the air as she drew me in for an embrace.

"Oh, dear one, it's good to see you." She placed a kiss on my cheek. "Your mother would be proud of your efforts."

I pulled her aside into the kitchen. I needed to ask her about her prophecy, the recipes backfiring, the missing pages. "I was trying to reach you. Something's gone wrong with the prophecy."

"I'm so sorry. I've been away tending to my aunt. She isn't doing well. What has gone wrong?"

I told her everything. She nodded, listening silently; all the while her smooth brow creased further.

"What do you think about the missing pages?" I asked.

"I agree with you that the damage in the book might have something to do with this. I'm sorry but Miranda didn't give me any loose pages, only the scarf and the book. So these three dishes that you cooked for tonight, are they the ones you think might return order?"

"Yes, I'm hoping this fixes everything," I replied. "Or at least gets us to where we were before I made things worse. I tried to find recipes that would create and restore harmony."

Miss Yu reached out to pat my cheek. "You have a kind heart like your mother and your grandmother before her. I also hope this works." She sniffed the air. "Judging by the aroma, you cook as well as your laolao. You have the same gift. The restaurant will surely be a success when it opens."

I had so many doubts that it made me feel guilty to hope. "Thank you, Miss Yu," I murmured. I wanted to continue the conversation, but with more guests filing in, I had to return to my duties. Perhaps at the end of the night, I might have another chance to privately speak with her and figure out my next move.

Celia hovered near the doorway. Despite her worried expression, she was radiant in a fuchsia frock with a hydrangea print. Lifting her hand in a half-hearted wave, she took a seat at the table without saying hello. Of everyone that I'd invited, she was the only one whose RSVP I wasn't sure of. I yearned to apologize again, but it wouldn't diminish her pain. Even now, Celia busied herself with her phone to avoid any eye contact.

The Chius entered together, but they might as well have come individually: it was clear from their stiff body language and distance from each other that they were still fighting. Mrs. Chiu wore a flattering floral-print wrap dress under a crocheted cardigan, and Mr. Chiu was in a light charcoal sweater and khakis.

Mrs. Chiu embraced me. "How are you doing? Do you need anything?"

"No, I don't need anything. Thank you for asking," I replied. "I'm really glad you could come."

"It's not a problem, dear. We all loved your mother." Mrs. Chiu's gaze turned toward her husband and she frowned. Mr. Chiu was already seated at the table talking to Older Shen. The two men were discussing the real estate market—a topic that now filled me with even greater trepidation.

I squeezed her arm while guiding her to the table. "Please have a seat."

Her smile vanished when her attention returned to her husband. Mrs. Chiu's glare could freeze the Pacific Ocean. She took a seat in between Miss Yu and Celia.

The last to arrive was Younger Shen, wearing a subdued shade of navy blue. "Hello, little one!" he boomed. "Thank you for the invitation. I hope I'm not late."

"Not at all." I gestured toward the table.

Celia never glanced up from her phone. Her knuckles glowed white, clutching the device tightly. She didn't want to be here, but I needed everyone to be present for this dinner.

They had to eat the three dishes and everything would be fixed; even Miss Yu agreed with my logic, which gave me hope.

When the last guest sat down, I took my place at the head of the table. The last time we had gathered together was for Ma-ma's funeral two weeks ago. Now, with the women on one side of the table and the men on the other, their eyes were on me.

I took a deep breath. "Thank you all for being here. I'm so glad you came. When I lost my mother, I thought I had nothing left. She was all I had. But you reminded me that all of you are here with me.

"While I was gone, you looked after my mother. You brought her groceries, kept her company, and helped her remember she was loved. You made her feel she wasn't alone. I know that she loved you all."

I motioned for them to start eating.

Everyone at the table tipped their head in acknowledgment before turning their attention to the feast. Celia lifted the stainless-steel lid of the tureen holding the watercress soup. Using the ladle, she served everyone a bowl while carefully avoiding eye contact with me. Mr. Chiu seized the platter of clear soda shrimp and helped himself before passing it across the table to his wife. She accepted the dish with a tight smile. To my left, Older Shen prepared his spring roll with more than a liberal sprinkle of the sugared crushed peanuts to satisfy his sweet tooth.

As soon as the symphony of eating began, I breathed a sigh of relief.

Food possessed the remarkable ability to heal and bring people together.

All would be well. It had to be.

"Don't eat too many of the prawn heads, Wayne," Mrs. Chiu said. "You have to watch your cholesterol levels."

Mr. Chiu dismissed his wife's warning and continued sucking the sweet prawns on his plate.

"Wayne!" She smacked his wrist. "Stop. There aren't enough fat blockers in my purse. Dr. Ong will be furious."

Prawn and lobster brains were considered a delicacy for their rich flavor. The Shen twins and Celia were engaged in the same practice, sipping the heads as if they were miniature cups of mead.

I winced as Mr. Chiu continued to ignore his wife, greedily consuming all the prawn heads he could fit on his plate. Sure enough, Mrs. Chiu launched into another tirade. No one at the table paused or intervened. Miss Yu watched with a wary eye. Older Shen busied himself with the soup I'd prepared. Celia and Younger Shen took turns filling their plates with samples from the various dishes while still not uttering a word of conversation.

Intervening now would bring attention to the bickering couple.

Instead, I glanced over at Older Shen. "When will you be done with the repairs at the bookstore?"

"Everything is almost done. It's almost ready for sale."

"I hope you considered what I said. To sell to the right people?" I asked.

"No, I've consulted with Melody and she said—"

"You are not to sell!" Younger Shen brought his open palm down against the tabletop. The resounding clink from the cutlery echoed, and the ensuing, invisible shock wave shifted the plates. "If you sell, you'll ruin us all. I don't care what that woman says. Our businesses do not have a price. We already settled this, Fai. You're not selling."

Older Shen rose to his feet, struggling with his crutches, and for a moment, towered over his seated brother. "It's my store. I can do with it as I see fit. Melody says I can be a millionaire if I sell now. You can't tell me what to do anymore."

Younger Shen rose to his feet and regained his physical advantage. "Yes, I can, because you're being a coward and an idiot. You have no shame. Our families worked to build this neighborhood."

One of the pendant lamps over the counter burst, burning out, but no one else noticed because the fireworks at the dinner table were more potent.

"Guang, Fai, calm down." Miss Yu rose from her seat. "Please."

She and Celia exchanged a glance and moved to the other side of the table, where the Shen brothers stood. Each woman chose a brother: Celia stood with Younger Shen and Miss Yu with Older Shen. As the women tried to calm them down, I managed the Chius, who were still fighting at the other end of the table.

Mrs. Chiu wagged a fork as if it were an extension of her finger.

"You never listen to me. You only do whatever you want. What about what I want or what our family wants?"

"I want what our family wants. Don't you think the boys deserve to inherit the business?" Mr. Chiu asked.

"There. Is. No. More. Money." She threw her fork down. Her cheeks were flushed and her breath was ragged. "You cling to the past like a ghost. We have to sell the business while we can still start over. If we do it now like Ms. Minnows says, we can retire well. There is no shame in this. Put aside your pride for once and—"

They were going to sell, like Older Shen had planned. How long until the others considered the same course of action too? The neighborhood was coming apart at the seams. I did this. I was the one holding the scissors.

Mr. Chiu stood up. "We're not moving. My family has been here for generations. I will not be the one to walk away. This is where we belong. I'm making the sacrifices to ensure the business stays alive."

Another bulb shattered. The glass burst into a fiery shower before turning into powdery ash when it landed on the counter. Once more, no one noticed but me.

How had I ever thought that cooking again would fix everything?

"What about my sacrifices?" Anita asked. "Why do you think I'm working four to five jobs? To keep your precious store afloat! I haven't seen my family in years! It's clear to me that you've made your choice. You don't love me as much as you claim to. I want a divorce, Wayne."

I winced. "I . . ."

My apology died on my lips, for words couldn't fix what had been broken.

Mr. Chiu looked into his wife's tearful eyes. "I love you, but if that's what you want, you can have it."

Mrs. Chiu closed her eyes. All of the bluster and anger left her as she pulled back, withdrawing.

Her husband turned to me and bowed his head. "This was a lovely meal. I'm sorry, Natalie, but I'm afraid I must take my leave."

I could do nothing but nod. What else could I say? Asking him to stay would be selfish and unnecessary. The damage had been done.

Mrs. Chiu opened her eyes and turned to me. "This shouldn't be a surprise to you. We've been trying for years to make it work." She grabbed her heavy, cherry satchel and turned on her heel, following her husband out the door.

"You always think you know better than me," Older Shen yelled. His index finger sank into his brother's chest as his other arm was held back by Miss Yu. "You never respected me, so why should I listen to you? You should heed my words because I'm the eldest."

"Like that matters. You're selling because it's the easy way out. For years, you let your business die instead of doing anything to change it. Now you're selling the carcass. You have no—"

Older Shen, though tethered by Miss Yu and restricted by his crutches, swung and connected with a forceful right hook to his brother's jaw. Celia's screams were muffled by yet another bulb shattering from the suspended pendant lamps. Younger Shen rubbed his jaw as his face mottled into the ruddy shade of a steamed Dungeness crab. His large hands balled into fists.

Miss Yu stepped between them, her hands pushing both men apart. "Please, gentlemen. No violence."

Younger Shen swung his meaty fist and connected, but not with its intended target.

Miss Yu crumpled to the floor. Older Shen managed to catch her in time. Celia sobbed, dropping to her knees. She cradled Miss Yu's head on her lap while Younger Shen hovered nearby with his hand covering his mouth.

I ran to the counter, fetched the phone from my purse, and dialed 911. The final bulb burst overhead, plunging the restaurant into darkness.

Chapter Nineteen

The day after the disaster, I returned to my futile study of Laolao's book. Every recipe specified what could happen if ingredients were adjusted, but there was nothing about potential disasters. As I flipped back and forth, I kept returning to the ragged edges of the three missing pages. What did they contain?

Since each page was written with such care, the ripped pages appeared like scars. If only what remained contained a hint of a letter or even a word, then I could guess what might have been written on them. I ran my fingertips along the edges, wishing.

My stomach rumbled. I had not eaten breakfast or lunch yet. Too tired to cook, I called my favorite Vietnamese place. I typically thought ordering in was lazy, but last night's dinner was still fresh in my memory, and I didn't know if I could trust my own cooking anymore. I needed a break. When my order arrived, I locked up the restaurant and ran upstairs to gorge.

I laid my feast out on the kitchen table. Draped over beds of jasmine rice, thin pork chops seasoned with lemongrass showcased charred stripes from the grill. Cold summer rolls with translucent rice paper glimmered with riotous colors from the mint leaves, vermicelli, and shrimp filling. Emerald coriander leaves peeked out amid slices of barbecued pork, in golden, crusty baguette sandwiches called banh mi. I placed a few pieces of the pork onto a plate for the cat. I bit into the cold rolls first. The thin wrapper yielded to my teeth, giving way to the crunchy pickled vegetables and plump shrimp underneath. The mint leaf inside complemented the sweet sauce with crushed peanuts. The two small rolls vanished into my belly.

I attacked the banh mi next. The crisp crust highlighted the varying textures of its filling: crisp from the pickled radish and carrots, tender from the meat, springy from the noodles. The symphony of textures sang on my tongue. Soon, golden crumbs dotted my fingertips and my lips.

I hovered my fork over the pork chops, ready to spear it into tender meat.

The telephone rang.

The shrill, metallic noise echoed in the apartment. No one had ever called me on the landline because this was Ma-ma's telephone. Another ring. My heartbeat accelerated, flittering like a pulsing hummingbird within my rib cage. I rushed to the ancient rotary phone on the kitchen counter.

"Hello?"

"Tan girl." The voice on the other end of the line was as ancient as the yellowed receiver in my hand. The nickname was strange, but I recognized the speaker. The last time I heard his voice, he had been screaming at me and practically chased me out of his restaurant. "This is Wu. Celia Deng came by last week and mentioned that you wanted to speak to me about running a business."

There was no point in this meeting. My neighbors' lives were a mess, so I couldn't open the restaurant yet. I didn't want to go, but avoiding the old man would tarnish Celia's reputation. I'd already damaged our friendship and I didn't want to do more harm. I had to go out of obligation to Celia.

I stammered out a yes.

"Hmph. Come by the restaurant in half an hour. I have time this afternoon before the evening rush comes in. Don't be late."

Old Wu hung up before I had the chance to reply.

The old man wanted me to come by and see him. My full stomach wobbled, protesting.

I must have checked my reflection a hundred times at the apartment before I left. The old man was a strict adherer to etiquette and tradition. My apprehension climbed, tugging the hairs on my arms upward into fine points. The loose hairs on my head, despite being sprayed down in a severe bun, stood up like porcupine quills. My palms moistened. I grasped the edge of the counter in an attempt to steady my breathing and heartbeat.

Old Wu hated me, yet he had acquiesced to Celia's request. If I decided to forgo this meeting, it would embarrass her. I had thought the meeting would be useful because I'd be ready to open the restaurant, but now it seemed like a waste of both of our time.

It didn't matter. I had no choice. I must go to his restaurant and undergo the equivalent of an unanesthetized root canal.

My chances of being decapitated by the Old Tiger were slim, but it wasn't physical wounds I was worried about. Though his claws and teeth were fearsome, his sharp tongue was his greatest weapon. I had felt its power firsthand when I came back. Nothing could diminish my foreboding that I was walking into flames.

Inside Old Wu's restaurant, platters of Cantonese dishes floated on trays above the servers' shoulders. Teapots emptied gallons of murky, low-grade jasmine tea for the noisy patrons who chatted in several languages. It was a concert of prosperity—the likes of which I wanted in my future, what I had thought Miss Yu's prophecy was promising.

Despite everything that had happened, having my own restaurant was still what I wanted—and I wanted it in *this* neighborhood, in Laolao's old place. Old Wu had managed it. Maybe talking to him would help me realize my next steps, if there were still any options available to me.

The old man wasn't standing at his usual post by the counter. A server emerged from the dining room and addressed me in Mandarin. "Mr. Wu is waiting for you at a special table. Follow me."

I nodded.

I followed her through the narrow path in between the packed tables, weaving, dodging, threading the needle until we arrived at a private table in the back, set up behind folded screens. A plate of fried tofu sprinkled with chilies was resting on a glass lazy Susan.

Old Wu sat with a folded newspaper at his elbow. His dark eyes assessed me over a cup of tea. I chose the empty chair across from him.

"Tan girl," he said. "I am surprised you came."

I attempted to meet his eyes. My hands shook, so I hid them under the table.

"Celia tells me you wanted to ask me something about the restaurant business." He leaned back and crossed his arms. "What do you want to know?"

In addition to respect and deference dictated by our culture—the old man would tolerate nothing less—this meeting must be approached with honesty. I was certain he expected me to ask about the restaurant business, so I proceeded as if things were running smoothly.

Diverging from the purpose of the meeting would incur Old Wu's wrath even more because I'd be wasting his time. I had only one important question to ask: "I have filled out the list of forms. One of them is the neighborhood application. I want to know if you will oppose me."

Old Wu narrowed his eyes. "Are you serious about opening a restaurant?"

I spoke from my heart. "Yes."

"It's a hard business. Much harder than anything you have ever done. Have you taken any business courses or other education?"

"I haven't, but I'm ready to learn. As I recall, my grandmother hadn't, either, and she managed well for herself."

"What will you do if you fail? Are you going to sell to those vultures who want to drive our people out of our own buildings?"

"I would only do that as my last resort, if I had no choice. And no, I wouldn't sell to the highest bidder. I would choose the right buyer."

He grunted. "I haven't decided yet if I will block your application. You're saying the right things. Time will tell if your actions prove it." He poured himself more tea. "I have to get back to work soon. Is there anything else you want to ask?"

The conversation so far had been civil—a stark contrast to our last encounter. This was my opportunity to ask about Laolao's recipes. Old Wu had been my grandmother's peer, and he must have known her.

"Is it true that you knew Laolao?" I asked.

Old Wu's posture shifted. His shoulders straightened, and his voice thickened like stirred hoisin sauce. "Yes. She was a leader in the community when she ran her restaurant. She was the best cook, and I say this with pride as her former rival."

"Did anyone ever get sick from her food or did something weird happen as a result of her cooking?"

"No." He frowned. "Qiao was an impeccable chef."

Warmth flooded my cheeks. "I mean, is it possible that—"

His lips clamped shut. "Are you questioning the legacy of your grandmother?"

A tremble crept into my voice, the kind of weakness I didn't want to show the old man. "No, it's not that. I was just—"

"You act as if it's your right to claim Qiao's legacy. She may have been your grandmother, but you and your mother forsook everything she worked so hard for. And you plan on reopening *her* restaurant? Running a business is not a hobby where you can take time off whenever you like. It requires great commitment. Did you even have financing in place?"

I wanted to say I was working on it, but the words stuck in my throat as if I had swallowed lotus seed paste.

"If you're going to run it like a hobby, don't bother. If that is the case, I will do everything in my power to block your application. Running a restaurant is hard work. Nothing your generation is used to. You don't even know how much money it takes to run the business and keep it afloat." Every point pricked, scraping the delicate skin of my collarbone hidden underneath my blouse. The tiny cuts bled, stinging.

Was I truly unworthy to inherit my grandmother's legacy? Was that the reason the recipes had failed to work for me?

"Tell me, Tan girl," he said. "Why do you want to run the restaurant?"

The answer eluded me. What had once seemed so clear was now lost in a fog of anxiety and doubt. My shoulders rolled inward. I wanted to disappear, to vanish like grains of sea salt into a hot broth.

The old man rapped his knuckles against the tablecloth. "Well?"

I blinked and stammered, "I care about the neighborhood."

He muttered something unintelligible under his breath, his inflection implying a curse. His hand on the table curled into a fist. Though Old Wu was in his seventies, he possessed a strength cultivated from a life with little leisure. As far as everyone in Chinatown knew, he'd never taken a day off. The restaurant never closed, even for Chinese New Year. His was one of the oldest and most successful businesses in the area. And I was nothing.

"You are lazy, irresponsible, and selfish." The old man spat out the words as if he were spitting out salted watermelon seeds. "All you ever did was run away. You left home and never looked back. You tell me you care about the neighborhood now? Where were you when your neighbors had to scramble to feed their families? Did you help then? No, because you were traveling, seeing the world, and not caring about what happened here. You abandoned them. You are a disgrace to your family's legacy. Just like your mother."

"I care about the neighborhood and the people in it." And my mother.

He scoffed. "You care about your guilt. You ruined their lives as much as you ruined your mother's."

Ma-ma. I wanted him to stop, but my cowardice rendered me mute.

"She threw everything away after your grandmother died. She should have honored her mother by running the restaurant. Instead, she closed it. She abandoned her duty and shut herself in to avoid the shame of disappointing the community. Your grandmother worked hard to make something from nothing, and then you and your mother profited from her while disrespecting her legacy. Selfish. So selfish. Everything you have, you did not earn. You, like your mother, are carrion feeding off your grandmother's corpse!"

I wiped my face with the back of my hand. His words cut into my skin, leaving a swath of tiny lacerations across my collarbones. Blood bloomed against the cotton weave of my blouse and mingled with the tears of my sorrow and shame.

I stumbled out of the restaurant sobbing with a wounded heart.

I ran home, over the fractures in the sidewalk, past the shops. I fished inside my purse for the keys to unlock the restaurant door. The criss-cross cuts on my collarbones stung, but the psychological wounds hurt even more. Old Wu's accusations held kernels of truth that I couldn't deny: I *had* ruined my neighbors' lives, Laolao's recipes *were* backfiring because of me, and I *was* underqualified to run a restaurant. Worst of all, I was responsible for my mother dying alone.

The door unlocked and I slipped inside.

Smoke!

Puffy dark clouds billowed from the kitchen, spilling into the dining room area. Under the thick veil of black, flashes of orange burst through. The fire was coming from the stove.

My grandmother's recipe book and her photograph were beside it. My family's history had begun with this heirloom, and I would not be the one to lose it. Shielding my eyes and nose, I plunged forward into the gray, gulping, gasping, burning with each breath. It was as if I were swimming through deep waters, my arms moving in strokes to clear the clouds while my lungs screamed for air.

The silhouette of the thick leather-bound book was faint against the rising inky billows of smoke. Laolao's photograph curled from the heat before bursting into flames. Laolao! Heat blasted my exposed skin as I reached forward, but my body convulsed in a series of coughing fits. The wall of smoke and heat proved impenetrable.

Suddenly, I was pulled backward into the dining room.

"What are you doing?" Celia demanded.

I blinked and coughed. "What are you doing here?"

"I smelled the smoke and ran over to check."

All I could see was Laolao's picture curling in on itself as it burned. "I lost her picture! But Laolao's recipe book. I have to get it back—"

"Your grandmother would rather the building remain standing and her grandchild still be alive than have her bloody book rescued. Don't go back in there." Celia held me back as I tried to surge forward into the restaurant again. "I already called 911. We need to get out of here, right now."

I stretched out my hand toward the gathering darkness. Laolao's precious book was gone.

The cat! What if the fire spread and reached the apartment? Meimei was upstairs. "I have to get my cat," I said to Celia. "I can't lose her."

She nodded. "Go quickly."

I ran up the stairs and unlocked the door. I had to find Meimei fast because the stairs would be the first route of escape the fire would attack if it were to spread. I would need to exit through the window and down the fire escape after I found her.

"Meimei!" I called out.

The cat wasn't in her usual spot on the chair. I could hear the fire crackling downstairs as my panic rose. I ran to my bedroom and the bathroom and she wasn't there. The door to Ma-ma's room was still closed, so she couldn't be there either.

"Meimei!" I screamed again, tears streaming down my cheeks.

I couldn't lose her. She was Ma-ma's, and to lose her now . . . There was too much I had lost already.

I lowered myself to my hands and knees and scanned the underside of the sofa. A ball of fluff curled near the back wall followed by a soft meow. She was terrified.

"Come on out, my love. We need to get out of here." I called out to her.

She mewed and didn't move.

I contorted my body so I could extend my reach. Without a word, I snatched her into my arms, tighter than she wanted because I heard a yelp, and ran to the window. I yanked it open and crawled onto the fire escape outside.

The heart of the restaurant was gutted. Ugly scars marred the galley kitchen from the ceiling to the floor: oily, angry, swallowing steel and the walls. Putting out the blaze had resulted in lingering water damage. The damp had seeped into everything porous. The fireman said it was an electrical fire from the old knob and tube wiring, and that it could have been worse—the entire building could have gone up in flames. The structural damage wasn't severe enough to compromise the first floor, which was a relief, yet the loss of the kitchen destroyed any chance of a future here for me.

Despite our fractured friendship, Celia dealt with the authorities and ordered me to stay inside what was left of the restaurant.

The cat climbed onto a stool, then onto the charred counter, and napped. I wished I had her ability to forget everything. I wanted nothing more than to fly away, far away from everything and everyone, or curl up in a ball beside the cat and slumber for a year.

A small crowd gathered outside, gawking. Unwanted pigeons. I spied a familiar blond real estate agent among the spectators. Extremely unwanted vulture. If only I had the energy to disperse them. My neighbors were on the other side of the glass, content to stay out.

They stared at me as if I were a zoo exhibit.

They stared at me as if I were my mother.

I was alone.

My dream had died in the fire and so had all of my hope.

Old Wu was right about me.

There was nothing left to do but run.

Chapter Twenty

I turned to the ruined goddess beside me. I had caused enough harm. I was the worst type of person. I had failed my mother. I had wrecked my neighbors' lives. And now, the restaurant was gone. In a culture where elders and the family came before everything else, destroying Laolao's legacy was unspeakable, the last of a long list of offenses to my name. Perhaps this was punishment for thinking I had been worthy of my grandmother's restaurant.

Maybe Ma-ma had been right. I was doomed from the beginning. She hadn't wanted me to open the restaurant. Had she foreseen my massive failure somehow?

Maybe it was more than that—the neighborhood, the building itself rejecting me. Yanking the Open sign off the window, I shut and locked the front door.

A hand appeared against the glass.

Daniel.

I placed my palm against his before unlocking the door.

He swept me into his arms, and I was enveloped in scents of laundered cotton, spearmint, and coffee. "I'm glad you're all right," he whispered. His hands rubbed my back in soothing circles as he continued to hold me tight against him.

I didn't deserve his comfort, but I took it, soaked it in. "The fire took everything. I've lost my grandmother's photograph and her recipe book," I murmured against his chest.

"It didn't take everything. You're still here. That's all that matters."

"Is it?" I asked. "I can't go through with opening the restaurant now."

"You'll find a way. There's always another solution—"

"No." Only hours ago, I had watched Laolao's picture burn along with her recipe book. There was no changing that. And as for the damage, I had no funds. I'd already cleaned out my bank account paying for the various permit and license applications. The fire had taken everything—including my will to fight.

I pushed him away. "This isn't some sort of coding bug. This is my life and it can't be fixed."

Daniel raised his hands. "I know you're upset and you have every right to be, but you can survive this. Don't give up."

I backed up against a wooden stool. My fingernails dug into the wood. "One of my neighbors told me recently that surviving isn't the same as living. There is no pride in that. I can't recover from this."

"If it's money you need, there are resources. You may not remember all of your grandmother's recipes, but you can create your own dishes. You are a talented cook. Isn't that the foundation of any successful restaurant?"

"You're not listening to me." The stool under my hands shifted, the wood splintering in the tiniest webs; not from the strength in my grip, but from the anger radiating inside me. The destruction of the kitchen, Laolao's burnt book, losing my only photograph of her, and my failure to achieve my dream swirled together, fueling a fiery anger I hadn't felt in a very long time.

He continued, "You can start over. It doesn't have to be here. Being a chef is a portable skill; you can work anywhere. I've tasted your cooking—any kitchen would be lucky to have you. You could do that for a while to save up until this place is ready to go again."

"No. I should have listened to my mother and found a different dream to chase. And now she's dead. Laolao's dead. And the restaurant is dead."

The world spun around me, whirling on its axis, vomiting its contents. The seat of the stool splintered, cracking in half, causing me to stumble back. Wooden shards littered the floor like tiny daggers with each sharp end pointing toward Daniel.

"You're still here. You are the agent of your own fate. It doesn't look like it now, but all is not lost," he said. His dark eyes focused on mine, pleading for me to reconsider.

He still wasn't listening to me.

The rest of the stool shattered with a thunderous crack. The legs and seat exploded in a mass of long needles on the floor. He jumped out of the way just in time. Wooden arrows arranged by invisible hands, interlocking in an intricate fanlike pattern, all pointed to where he stood. I lowered my chin, spent from the release of my anger. "No, Daniel, I'm leaving. There's nothing left for me here."

"Nothing?" His hands clenched. "So you'll run away? Because it's so much easier? I thought you were better than that."

"This is what I'm good at. I screw up, then I leave. And that's what I'm going to do now."

Daniel flinched and then stared at me with a gaze that seemed to me like a final goodbye. It was how I must have looked when I'd left Ma-ma for my travels.

"When you're finished flying away from your problems, you know where to find me," he declared before taking his leave.

I let him go. Time and distance were the cure for any pain. And he would forget. The girl in white would fade from his memory, like a dream leaving fleeting impressions.

I glanced at the devastation in the kitchen. Seeing darkness claim the heart of the restaurant was causing me physical pain. I had transitioned from destroying lives to destroying property. If this wasn't a sign, I didn't know what was.

I approached the spot on the counter where I had left Laolao's recipe book and her photograph. There was nothing here but darkness.

I wished I had brought them upstairs to keep them safe. I wished Ma-ma were still alive. I wished the recipes had worked the way they should have. I wished I'd never meddled with things I had no business involving myself in. So many wishes. My mother had once told me, "Wishes are worth nothing because there's so many of them. If they turned into stars, there would be no sky left."

I couldn't stand the sight of the wreckage any longer. I picked up Meimei and headed upstairs.

I was entropy's handmaiden, bringing destruction to every life I touched. Although it was Younger Shen who'd thrown the punch, Miss Yu was in the hospital with a concussion because of me. Wayne Chiu, Anita Chiu, Older Shen, Younger Shen, Celia, Daniel, and even Ma-ma. I ruined lives—who was to say I wouldn't have made Ma-ma's *worse* if I'd stayed all those years ago?

Her letter still sat on the counter. I returned it to its spot in the toaster slot. The image of Ma-ma placing it there was one I wanted to remember. My mother had written a letter before she died, used the toaster as a mailbox, and hoped it would deliver her message to me.

I tossed my purse onto the coffee table.

The cat rubbed herself against my leg, stopped, meowed, and stared up at me, waiting to be picked up.

"Oh, Meimei," I said, clutching her to my chest. I carried her to the sofa, where I curled into the fetal position. Warm tears trickled down my cheeks, spilling onto the sofa cushion, crystallizing into sparkling teardrops. I gathered the crystals and deposited them into one of Ma-ma's bowls. The cat nestled her head against my neck. Her purrs made me cry harder. This little creature still loved me despite my failures. "You don't choose the ones you love, do you?" I asked the cat through my tears. "I'm so sorry. You deserve better. I know you miss Ma-ma because I miss her, too, now more than ever."

I handwrote a stack of letters, all apologies, ready to be mailed at the nearest post office before I headed for the airport.

Selling the building and its contents would have to wait. Mrs. Chiu and the lawyer could sort out the details. Ms. Minnows would not be involved: I would be sure to include specific instructions about who the ideal buyer should be as I owed the neighborhood that, at least. After I got a new job, I could pay for a professional packing company to come in and tuck Ma-ma's things in storage. There wasn't anything else left in the apartment that was valuable aside from my mother's belongings; even those were only sentimental.

Exit plans were my forte: I always had my eye on the door from the moment I entered any room. I had my father to thank for it. He'd abandoned me and Ma-ma and left an indelible mark, teaching me that leaving was a viable solution to any problem. Fleeing was in my DNA. I'd often wondered if he had started over with a new family somewhere, if I had half siblings out there like me, but bringing up that particular line of thinking had only hurt Ma-ma. I'd always had the impression that as much pain as he had caused her, somehow a part of her had still managed to love him. I carried no such affection for the man whose genetic material contributed to my being.

He wasn't here.

He had never been here.

He had left.

Maybe I was more like him than like my mother or Laolao.

He'd done us a favor by leaving.

And so would I.

The neighborhood was better off without me meddling in it and sticking around to rub my failures in their faces. I fell asleep with my passport on my pillow and the cat asleep on my stomach, hoping to dream about anything but what I was leaving behind. Sleep came with the heaviness of my world disintegrating. It pinned down my heart and soul until even hope couldn't escape.

Chapter Twenty-one

The taxi pulled up as my finger was hovering over the send button on the message to Celia regarding my situation. I resolved to send it when I reached the airport. I'd bought a ticket back to Montreal, a city I'd wanted to spend more time in anyway.

As I glanced around the apartment, the cat rubbed against my legs. I picked her up and held her against my neck. "Oh, Meimei, I'm sorry, but I can't take you with me. I'm asking Celia to take care of you. I'll miss you. I'm sorry I couldn't stay."

The cat purred, sending gentle vibrations up my arms. If I could smuggle her into my shirt and past security, I would. It wasn't fair that my mother had died, leaving her alone. It wasn't fair that I was about to do the same.

Celia would take care of her. Meimei would be better off without me.

I wheeled my rolling luggage down the stairs. Each thud felt like another nail in the coffin. When I opened the door, I was surprised by who stood between me and the taxi.

"I knew you were going to run," Mr. Kuk Wah said.

There was no sign of his erhu or its case. He crossed his arms over his chest; the writhing, tattooed dragons on his arms tightened into coils. The dragons were so lifelike I could almost hear the hiss from the rubbing scales. I waved the taxi off. I could always call another one later. I owed it to Mr. Kuk Wah to explain.

"There's nothing left for me here," I said.

"What about the restaurant? Your heart's wish to open it?"

"It's too late for that now. I've ruined my neighbors' lives, and the fire destroyed the kitchen. I'm out of money. Even if there wasn't a fire, Old Wu said he might block my permit application."

He didn't budge. "And you would let that stop you?"

I couldn't answer. Instead, I walked toward the door of the restaurant and unlocked it. "You can see for yourself how hopeless it is."

We both stepped inside. I was certain that once he saw how bad the damage was, he would understand why I chose to leave.

The thick stench of smoke still hovered in the air like an unshakable, oily blanket. I left the door open, hoping to disperse some of it.

"Where will you go?" The street musician's dark eyes bored into mine. "You want to disappear again?"

Like my father, the one I hated the most in this world, the one wandering around in some city who probably didn't care that his wife had died, the one whom I'd spent my entire life trying not to be.

"Your neighbors need you and so does the neighborhood. What do you think will happen when you leave?"

I didn't want to answer his question because it meant confronting my own cowardice. The street would be fractured when Older Shen and I sold. Ms. Minnows and the others would descend on the opportunity and begin the process of gentrification. Gentrification would turn the Dragon's Gate into a grave marker of what was once here. But my best efforts had created more harm than good, so I straightened my shoulders.

"What will happen, will happen. For seven years, I was gone. They didn't need me then. They don't need me now," I replied.

"It sounds like this is what you want to believe. What do you actually want?"

I bared my soul. "I want this neighborhood to be as prosperous as it once was. I want my neighbors to be happy and to be able to provide for themselves and their families. I want my mother back."

"What about your restaurant?" he asked.

My heart constricted. I shook my head, unable to speak.

"If this had happened to your grandmother, do you think it would have stopped her from running another?" The street musician didn't wait for me to answer. "She came to this country without much. She only had herself and her skills. Her restaurant isn't a physical building made of brick and mortar. It's her heart and soul."

He was right. Laolao would have found—*made*—another spot. It wasn't *where* she cooked that was important; it mattered *that* she cooked.

"Cooking is your gift. You can't ignore how well your food has been received. Do you fear that you are only able to cook from your grandmother's book?"

"I cooked before I was given Laolao's book. I've cooked my own dishes since," I replied.

"Then the need to cook will continue to burn inside of you. If this is so, why give up on the restaurant?"

"Look around you. I don't even want to know how much it will cost to fix," I said, gesturing to the damage.

"It looks bad now, Xiao Niao, but it will all work out. I didn't believe it could happen, but I have my wife back. Miracles can happen if you allow them to." His smile lit his face, highlighting its handsome angles. "Perhaps if you take a closer look, you can see that there's still hope in the most unlikely places."

I walked to the burnt wreckage that was the kitchen. The darkness intimidated me. The memory of the angry flames devouring everything in sight was still fresh in my mind. There was a strange, dark lump on the counter. I moved closer and dragged my fingers across it, coating them with soot. When I pulled my hand away, a streak of brown appeared against the black. Odd. Using both hands now, I rubbed away the grime, channeling Ma-ma's motions when she attacked her scratch-off lottery tickets. Something was emerging from the darkness . . .

My mouth fell open.

Laolao's recipe book.

It should have been destroyed.

Yet the leather-bound book showed no signs of damage. It was as if it had been sitting on the coffee table upstairs instead of here. Traces of soot peppered the ornate grooves of the cover and the leather, but wiped off easily. My grandmother's book had survived.

What did this mean?

I pulled the book against my chest, not caring that the last bits of soot stained my white sweater dress.

Everything else might have been lost, but at least I still had this.

This was a connection to my past.

Perhaps Mr. Kuk Wah was right: I really was meant to honor and follow Laolao's legacy.

There was no other reason why the book would have survived. Laolao faced overwhelming obstacles and built a life for herself and her family here. She found her purpose. All my life, I had been searching for mine. Running a restaurant was what I always dreamed of and it had cost me years away from Ma-ma.

This was what I wanted.

If I gave up now, I would be left wondering about what could have been . . .

If only.

Twenty-eight years of *if onlys*.

This was enough.

My destiny was mine to shape.

Laolao's book had survived this and so would I.

"This is a sign that you are meant to stay," declared Mr. Kuk Wah.

"Yes, I think it is. You were right, and finding the book confirms it: I do need to stay and finish what I started. And now that I have the book back, I need to find out why the recipes aren't working," I said. "Once I do, I can start figuring out how to get financing to fix up the restaurant."

"There must be something we have missed." Mr. Kuk Wah nodded. "It is a shame you can't ask your mother for help."

"Yes, I'm sure that if Ma-ma were alive, she could shed some light on this. She knew Laolao the best."

"So your days of running away are behind you after all?"

I didn't want to be the person who ran away from people and from love. I wasn't my father. His habit of abandonment was no longer mine. I wanted to be the person who wasn't afraid to seize my dreams. I wanted to be the woman that Celia had called her friend and the one Daniel had believed in.

"Yes. I'm not going anywhere. Besides, it's time for another woman in my family to cook for this neighborhood," I replied.

After saying goodbye to Mr. Kuk Wah, I headed back up to the apartment. If Ma-ma were alive, I was certain she would know why her own mother's recipes were backfiring. I missed her so much. I wanted nothing more than to eat one of her special peanut butter and jelly sandwiches on toast.

But before I could make one, I had someone to apologize to. I hugged the cat and told her I was sorry for almost leaving her before.

In response, Meimei licked my cheek. I took it as a sign of forgiveness.

But the cat wasn't the only one I owed an apology to. I pulled out my phone and sent a text to Daniel: **I'm sorry.**

I waited three minutes, then I left the phone on the coffee table in the living room. I didn't expect him to respond after how I treated him, yet I still hoped he would. For now, fixing the neighbors' issues and my friendship with Celia seemed more achievable.

After I unpacked my suitcase, my stomach rumbled. The memory of Ma-ma's peanut butter sandwiches burrowed in my mind, and my craving for them strengthened. I walked to the kitchen, took out the loaf of sliced bread from the fridge, and peered into the toaster. There was something in the other slot that I hadn't noticed before: another sheet of crumpled paper. I fished it out and began reading.

> *Mother.*
> *Why did you die and leave me?*
> *Mother!*
> *Darkness came for me. Swirling, tugging, drowning me*
> *with the thickness of sesame oil. Captive by paralysis of grief.*
> *Spending days in the tub submerged by the weight of my*
> *tears. The pain nullified every other sensation.*
> *Mother.*

There was so much I wanted to say.

Mother.

Come back. Awaken me from this nightmare.

But you can't.

At least you didn't leave me alone.

He pulled me out of the deep.

He reminded me of after, that there was an after: children, our family, a future.

He wants to have a child.

I want it too.

I want to have a daughter, nourished with joy and youtiao. She will be like you, Mother: strong, confident, capable. No demons will haunt her steps. My curse will not befall her. She'll smile because she wants to. Succored on kindness and wonder, her imagination will be boundless, and her lightness of being will outweigh the darkness of mine.

She will not be me.

She will be like you, her grandmother.

She will be like her father.

Him.

The one who saved me from myself. He who accepted the darkness and instead of banishing it, acted as a beacon so I could find my way back. My love. My match. My other.

Oh, I wish you could be alive to meet your future grandchild, Mother.

The wrinkled page crinkled under my fingertips, undulating like a wave. Even now, the paper had marks on the places where my mother's tears had fallen.

I cried now, too, for my grandmother, for my mother, and for me. Drop by drop, my tears joined Ma-ma's, changing the stains into brushstrokes as my sadness mixed with hers. The pattern of miniature puddles resembled the Chinese word for sorrow: *bei-ai*.

I wept for the grandmother I had never known, the woman whose recipes I cooked and whose words I cherished, whose face I had the fortune of seeing before the photograph was lost in flames, the one who traveled across the ocean to raise her daughter alone and help those in need.

I cried for Ma-ma, whom I missed more than anything in this world, the person whose words reached me from beyond the grave.

I cried for myself, who was alone, uncertain, and yearning for those who had been taken from me.

I had lost them both.

Ma-ma's voice spoke through the page. Her thoughts and hopes reached across time to me. It was as though we were still together drinking an afternoon tea. This piece had been torn from a notebook of some sort. A diary, perhaps? Had my mother kept a journal?

The tangible possibility that I could reconnect with Ma-ma eased my sorrow.

If I could find other pages, who knew what else she might have written. Maybe there was something in them that would help me figure out why Laolao's recipe book wasn't working. I needed to find the rest. My mother was meticulous, and odds were that if she had kept these books, they were in immaculate shape.

I called the cat. "Come on, Meimei! Let's go looking for treasure."

Chapter Twenty-two

Ma-ma's room was the only place in the apartment I had not been in since I returned. I hadn't opened the door, for I'd been too afraid that the painful memories of her would overwhelm me. Since the apartment had two bedrooms, I had avoided this for as long as I could. But if Ma-ma had kept journals, she would have hidden them in her room. I needed to face my fears and enter. The doorknob was cold to the touch. It rattled as I tried in vain to twist it open with my hand, sweaty from nerves.

Opening a door shouldn't be difficult, but this simple act had become complicated. It was the admission that my mother was truly gone, that she could no longer pop out of her bedroom in time to watch her Korean soap operas or share in a long, languid conversation over cups of tea. Even now I craved a cup of oolong, but only if Ma-ma were here to share it with me.

I twisted the knob again and pulled the door open.

A lingering miasma of pungent, traditional Chinese ointments assaulted my nostrils. My mother had used a heady mix of creams and liquids to treat anything from headaches to menstrual cramps. She had applied medicated bandages smelling of menthol and eucalyptus for any muscle aches. Odd stripes of white across her shoulders or neck had been a common sight.

Small circular mirrors nailed all over the walls reflected my face back at me. My mahogany dark eyes, wide forehead, and small nose were replicated over and over as a hundred versions of myself stared back. These mirrors were not a product of vanity, but of superstition. According to Ma-ma, they warded off the demons and ill spirits. If each mirror represented an individual demon, my mother must have feared legions of them.

The queen-size bed dominated the modest bedroom with its mismatched sheets, ancient because of my mother's frugal nature. Their cotton was pilled and thin from far too many washings, but they were the most comfortable bedding I had ever known. A bad dream always guaranteed me admission into Ma-ma's sanctuary. She would drive the ghosts and bad demons away by humming arias from *La bohème* in my ear until I fell back asleep.

I sat on the lumpy mattress. Meimei squirmed out of my arms and settled herself on the bed. Nothing much had changed in the years I was gone.

No. The birds . . .

The birds had multiplied. She'd installed rows upon rows of floating melamine shelves above shoulder height to accommodate the expansion of her once humble collection. Though she'd had bird figurines all over the apartment, the bulk of her prized collection was confined to her bedroom because it had given her joy to wake up to them every morning. Before I'd left, I had a tradition of gifting her with bird figurines. It began with a storm petrel, a Wakamba carving of ebony wood from Kenya I had picked up at the museum gift shop from a sixth-grade school field trip. She'd adored the unexpected birthday present, and I had hunted for them since.

Clusters of ceramic birds were perched on every shelf. Her obsession had brought her happiness, so I'd fed it. The tiki bird from French Polynesia nested beside a delft bluebird from the Netherlands. One of my favorites was a glass rainbow macaw from an Argentinian artist that mimicked the vibrant barrios of Buenos Aires. Since the sixth grade, I'd given her one every year until I'd left: eight birds in total.

As I lifted each member of her extensive bird collection, I imagined Ma-ma was with me, telling a story about each one. There were no signs of dust anywhere; cleanliness had been her religion. I counted eighty-eight birds in total. Ma-ma had been busy collecting while I was gone.

I couldn't deny that every time I saw a beautiful feathered creature in figurine form, I thought of my mother. If only I'd sent her one, even a single bird, from my travels, it could have been the precursor to establishing communication once more.

Ma-ma had spoken to her birds often, especially when she cleaned them every Saturday morning. I had imagined she was some fairy-tale princess in the Black Forest holding court over an avian kingdom.

I was tempted to speak to them now, but I didn't want to be the one to convey the loss of their queen.

Suddenly, however, Ma-ma's collection stirred.

It began as a single chirp, a mournful cry swelling into a chorus. The figurines burst into song, tiny beaks opening, chests puffed, to release a somber tribute to their departed beloved. The tune was unfamiliar, yet its melancholy was palpable, rising, surging until the final trill when every bird bowed their heads toward the empty bed, frozen as if they hadn't sung seconds before.

I thanked them for the happiness they'd bestowed on Ma-ma.

I fell backward onto the bed with my arms spread-eagle. A soft purr rumbled near my ear. Meimei had hopped across the bed to join me, and curled against my side. "She's really gone," I whispered to the cat. "I bet you miss her as much as I do."

The ache in my heart swelled, pushing against my ribs. Ma-ma should have been here waiting for me. If I had returned while she was still alive, would she have flitted to the toaster, happily tearing up the letter before I could see it? My chest rose and fell in ragged breaths. Tears threatened to drown me again, so I gathered my thoughts and remembered why I'd come in here: to search for the rest of Ma-ma's journals.

I rose and crouched down to my knees to peer under the bed. Labeled shoeboxes formed an impenetrable wall. Every single one had my name on it: artwork, report cards, essays, and school projects from over the years.

She had saved them all.

I opened more boxes and unearthed all sorts of financial records. Everything was organized with multiple copies. She had even kept Laolao's old permits and licenses for the restaurant. I set that folder aside for further study.

Ma-ma had squirreled an unlabeled box between a fortress of tax returns and old *Time* magazines. I opened it and counted fifteen black spiral notebooks chronicling her life from her teenage years up until her death a few weeks ago. The crumpled page I'd found in the toaster must have been ripped from one of these books. I wondered why she decided to place it in there. Was it a bread crumb to lead me to find the others?

Judging from the last journal's entries, she had written on an erratic schedule, but nevertheless, it was regular enough to fill all these books.

I pulled the box out from under the bed, placing Laolao's folder on top. Meimei, being the cat she is, hopped onto the box, and came along for the impromptu ride to the living room.

How should I read Ma-ma's life? From the beginning, as I would any story, or from the end where we had parted? Her letter answered any questions I'd had about whether she'd regretted the past seven years of silence between us. My eyes traveled to the worn folder full of permits. The restaurant. Laolao. Ma-ma had mentioned in her letter that she, too, had quarreled with her own mother.

On the coffee table, I arranged the journals into stacks with the oldest first. Perhaps the earlier ones would contain a clue about Laolao and her recipe book. I pulled the first book from the pile and began to read.

> *Some of the most magical times are when I watch Mother and Mr. Wu cook together in our kitchen. It looks like they're culinary wizards performing some sort of alchemy.*
>
> *Oh, the aromas they can conjure.*
>
> *They often allow me to taste the new dishes after they both critique them. Mother makes adjustments and writes them down in her book.*
>
> *Mother, I wonder if you know how Mr. Wu looks at you.*
>
> *He holds you in the highest regard. I'm sure he would present you with his heart if you'd give him a chance. He has never said anything, probably because he fears it would jeopardize your friendship.*
>
> *Why doesn't he say anything?*
>
> *Does he need to?*
>
> *Mother, do you already know?*
>
> *This must be one of those situations where love can never be.*

Old Wu. He was here testing recipes with Laolao. And he knew about the recipe book, but wouldn't answer my questions. Why? Perhaps because I hadn't earned his respect yet.

He loved Laolao. No wonder he snapped when I started questioning her cooking.

With Ma-ma gone, he was the only one left who knew my grandmother. He cooked with her. He'd been there when Laolao wrote down her recipes.

I had to try. I had nothing left to lose. My fingers flew to my collarbones. The crisscross marks there had already healed. I wouldn't allow him to wound me with his words again. Perhaps the Old Tiger needed to see I shared the same claws as Laolao, though mine were still growing in.

Chapter Twenty-three

I headed to Old Wu's restaurant.

The afternoon crowd had dwindled to a handful of tables. I slipped past the folding screens and walked over to Old Wu at his customary seat, sipping his tea and grazing on a cold plate of spiced chicken and sliced pork hock. He ignored me as though I didn't exist.

I slammed my palm onto the table. The force shook the plates and sloshed the tea from his cup. Old Wu finally raised his eyes. I had been nervous walking in, but now my nerves were overtaken by a kind of bravery borne from desperation.

"The restaurant didn't survive the fire, but I did. I came to you earlier for help and I let you speak. It's my turn now and you will listen." I pressed both hands against the table. Old Wu stared, his lips pressed into a thin line. If it weren't for the soft rise and fall of his chest, I would have thought I was speaking to a statue.

"I want to open the restaurant, but I can't because something's wrong with Laolao's recipe book. I don't know what it is. You're the only one left that knows her as well as Ma-ma did. I'm doing this to help my neighbors and myself. I can't walk away from them when they need me."

The old man said nothing.

"You say you want to save the neighborhood. But even before the fire, you said you might block me. But as one of the leaders of Chinatown, you should be better than that. You're supposed to look out for what the community needs. Maybe I messed things up, but at least I'm trying to help us all. You're nothing but a hypocrite."

With my final words, my bravado fled and my voice faltered. Then the song of my heartbeat returned, thumping in a steady rhythm, marking the passage of time. One. Two. Three. No answer. I raised my chin and turned to leave.

He lowered his teacup onto the table. "Are you done speaking?"

I nodded.

"Please." The old man gestured for me to stay.

I pulled out a chair and sat down.

"When you came back, I was certain you would sell the building and cut the last ties you have here. You'd been gone so long, what reason was there for you to stay? Then you started cooking. Fai, Anita and Wayne, and especially Celia sang your praises to me. It sounded like Qiao had returned. I wasn't sure what to think or believe. But if even a fire cannot drive you away, perhaps I was wrong about you. Maybe you do care after all."

He rose to his feet. "A true test of a cook is her skill. Show me, Tan girl. Let me see if you can cook. Prepare me a dish tomorrow in your kitchen. If I like what I eat, I promise I will answer all your questions about your grandmother."

The next day, we met at my apartment. The cat took one look at the old man before bolting off into one of the bedrooms to hide. As Old Wu busied himself reading from a stack of Ma-ma's old issues of

National Geographic, I turned the kitchen into my kingdom. No nervousness or uncertainty. I focused on the joy of creating.

I began the process of transforming the slab of pork belly in the fridge into my version of a Shanghai-style dish. I chopped the lean meat into bite-size pieces, and then blanched and browned them in demerara sugar and sesame oil. The sizzle and occasional pop accompanied the incomparable, savory aroma of rendering fat. As the meat stewed in its juices, I created a sauce comprising pink peppercorns, star anise, cloves, sweet soy sauce, and Chinese rice wine in the hot wok. I braised the pork belly, checking in at intervals to ensure the tenderness of the meat.

One hour later, I served the dish in a shallow clay bowl with diced cilantro as a garnish.

Old Wu closed his eyes. His nose twitched as he inhaled the delicious aroma. He used his chopsticks to pluck a piece off the plate. The sticks dripped with the viscous sauce as he bit into the tender pork. He nodded, bobbing his head to a phantom melody as he chewed with deliberate bites. After four more pieces, he wiped his mouth with a napkin and finally spoke. "Is the dish done to your satisfaction? Would you change anything in how you prepared it?"

"Yes, it turned out exactly how I wanted it. The pork is tender and the spices, the right balance. I wouldn't change how I prepared it. I could have used a traditional clay pot, but the results would be the same."

"I see." He struggled to keep his expression blank. A cough escaped his clamped lips, followed by another, until he was overcome with a bout of coughing.

I rushed to fill him a glass of cold water. "Mr. Wu, are you all right?"

He held out his hand. After the last cough, he burst into laughter. Tears escaped the corners of his eyes. His lean body convulsed with every guffaw. What was happening to him? Meimei padded out of the bedroom and stared at him from across the room.

"Mr. Wu?" I asked. "I don't understand."

After his laughter died down, he sipped his water. A smile lingered on his lips. "Tan girl, you can cook. Oh, how you can cook."

He liked it. He *liked* my food. He was smiling at me. I couldn't have imagined this even if I tried. Of course, I had used my own recipe. Serving something to him from my grandmother's book would have been foolish.

"It reminds me of hong shao rou, but your preparation is different," he said.

"I tasted this in my travels and loved it. I think the added sweetness complements the spices I chose." Though my voice was steady, I linked my fingers behind my back to prevent them from trembling from excitement.

"Very good, and unlike your laolao's style. Different but in a good way. You have convinced me that you have what it takes to continue your grandmother's legacy. I will answer whatever questions you may have for me." The tone of his voice had changed. I recognized it, for it was the same one he reserved for Celia.

The animosity I had grown accustomed to was gone. Tension melted away from my neck and shoulders. Perhaps I would get the answers I so desperately hoped for. "I want to ask you about my grandmother."

"Is this related to you opening the restaurant?" he asked.

"Yes. It's all related. However, I can't open anytime soon. The damage is extensive. I was lucky the fire didn't reach upstairs, or spread," I confessed.

Old Wu took a sip of the tea. "If you want to, you can make the impossible possible. The women in your family are steel because they refuse to bend under the direst of circumstances, Ye Ying," he said.

Ye Ying. Nightingale. Its songs were the most beautiful in the bird kingdom, and legend had it that its magical song had cured a dying emperor. It was a name worthy of a new beginning. Meimei slinked her way onto Wu's lap. I expected him to push her off, but he surprised me by smiling and rubbing beneath her chin. She mewed happily.

Wu smiled. "It's funny that you mention Qiao. You remind me so much of her. You have inherited her spirit."

Was this the beginning of a strange friendship between nightingale and tiger?

"Before I can speak of her, I want to apologize," Old Wu said before sipping his tea. His dark eyes were direct. "I am a bitter old man. I have never been fair to you or your mother. I judged Miranda harshly. To compare her to Qiao was not fair. Miranda was her own person.

"When she decided not to continue with the restaurant, I was angry because I was there when Qiao arrived from China with nothing. I was a new immigrant myself having come from Hong Kong four months earlier. Qiao and I became friends at the market. We'd always fight for the best vegetables and fish. She lived in an apartment with three other women near where you live now. Her roommates were seamstresses. When she spoke about food, I knew she was a cook.

"But in this new world, life was hard and jobs, scarce. I'd been lucky. My uncle helped me get work at the restaurant. Qiao had no family here to advocate for her. No one wanted to take a chance on her, but she prevailed. She proved them wrong with one taste of her cooking. I thought Miranda was throwing away everything Qiao had worked for, but I realize now, she was saving it for you."

"You really were close to my grandmother," I said. It confirmed what I'd read in Ma-ma's journals.

A wry smile crossed his lips, softening his usually stern countenance, and I caught a glimpse of the man who might have been a good friend to Laolao. "Qiao was not perfect. Her temper was legendary."

The faraway look in eyes suggested he was losing himself in nostalgia. "When she was hired as a cook in one of the busiest restaurants in Chinatown, she found out that she was earning only half of what the other cook was making. The other cook was a lazy man—the son of the owners. She was furious. She quit the same day and sought out her former employer's rival, offering her services for a low wage with the caveat that if business doubled, so would her pay."

"I'm guessing she triumphed?" I asked.

"No. Her new employer was as shifty as her former one. Business doubled but she never received what she'd been promised. So she cursed them both. In her anger, she went blind for a week. The two restaurants suffered so much ill luck afterward that, eventually, they went out of business. Even though Qiao regained her eyesight, her anger never subsided, so her curse remained. There was another restaurant across the street, but as you can still see, nothing survives there."

Curses were like salting the earth. Hearing about Laolao from Old Wu's perspective filled in the gaps for me. He was the connection to the woman I'd never met but had always wanted to.

"You eat up my stories about your grandmother like a child nibbling on sweets. Did Miranda not tell you much about your laolao?" he asked.

I shook my head.

"I think it is because she might have found it too painful to speak of her. I was the same way for years after Qiao died. Such is the case when one loves too much."

"So you did love her?" I asked, recalling that my mother had thought the same thing.

He cradled his teacup. "How could I not? I was one of many that loved Qiao. She had a way about her that attracted people. Her temper was as famous as her capacity for kindness. Qiao welcomed all new immigrants into the area with a meal and connected them to what they needed. Helping people was one of her many specialties. Yes, I loved her. I have always loved her, but she only saw me as a good friend."

"Was it because of my grandfather?" I asked.

He refilled his empty teacup. "The day she told me she had lost her heart to the Shanghainese hotelier, all I could do was be happy for her. I could tell by the way she looked at him, everything and everyone else disappeared. At the time, I would have given anything for her to see me in the same way."

The old man's voice softened like fresh pork buns from the steamer yielding to a fork.

"When Qiao found out she was carrying Miranda, I knew she'd made her choice, and it wasn't me. She never ended up marrying the hotelier because she didn't want to move back to China. She was determined to raise her child on her own. I'd been foolish in thinking she'd accept my affections, but when she refused, I didn't take it well." He paused, lowering his eyes for a brief moment. "I was also very upset when your mother decided not to continue with your grandmother's restaurant. The neighborhood needed it. It felt like Miranda had turned her back on all of us. But I shouldn't have been so harsh on her. She had a sickness that prevented her from leaving the house after your laolao died. In retrospect, I should have been kinder to her."

I swallowed before mustering a nod. Old Wu inspired fear, a remnant from my childhood that had never faded over time. But here he was, petting the cat and saying more to me this afternoon than he had during the span of my entire life.

"Misplaced anger is an old, bitter habit, one I am ashamed of having. I behaved terribly when you came back into town and when I invited you to the restaurant. I thought that if you were home, Miranda's death could have been prevented. But I only blamed you because I could not blame myself."

"You're right. I should have been home. I blame myself for her death."

"No, it wasn't your fault. Miranda's death showed me how much I'd failed Qiao. When Miranda died, I was there when the ambulance came. All of us were shocked that she walked out of the building. I hadn't seen her in years but knew she was still alive. Every week, someone in the neighborhood visited her, and as long as they did, I did not worry. She was still young. But it all changed that morning."

Yes, my life also had changed that day, and I still didn't know why my mother stepped outside.

"Since it is too late to help your mother, I want to help you. You are what your neighbors need. You said earlier that the recipes were going wrong, but now that I have tasted your cooking, I do not believe it is because you failed the execution of them. You mentioned the fate of the restaurant was tied to these recipes somehow?"

I told him about Miss Yu's prophecy and its conditions.

"May I see the book?"

I placed the heavy book onto the table and pushed it toward him.

Old Wu marveled at the cover for a brief moment before flipping through the pages. He seemed to be searching for something specific, finally stopping at the spot where the three pages were missing. He gently pushed the opened book toward me.

I straightened the book before me. "Ah, you've seen the damage. I don't know what was in these missing pages, but I am hoping you might. I think it could be related to what's going wrong."

"Miranda ripped these recipes out when Qiao told her she had to run the restaurant. They were special dishes she and her mother had cooked together. She burned them in defiance. Qiao told me about it years ago. She was very upset at the time. I agree with you: this represents a severing of harmony that must be the reason the recipes aren't working as they should. If you can repair the book, I am certain the troubles with the neighbors will be solved."

I was shocked. Ma-ma had *burned* the pages. Yet Ma-ma's relationship with Laolao had been complicated. I had known this for years. Ma-ma's delicate temperament would never have allowed her to run the restaurant. She must have been horrified when her mother insisted she follow the family line. The family business became the point of contention between them.

"I have confidence that you will solve the problem with your grandmother's book, and once you do, the restaurant needs your attention. I will not stand in your way. Ye Ying, if you will allow it, I want to help you. You have the skill and passion to succeed."

One of the most successful restaurateurs of Chinatown was offering me his aid. I would be a fool not to welcome his valuable advice. Hours ago, I'd thought I had lost everything, but now I had purpose again, a clear path to my goal, and support from the most unlikely of places. Faith rushed in from every direction, like water gushing from a broken dam.

"I can't possibly accept such a generous offer," I blurted.

Meimei mewed at me as though she was calling me an idiot.

Old Wu smiled. "I insist. This is something I can still do for Qiao. What I'm offering is a mentorship."

No hesitation. This was a gift. "I'm honored to accept your help, Lao Wu," I said. "Thank you."

He set Meimei down and rose to his feet. "Then let us start now. Show me the kitchen that was damaged by the fire."

We headed downstairs to the restaurant. Inside, Old Wu conducted a thorough inspection of the damage, and we discussed our options while he took copious notes in a small notepad he kept in his back pocket. Now that he was not taking the role of antagonist, he proved to be quite the ally.

I slipped *The Barber of Seville* record into the Victrola and lowered the volume to ambient level. Old Wu walked to the counter and examined the ruined goddess. He reached out to touch her, but pulled back at the last moment.

"She was beautiful once," he said. "Qiao had her displayed in the same spot. She was the symbol of prosperity in the neighborhood. I hope when you take over, we can see her restored."

I blushed. "I wish for the same thing."

"As for the kitchen, I am going to be honest with you," he said. "I estimate the repairs will cost at least one hundred and twenty-five thousand. When you factor in new electrical, plumbing, and possible structural damage, updated appliances, and redesign for a more efficient space, it's a reasonable figure."

My heart sank. The bank would never loan me that much. I wiped my damp hands on my white skirt.

"Do not lose hope. I will give you the loan on three conditions: first, that we have a weekly meeting to discuss your progress; second, that you will cook me a meal once a month; and third, the full amount must be paid back in five years. The meetings will facilitate our mentorship, the meal will act as a trial run for the new dishes you want on the menu, and the last item will motivate you to succeed. A time frame shorter than that would be insurmountable, and a longer one would be more like a gift than a loan." He leaned forward. "This is a means for you to make your own way, Ye Ying."

His terms were more than fair.

"I accept your generous offer, Lao Wu," I replied.

"By the way, I prefer not to be reminded of my age." A rusty chuckle escaped his lips. "If you want to, you can call me Lao Shi since I will be your mentor."

Teacher. I smiled and found I was no longer surprised to see his rare smile in return.

The universe unfurled in such unpredictable ways. We all moved in a constant celestial dance. The song ends and the music and our partner may change, but in order to survive we must continue dancing. I would prevail, and I would succeed.

"Qiao was an excellent chef with a long shadow. In order for you to succeed, you need to walk alongside her, not behind her. Cook from your heart." He glanced at his watch. "I am afraid I must return to the restaurant. I have been gone far too long already. Come by and pick up the check next week. I'm confident that you will find a way to solve the problem with the neighbors."

I tipped my head. "Thank you, Lao Shi."

I didn't know yet how to fix that issue, but I was hopeful that I would figure something out. Working out a solution was easier now that the problem had been identified.

"No, thank you for the wonderful meal," he said. "You have a gift, Ye Ying, and a vision that is your own. You need both to succeed."

I migrated back upstairs to think about the missing pages. The mystery of what had happened to them was solved: Ma-ma had burned them out of spite. Though I was grateful for the insight, I still had a dilemma. Miss Yu had told me that the fate of the restaurant was tied to cooking from the recipe book. With Old Wu's help, I could restore what had been lost, but with the book still damaged, I wouldn't be able to prosper.

The sounds of Meimei gnawing and chewing greeted me. "Meimei?" I called out. "What are you up to?"

I checked the hallway and the bedrooms, but no cat. The sounds originated from the living room. Lowering myself to my hands and knees, I peeked under the couch and caught the furry criminal in the act. I reached out to see what she had in her mouth, inadvertently beginning a slobbery game of tug-of-war with the cat.

Meimei sank her claws into me and I winced, annoyed. This wasn't like her. After extricating the cat's needle-like claws, I stretched out what I had managed to grab from her. It was a woven bracelet I'd bought in Boracay, a memento of my first vacation with Emilio. I gathered the edges and contemplated whether it could still be saved. As I separated the loose strands, a memory resurfaced of when I had seen this similar kind of damage.

When I was little, while crossing the street, I'd dropped a cloth doll my mother had made for me. Part of it was run over by a passing vehicle, and one of its arms was torn off. When I came home crying, Ma-ma scooped me into her embrace and calmed me down with kisses and hugs. "Sometimes when something is broken, we can't fix it. Instead, we can make it anew." She made a new limb from a fresh piece of fabric, stuffed it with batting, and reattached it. The doll was made whole again. My recollection gave me an idea. What if I wrote down three of my own recipes and added them to Laolao's book? What if I contributed something brand-new instead of trying to replicate what was already there?

Would it work?

The same blood flowed in my veins; theoretically, so did the same magic. Maybe adding new recipes of my own could heal the heart of my grandmother's recipe book. This was an educated guess at best, but it was the only solution I had.

My grandmother had created it.

My mother had damaged it.

I would restore it.

I rushed to the book on the kitchen table and opened it to the section where the three pages were missing. I used a scalpel from Ma-ma's utility drawer to cut away the ragged edges, leaving enough of a margin to attach my addition later.

The instant I finished, an invisible wind stirred the pages, flipping them, releasing all of the aromas of the dishes in the air. I closed my eyes to drink in the unseen feast. When I opened them, the book had returned to its normal state, open to the place I had trimmed.

Was this a sign I was on the right track?

Three of my recipes. No, three of my *best* recipes.

The tiniest speck of hope arose from the ashes of my failure. My grandmother had learned to stand on her own after crossing an ocean. My mother had raised me alone even while tormented by her lingering demons. I was a product of these strong women. Ma-ma's final request to follow my dreams was within my reach.

Would my idea work?

Only one way to find out.

Chapter Twenty-four

Sitting at the kitchen table with my grandmother's book beside me, I wrote out the recipe I would cook for Celia on a piece of paper I'd found in Ma-ma's stationery drawer. The parchment matched the pages in the book, so it must have belonged to Laolao at one point.

I followed the format of Laolao's recipes. I wrote down the ingredients and instructions before moving on to the final part of the recipe. What was my wish for this dish? I pulled out a notebook and revised the words until the note conveyed what I wanted.

Writing the recipe was the easy part.

I had to call and invite Celia over. What if she said no? She had been there for me when the fire happened, but that could have been out of duty or common decency. I hadn't heard from her since.

I shook my head, trying to dislodge all of my growing doubts. I dialed her number and waited.

"Hello?"

"Hi, Celia," I said. "I need to talk to you. Can you drop by tonight at my place for dinner around seven?"

"I . . ." The hesitation in her voice wounded me. I'd done this.

"Please. Allow me the opportunity to apologize in person."

I heard a soft sigh. "All right. I'll be over for dinner."

She was coming.

Using a strong adhesive, I attached the recipe I had finished writing to the clean edge I had left in the book. By the time I completed the other two pages, it was five o'clock. The market was still open and the night young. I headed out to collect the ingredients I would need.

Arroz Caldo
(Natalie's Recipe)

Cooking oil
Ginger
Chicken wings and drumsticks
Fish sauce
Chicken broth
Short grain rice
Saffron threads
Chopped green onions

Add the cooking oil and crushed ginger in a stockpot. Once it is sizzling, add the chicken and the fish sauce. Stir-fry to avoid burning. When the chicken skin begins to brown, introduce the chicken broth and the rice to the pot.

Bring to a boil for thirty minutes. Stir every two minutes to make sure the rice does not stick to the bottom of the pot.

When the rice is cooked, add the saffron threads and stir. Serve with chopped green onions.

Note:

To bring comfort and warmth to those you love.

I cooked this for Celia, a treasured friend. I wanted her to know how much I love her.

This was a recipe I learned from my travels in the Philippines.

Arroz caldo was comfort food, a Filipino-style congee. The dish was golden, warm, comforting—just like Celia herself.

My note for her was simple—I wanted to show her that I valued her friendship and I was grateful for her presence in my life. There would be no more errant meddling or ill-conceived notions of what would bring her happiness.

After I finished preparing it, I sprinkled on a garnish of minced green onions as the final touch. The confetti of green accented the yellow porridge. It wasn't the fanciest dish, but its bold flavors sang on the tongue.

I placed a round, raised lid over the small bowl to trap in the heat.

From the moment I arrived after my mother died, Celia had welcomed me. I had never truly thanked her for everything she had done for me. I vowed to myself that this dish would be the first of many gestures I would make.

She arrived a few minutes later, coming up the steps and through the door with the tentativeness of a wild fawn. I had ruined the effortless intimacy we had once shared in our friendship. I had to fix this.

"What did you cook?" Celia unloaded her satchel on the counter and headed for the empty seat I pulled out for her.

"First, I want to apologize again for how I treated you. I was so wrong and I hope, in time, you can forgive me." I took the seat across from her. "Before you eat, I want to tell you something."

She crooked an eyebrow. "Are you about to warn me that you're going to perform some sort of strange experiment on me? Again?"

"No," I replied. "This isn't a dish made with the intention of meddling. I don't want to change you. I think you're perfect the way you are."

Celia's cheeks turned rosy pink.

"This is me showing my appreciation for the friendship you have given me. I can't thank you enough for your kindness and generosity in the wake of Ma-ma's passing. You have been my kindred spirit, and I hope to earn that trust back. I'm hoping this dish will bring you a small measure of the happiness that you've given me." I lifted the lid, revealing the steaming arroz caldo.

Celia's eyes widened. Her tortoiseshell glasses began to fog up from the steam, and her stainless-steel spoon blushed from the heat. She took a spoonful of the porridge, blowing on it to cool it off before taking a small bite.

Two tendrils of steam rose from the bowl, traveling along her shoulders until they joined together at her back. Celia let out a sigh, a contented purring sound that vibrated the hovering line, changing it into a thick, glowing strand of yarn. The yarn multiplied, falling downward as if invisible knitting needles had purled and cast a materializing shimmering blanket. Each murmur from Celia extended the material until it fell to the floor. Once finished, it tightened around Celia's body in a comforting embrace.

"This makes me feel so warm inside," she said in between bites. "It reminds me of snuggling under afghans on rainy days with my mother. I loved those moments."

As she finished the dish, the wispy covering dissolved into the air.

"Thank you," she murmured, wiping her mouth.

"You're very welcome." It worked. I had done it! The best part was being able to make reparations to this person I had come to care about so deeply.

"Why don't you make some tea?" Celia asked. "We're due for a chat."

I made my way to the cupboards and chose jasmine tea. I craved its light, floral scent and flavor, for I needed a sense of levity and normalcy. Celia got up from her seat and busied herself watering my mother's orchids by the windowsill. It was clear she had been here often enough that she knew where the spray bottle was. I realized at that moment that the stack of magazines on the table were from Older Shen and the stocked fridge when I arrived, from his brother. The brand-new tin of jasmine tea in my hand was from Miss Yu. They were all here all the time, yet I had never seen it until now.

"Didn't you have your date with Daniel recently?" Celia asked, setting down the spray bottle.

Daniel hadn't responded to my apology text. I was afraid that I would never see him again.

I dropped scoops of tea leaves into an empty pot. "I did and it went well, but after the fire . . . we fought. I'm pretty sure I screwed up any chance of being with him." The kettle on the stove whistled. The high-pitched sound pierced the peaceful air in the apartment. I lifted the kettle off the stovetop and poured the steaming water into the teapot. I placed the pot and two earthenware cups on a wooden tray.

Celia's mauve lips opened while her hands moved to frame her hips. "Why would you do something so stupid?"

I almost dropped the tray on the way to the coffee table. The cups clinked from the sudden movement.

"He's cute, decent, and you like him." She huffed. "Need I remind you about the best part—he's not married."

"With all of the neighbors' problems blowing up around me and the fire gutting the restaurant, I thought I had nothing to stay for." I poured the tea into two cups. The steam rolled off the rims. I glanced in Celia's direction. She sank into her chair, cradling her cup.

She narrowed her eyes at me.

"I had a high body count already. I didn't want to add to it," I reasoned, then buckled under her glare. "Fine, I pushed him away so it would be easier to run. I'd even bought a plane ticket, but a wise friend stopped me. But before I can even think of Daniel, I need to focus on undoing the harm I did around here. Maybe opening the restaurant will show him I'm serious about staying and he'll forgive my stupidity."

"It sounds to me like he is your match. When you talk about him, there's so much hope in your voice, like you think this one is different from the others."

I sighed. The thought had crossed my mind. "What if he doesn't forgive me? What if the only thing that kept him coming was the magic of the recipes I cooked for him?"

"We both know it's more than just the food."

"Well—"

Celia held up her hand. "If you're going to say that your laolao's food is more powerful than love, I beg to differ. Her cooking was amazing, but to say it's greater than love, even I have to disagree. Anyway, Daniel sees something wonderful in you and I see it, too, you know."

I lowered my eyes. "Even after the damage I've caused?"

"Yes, and if you had left without saying a word . . ." She met my eyes. "I forgive you for what you've done. I missed you, my friend."

First she had given me kindness and now, forgiveness. I was very lucky to have Celia in my life.

"Thank you. I should probably also confess that I was going to send you a message and leave you the cat."

She whacked me in the arm. "If you had done that, I'd have hunted you down and dragged you back here myself."

I still had two more recipes to write. Celia agreed to accompany me to a late-night market across town. We returned to the apartment with four overstuffed bags of ingredients. Celia, ever the enabler, had pointed to everything in sight, shoving items into the shopping cart as if we were preparing for an apocalypse. I hadn't the heart to dissuade her; as a result, I had to play a game of Tetris to fit everything into the fridge when we got back. I started to experiment in the kitchen as we chatted; Celia would be my taster as we figured out the best recipes to use.

"Are these your notebooks from your school days on the table?" she asked.

"Oh, those are my mother's journals. I didn't know she had them. I found them in her room; I'm going to read them all eventually," I replied.

"Miranda did like to write. I remember that her penmanship was beautiful. I guess reading them would kind of bring her back in a way."

Celia was right. There was a measure of comfort seeing Ma-ma's words. I should make time to read more tonight after I finished cooking.

"So once you decide what to cook for Fai Shen and the Chius," she said, "have you figured out how you'll get them to come here?"

I stopped midchop. The garlic cloves on the cutting board almost rolled away from the abrupt motion. "I hadn't thought about that part yet," I replied.

"The last I heard, Wayne and Anita weren't talking. At all. You'll need to contact both separately. It'll be trickier to get Wayne out of the convenience store than to get ahold of Anita in between appointments." Celia sipped her glass of cranberry juice. "Wayne did come out of the store that afternoon when he saw the fire truck. He was going to drop by, but I told him you were all right and that it wasn't a good time. Maybe if you ask him to stop by tomorrow, asking for help with something, he'll come?"

"Celia, are you asking me to lie?"

She rolled her eyes and snorted. "It's for his own good. Those two need to sit down and talk instead of yelling over each other. Leave Anita to me. Tell me the time and I'll make sure she's here. As for Fai, he's cleared his schedule to entertain Melody Minnows. You'd think he was dating the woman. It's a shame that he's decided to sell. I'll leave you his number."

"Thank you," I murmured. "What would I do without you?"

"Your life would be far more miserable," she replied.

"You're right, it would be."

Celia and I made more plans that night. Once we had selected the meal for the Chius, she began to nod off, and I sent her home. I should have been exhausted after what had happened, but I was just awake enough to create the perfect dish for Older Shen.

It was well past midnight, but I had my final recipe. All three were written and placed carefully into Laolao's recipe book. With that done, I decided to read some of my mother's journals before succumbing to sleep.

Mother wanted to add a new item to the menu. She wasn't satisfied with the current repertoire. I told her that her dishes were already famous. She insisted it wasn't enough.

I still laugh when I remember how she looked that day.

She waved her wooden spoon like a saber, like some warrior woman of old.

"You are only as good as your last creation. You need to grow and get better. Do you think my competitors are sleeping? They're waiting to capitalize on my mistakes. To be the best, you have to be in a constant state of hunger."

"Always being hungry sounds like torture," I said.

"Anything worth having involves some measure of pain and work. Because of this, you treasure it more. Now eat your noodle soup before it gets cold."

I smiled and closed the book. I wished I had the chance to know Laolao. I would have learned so much from her.

Outside my window, night descended on the city, with its lights obscuring the heavens.

My dreams were fueled with stars that evening: swirling galaxies of wonder, radiant colors with no earthly names, the weightless sensation of traveling through universes with the task of collecting wayward comets and wispy nebulas, showing me the infinite possibilities of my fate.

Chapter Twenty-five

I awoke the next morning energized by my nocturnal reverie. Today, I would start fixing my neighbors' dilemmas—starting with the Chius' marriage.

After texting Celia the scheduled time for Mrs. Chiu's arrival, I started the preparations for the dish. I planned on calling Mr. Chiu with a faux emergency when the meal was almost ready.

Snow Pea Leaves
(Natalie's Recipe)

Garlic
Oil
Snow pea leaves
Salt
Pepper

Mince the garlic into tiny cubes. Heat the oil in the wok, then toss the garlic in. Watch the color change from pale yellow to gold. This is the indication it is ready. Too soon and it will lack the crispy texture. Too late and it will become bitter. Scoop the pieces out of the oil and set aside.

Rinse the snow pea leaves under cold water. Stir-fry the leaves in the hot wok for about a minute until they wilt into a mountain of emerald. Add salt and pepper to your taste.

Garnish with the toasted garlic on top.

Note:

My mother made this dish for me one Sunday afternoon. We didn't have much, but it was enough. Nothing gave me more comfort than this humble dish. No other dish reminds me more of home and Ma-ma's embrace than this.

Cook this for those who are in disagreement. The simplicity of the ingredients will facilitate communication. I served this to the Chius to help them remember the love that was the foundation of their marriage.

Using my mother's cleaver, I minced the garlic, tapping the knife's edge against the wooden chopping board to a woodpecker's rhythm. The pale yellow bulbs dwindled into tiny cubes. I transferred them to a sauce bowl. I rinsed the emerald green snow pea leaves in the sink before placing them in a stainless-steel colander.

The recipe called for only a handful of ingredients: garlic, salt and pepper, oil, and the snow pea leaves. Despite its simplicity, the flavor was profound, and the dish was a favorite of mine. I adjusted the heat of the stove. The temperature was key for success. Too hot, and the dish would burn. Too cold, and it would grow soggy and be ruined. I dipped a chopstick into the drizzle of vegetable oil in the wok. The tip bubbled from the heat—it was ready. The minced garlic took the initial plunge, bathing in the heat, tanning into crisp golden brown before I scooped the pieces out to toss the greens in. With a sprinkle of sea salt and pepper for taste, I continued to stir to avoid burning them. The green leaves wilted, changing into a deeper hue, the shade of moss on the forest floor. The color signaled peak tenderness and texture.

I scooped the cooked snow pea leaves out of the wok and onto the two plates, arranging them over a bed of fragrant jasmine rice, and adding the toasted garlic as a garnish. The dish wore a palette of gold, green, and white.

It smelled delicious. Sometimes, it was the simplest things in life we needed most.

I picked up the rotary phone's receiver and dialed the number for the convenience store. The dial rotated, making a whirring sound, clicking as each number registered.

"Hello?" Mr. Chiu called out over the line.

"Mr. Chiu, it's Natalie," I said. "I need your help. There's a problem in the apartment. I think I have rats."

"Aiyah!" There was muffled shuffling on the other line. "They must have come out because of the fire."

"Please help me. I think I saw a few of them running around. I'm terrified of them," I pleaded.

"I'll be right over." Click.

I returned the receiver to its cradle. Rats. Celia would be impressed at my fibbing ability, but horrified by the subject of the lie. I let Mr. Chiu into the apartment five minutes later. He'd come armed with traps.

"Where did you see them last?" His eyes darted to and fro, scanning the apartment, moving in a frenzy rivaling the action of the ball in an Olympic Ping-Pong match. "Kitchen? They always migrate to where there's food."

I made a vague motion toward the bottom cupboards.

Mr. Chiu lowered himself to all fours to check the baseboards. "The cat should have caught one. They're really effective in keeping away rodents. My cousin in San Rafael is a cat breeder. He breeds those fluffy white pancake-faced types. Persians, I think they're called. Your mother bought her cat from him."

I smiled. Of course, it made sense that Ma-ma had done this.

There was another knock on the door. I excused myself and ran down the stairs to open it. Mrs. Chiu was waiting for me. The corners of her eyes were deepened with creases, her shoulders drooped, and she could barely handle her massive quilted tote.

"Celia told me you were in trouble. Something about misplacing the insurance papers?" Weariness permeated her voice.

"Uh, yes, I can't remember where you said you left them. I'm sorry, Mrs. Chiu. I know you're busy."

"It's all right, dear. After what you've been through, it's natural to forget things."

She followed me up the stairs.

I walked to the kitchen and pulled out the two chairs I'd set for the couple.

Mrs. Chiu dropped her purse when she saw her husband crawling on the floor on his hands and knees. "Wayne! What are you doing? Get up."

Mr. Chiu bumped his head against the edge of the counter. "Anita, what are you doing here?"

I gave the couple my sternest glare. "Both of you, please sit."

"There are no rats, are there?" Mr. Chiu asked, rubbing his head.

"No. Please, sit. All I'm asking for is a meal. You don't need to talk."

Mrs. Chiu sighed. She took the seat on the left. Her husband took the seat on the right. They avoided each other's eyes and focused on their plates. I noted that, for a couple in disharmony, they still took their first bites at the same time.

I stood back, my heart in my throat, watching, waiting, hoping for a sign. If nothing out of the ordinary happened, everything I had done before this was for naught. And then, after the third bite, something happened, a most subtle change that would have gone undetected had I not been so vigilant.

A fine thread made of shimmering gold appeared, connecting the top of Mr. Chiu's salt-and-pepper hair to Mrs. Chiu's dark brown hair, then another connecting each of their shoulders, more and more of these nearly translucent threads materializing, encasing the couple in a beautiful display of a cat's cradle. The couple was connected by strands of starlight, as lovely as any constellation in the night sky.

Once the food had disappeared off their plates, they both looked up, meeting each other's eyes. Their mouths opened, but no sound came out, or none I could hear. I turned away to give them privacy. They were speaking and listening to each other, although silently.

The dish was working! I walked to the sofa and opened a magazine, skimming an article on the hidden beauty of Micronesia. I must have escaped through the pictures because I was startled when I felt a tap on my shoulder.

"Natalie?"

I snapped the periodical closed. "How was the meal?"

"Quite delicious," Mrs. Chiu said.

The couple was holding hands, fingers intertwined, wedding rings glinting off their respective ring fingers. Mr. Chiu looked at his wife with the same longing I had seen when he'd confessed the situation of his marriage to me.

"We talked," he said. "It was good."

"Better than I hoped," Mrs. Chiu added. "Not perfect, but it may get there again in time."

"It will," Mr. Chiu said before placing a kiss on his wife's temple. "We both want it to. We decided to retire and spend more time with family."

I smiled.

Perhaps I should have been more cautious, but I had no nagging doubts this time. My recipe had worked, and I couldn't be more pleased. It was as if the Chius had shared their happiness with me. This must have been how Laolao felt when she helped others. A familiar shot of adrenaline coursed through me along with a thrumming sense of joy; an exhilarating jolt of vitality.

Yes, this was what had been missing from the previous botched attempts.

I still had to cook for one more person. I ushered the happy couple out of the apartment and readied the kitchen for the next round of cooking.

Older Shen's predicament required me to think of not what was best for the neighborhood, but what was best for him. If he wanted to sell and leave, he should, but with eyes open to all consequences. The recipe for courage had unearthed a restless streak in him that could lead to unhappiness if untempered.

Minced Pork in Lettuce Cups
(Natalie's Recipe)

Carrot

Ground pork

Mushroom soy sauce
White wine
Green peas
Mushrooms
Salt
Pepper
Iceberg lettuce

Sauce:
Mustard
Hoisin sauce
Hot sauce

Chop the carrot into tiny cubes. In a heated wok, add the ground pork, mushroom soy sauce, and white wine. When the meat has been cooked, add the green peas, mushrooms, and carrots and stir for a minute. Sprinkle some salt and pepper to taste.

Pull the iceberg lettuce apart, rinse, and let dry. These will act as the cradle to hold the filling.

Mix equal parts mustard, hoisin, and hot sauce into a small bowl. Stir the yellow, brown, and red until they turn into a rich brown.

Serve the iceberg lettuce, filling, and the sauce.

Note:
This dish is a marriage of different textures: the crispiness of the lettuce, tenderness of the pork filling, and silkiness of the sauce.

This dish is to encourage temperance. Serve it to those

who need restraint added to their impulses—just as the
lettuce holds the filling together and keeps it from falling out.

I hovered over the sink and pulled the washed iceberg lettuce head apart. The crisp leaves squeaked under my fingers. A firm but delicate touch was required to retain the integrity of the leaf—the perfect receptacle for the minced pork filling.

A snowfall of white pepper floated down from my fingertips into the hot wok where the minced pork, shredded carrots, and sliced Chinese mushrooms sizzled. Puffs of steam bloomed upward, prompted by the turn of the wooden spatula. More spices, more steam, more flavor. I prepared my own version of hoisin sauce to include with the dish.

It was three in the afternoon and time to call in my final visitor.

I dialed the number Celia left for me. "Mr. Shen?" I asked as the call went through. "It's Natalie."

"Oh, hello there. I saw the fire trucks. I wanted to come by, but Celia said you needed space. I didn't want to intrude. It must have been traumatic. Are you all right?" The concern in his voice touched me.

"Yes, I am," I replied. "Can you please come by the apartment now? I have something for you."

"Of course. I just finished with an appointment. I'll be right over."

Older Shen appeared in under five minutes at my doorstep with an unopened bag of White Rabbit candies as a gift. "These are for you," he said. "I hope they cheer you up."

"Thank you," I murmured, accepting the gift. Though I was in my late twenties, my joy at seeing these candies was undiminished.

I helped him up the stairs because of his crutches. His gaze fell upon the potted orchids on the windowsill, then to the stacks of magazines. Older Shen picked up the current *National Geographic* issue and smiled. "Did you know Miranda didn't even know these existed until I gave her a copy years ago? I was so pleased when it became her favorite."

"Celia told me that you'd all helped Ma-ma when I left. Thank you," I said.

He set the magazine down and made his way to the kitchen table. "Miranda was one of us. We try to take care of our own." Older Shen took his seat and marveled at the meal I'd prepared for him. "This looks lovely, thank you."

"You're welcome. I hope you like it."

A shy smile emerged from his face, one I recognized from before his transformation; as much as I liked the current version of Fai Shen, I missed some aspects of the previous one. My prescription for this dish was one I thought was perfect for him.

Cradling the curled lettuce leaf in one hand, Older Shen spooned the minced pork filling into it with the other and drizzled the hoisin sauce on top. The touch of added sweetness completed the savory profile of the dish. The contrasting textures might be the reason I had chosen this. The crunch of the lettuce combined with the juicy, tender filling created harmony for the palate.

Older Shen took his first bite.

A discordant symphony rose from each nibble; the kind one would expect on the first day of band practice. If Shen heard the cacophony, he made no indication. Tiny balls of light appeared over his head, all mimicking the audible chaos by pinging this way and that. With every chew, the noise became more organized as if each hapless instrument were being replaced by a skilled performer. The lights followed, falling into an ethereal formation—that of an unbroken circle.

Temperance.

And then I felt it, the adrenaline, the joy.

I refilled his cup of tea and took the seat across from him. "Have you sold the store yet?"

"No, but I have offers already. I haven't made the final decision," he replied. "I'm sorry, Natalie, I know you wanted me to stay and run the bookstore, but I don't have the heart to do it anymore. I can't keep doing this when I know someone else can do a much better job."

"What do you want to do after you sell?"

"I don't know yet. I thought about getting an apartment nearby, somewhere close enough to visit, but far enough so that I get a change of scenery. Maybe travel? It was a luxury I denied myself for years."

Though I was saddened by his departure, the mention of visits comforted me. When he did leave, I would cook him a worthy feast as a send-off. "Our street won't be the same without you and the store. We'll miss you," I said.

Older Shen sipped his tea. "I'll make sure whoever takes my place will bring life back into the neighborhood."

"Maybe it should be a young family?" I suggested. "New blood. It'd be nice to see children again around here."

He laughed. "Yes, we're all getting older." He nodded as if contemplating my suggestion. "The street does need the influx of new blood. I'll make sure to keep an eye out among the prospective buyers. Although I'm not looking forward to Melody's reaction when I tell her what I have decided."

The neighborhood would be saved. Seeing younger families take over for the retiring shopkeepers would be a blessing to my community. In time, I might be able to see it prosper. This gave me hope for the future: I felt excited at the prospect of meeting this next generation of neighbors.

I'd been wrong in thinking that shackling the shopkeepers to the neighborhood was the answer to their problems. It had been *my* misguided solution. Helping them was to allow them to move on to wherever they needed to be. Like Older Shen and the Chius, it was to retire and make way for others.

"She shouldn't complain if she's still getting a commission from the sale."

"And what about you? How are you faring? I hope the fire hasn't dashed your goal of reopening the restaurant."

I told him about Old Wu and my mentorship.

"You have the best teacher in Chinatown," he said. "You will do well. What about your beau?"

"Who?" I asked.

He winked. "The young man I've seen come and go by the restaurant. Forgive me if I've overstepped, but one of the hobbies of the aged is to stare out the windows. Celia calls it gossip but I call it mindful observation."

Daniel. I blushed when I remembered the terms on which we parted.

"I messed it up between us," I replied.

"For someone as eager to fix things as you are, I find it hard to believe that you wouldn't at least try to make it work with your sweetheart. Love is one of those rare things that may seem fragile, but it's stronger than it looks. Much like me." He patted his chest.

I smiled.

Older Shen leaned across the table and lowered his voice. "You never know, he might come back. Love, like life, has the highest risk, but the greatest reward. If you jump and fail, the chasm below is endless, but if you fly, the sun will be yours."

"I'm not aiming for the sun, Mr. Shen," I said.

"Maybe you should be."

Chapter Twenty-six

With the neighbors and my friendship with Celia in a better state, and the renovations for the restaurant about to start, I settled in that evening to read more of my mother's journals. I picked up the next in the stack. There was so much of her past that she had left unsaid.

> Mother, when I told you about him, you were disappointed.
>
> Not the proper husband. Not secure enough. Not good enough.
>
> He wasn't what you wanted.
>
> He wasn't what you expected.
>
> He knew nothing about the restaurant. It infuriated you that he agreed with me about leaving Chinatown.
>
> All you saw were his imperfections. The cracks, the inelegance, how un-Chinese he was. His skin was the same as ours and his name, written in ink brushstrokes. He was born in San Diego from a respectable family, yet it wasn't enough.
>
> What did he need to be?

Like the father I never knew? The man you never married. I have heard the whispers about the one who stole your love and brought it back with him to Shanghai when he left. How you wanted to follow, but your pride kept you planted on this side of the ocean.

You never told me, but I knew.

How he sent letters but you never replied. Instead, you burned them so I couldn't find them.

But I knew.

My love is different, for I have chosen well. You will see, Mother.

You finally met him. It was as inevitable as the sun rising over the horizon.

I had feared this meeting from the moment I decided he was mine.

You didn't find him suitable.

I love him.

I love you.

I don't want to choose.

Mother, you will make me choose.

I can't.

I will break your heart because I will choose the future.

I will choose him.

I want to spare you this heartbreak, Mother.

Don't ask me to choose.

Please.

Ma-ma's choice. I couldn't imagine how hard it must have been for her. I didn't blame Laolao for her disapproval—my father had ended up abandoning Ma-ma. He should have loved my mother as much as she had loved him.

There was no trace of her agoraphobia back then. Miss Yu and Celia both concluded that it had been Laolao's death and my father's desertion that triggered the condition—or at least the severity of it, since the seeds of it were within her since girlhood.

I pulled my phone from my purse and sent Celia a message.

Me: So I have been reading my mother's journals . . .

Celia: Hahaha. Do I want to know?

Me: No, nothing like that. She's writing about my father.

Celia: Heavy subject. Do you want company?

Me: Yes. Part of me is nervous about reading them.

Celia arrived three minutes later. She sat in her favorite chair with her arms crossed over a frock printed with white cats. "Why are you so nervous?"

"I have a feeling there will be more about my father," I replied.

"Oh." She frowned. "I never met him. I was away when they were dating. Then I traveled around Europe after that, and by the time I got back, he had left. I asked Miranda if she wanted help in tracking him down, but she adamantly declined. She said she knew where he was and that he had made his choice clear. We left it at that. The neighborhood doesn't talk about him much for obvious reasons, mostly out of respect for her.

"Miranda was always one of those people who spoke little, but she had a sharp mind. I often wondered what she was thinking at any given time. I imagine that what she wrote in those diaries will give you some sort of closure, or even a better understanding of who she was as a woman. And maybe it'll show you more about her relationship with your father. It was too painful for her to tell you when she was alive."

"I suppose," I said.

"Since I don't have a hot date tonight, I'll keep you company." Celia pulled out her cell. "I'll cook. Do you want pizza or Thai?"

I went through three more journals with no additional insight into my father. They seemed to jump back and forth in time to reflect whatever was on Ma-ma's mind. However, there were many entries detailing her depression, which were heartrending to read.

> Sadness isn't something I can ever shake.
> Wherever I go, she follows.
> She ties me to the bed and holds me down until I have no
> energy to get up. She robs me of any small joy like stealing
> the sweetness away from sticky sesame balls or the tangy
> note from sliced green mangoes.
> If I could banish her, I would.
> Yet I'm afraid.
> I fear she is a part of me.
> We will never be separated.

I reached for the kettle to pour myself another cup of tea. "I wish Ma-ma had gotten help."

Mental illness was a foreign concept in my culture. To my people, superstitions were more real than depression or anxiety. Instead of therapists, we saw doctors, herbalists, feng shui consultants, and acupuncturists. We would rather believe in spirits, luck, ghosts, and demons than the discipline of psychology. Perhaps it wasn't that my grandmother had refused to see my mother's condition, but rather that she *could* not see it.

"Your grandmother was from another generation. Was it possible? Sure. Unlikely? More so." Celia sighed. "The only thing you can do for Miranda now is to listen."

After the pizza ran out and the hour grew late, I sent Celia home with the reassurance that I would contact her if I needed anything. Besides, I wasn't alone. The cat curled around my belly as I read. The more pages I consumed, the more I began to realize that I was more like my grandmother in terms of personality than I was like my mother. Laolao found happiness in cooking and felt the call to help those around her. If my grandmother had been alive when I was a child, perhaps I could have helped heal the fracture between her and Ma-ma.

The second to last journal meandered back and forth in mood between anxious ramblings and Ma-ma's depression after Laolao's death. As painful as it was to read, I kept turning the pages, hoping and wishing that I would read about Ma-ma experiencing joy again. The tone of her writings changed at the end. I sat up, jarring the napping cat from my belly.

> Oh my love, you give me such joy.
> I knew you were the one when I first heard your voice.
> Nothing made me happier.
> I never thought I could ever be in love.

This could only be about my father. My stomach clenched at the thought of what I might find in these pages. I didn't want to learn about him, but I couldn't help but keep going. As I read, I was submerged into my mother's first foray into love—happy, hopeful, infatuated. The journals existed out of time, with stories of their courtship intermingled with vignettes of their marriage. He'd made her happy once, only to break her heart afterward. All I remembered was Mama's sorrow, pain, and anger. The triumvirate of emotions tugged at my throat, reaching down into my heart as it locked my limbs into place.

Chapter Twenty-seven

Mother, if you could only see what I see.
Push aside your rash judgments.
Give him a chance.
He makes me so happy.
Please.

"Laolao didn't approve of Ma-ma's husband," I murmured to the cat before taking another sip of the tea. "Can't say I'm surprised, since I don't like him either."

The cat placed a paw of solidarity on my chest.

"He should have been there for her. She needed him."

Meimei tapped her paw.

"I know that I should let it go. Anger poisons."

Father. No other word caused me more rage and anguish. As a child, I'd fielded questions about my absentee parent, swatting them away like fruit flies in the heat of summer. The questions stopped when I claimed he was dead. It wasn't a lie because it was plausible. And while I had asked the neighbors about my grandmother because I wanted to know more, I never asked about my father because I was afraid of what they might say: that he never really loved my mother, and that he wouldn't have loved me.

My fingers found the place where I'd left off. Ma-ma's diaries shone a spotlight on the creature I kept in the darkness, fattened by hatred and bitterness. Since I was a child, I had considered my father a monster. It seemed it was time for me to confront him through my mother's eyes.

Mother, do you remember the morning we decided to elope?

I wanted to leave, but he wouldn't allow me to go without telling you. He insisted. He didn't want our relationship to suffer.

You never cared for him, but he held you in great esteem.

So I stayed and waited until you came home from the restaurant.

I spoke my heart's desire.

You said it was too soon.

But this was what I wanted.

And then you withheld your blessing.

The dishes smashed. The apartment shook with the thunder of exploding ceramics. White powder sprayed from the opened cupboards, creating an impromptu blizzard. False snow created from the debris of the dishes.

I burned the pages we wrote together in your recipe book. I destroyed what I knew would hurt you the most.

This was the consequence of your anger, Mother.

In a last bid, I prostrated before you, but you cast me away.

You never saw me leave.

I found out later from the neighbors that you lost your sight for a week.

This entry was out of order. Old Wu had mentioned how much of a temper Laolao had had. Although I hated my father, I felt horrible for Ma-ma. This was the time she ripped out the pages in the recipe book to hurt her mother. It confirmed what Old Wu told me. Ma-ma fell in love with someone Laolao deemed unworthy and had lost her mother in the process. She must have been as angry as my grandmother. This explains why Ma-ma had been so supportive about anyone I'd decided to date. She'd wanted to spare me the sting of a parent's disapproval over my heart's choice.

She had tried her best to be the mother she'd wanted, the one Laolao couldn't be.

I read on with a sense of dread, bracing myself against the revelations regarding the man whom Ma-ma had given her heart to.

My husband.

You love me for who I am.

You found me when I suffered in darkness.

You charmed me with your love for Teresa Teng and parcels of glutinous rice with Chinese sausage wrapped in banana leaves.

When you played "Sono andati?" from La bohème, you collected my heart.

Your talent, my love, was one of the many marvels I saw.

As long as we are together, happiness is within my reach.

I love you, Thomas.

My Thomas.
Thomas Kuk Wah.

The diary slid off my lap, slamming with a thud onto the floor. My hands shook. An earthquake vibrated from my bones, trembling, causing my teeth to clatter together. I wrapped my arms around myself to suppress the tremors. The cat jumped off me.

I closed my eyes.

Mr. Kuk Wah was my father?

The musician whose erhu played to my soul.

The man who refused to let me run away from the mess I'd created.

My father.

Starlit fireflies danced before my eyes. I calmed my breathing to stop the Tilt-A-Whirl sensation brewing in my stomach. I wondered whether I could ever regain my balance. I didn't understand it. He had never said anything. Mr. Kuk Wah had begun appearing on Grant Avenue when I was six. We'd become friends when I was on my way to pick up mail from the Chius' convenience store. He'd played my favorite piece from *La bohème* for me. *La bohème.* Ma-ma. He'd never said anything about it or acknowledged me as his child. All these years and all our talks about everything from music to love. I found him so easy to confide in.

He was my friend. I'd even told him about the bullies at school. He had listened to me and comforted me with a rendition of "Three Little Maids from School."

He was my father? But my father was the beast. A horrible creature who'd abandoned my mother and me. He'd never cared about his family. My hatred for him was a tattered cloak—woven with vitriol and aged by habit.

I took a deep breath to calm myself. If there was someone who I'd wished was my father, I might have chosen Mr. Kuk Wah. In hindsight, I could see what his appeal was and why Ma-ma was smitten. He'd been here all this time, and Ma-ma couldn't see him because she never got out of the house and he had always been a little farther down the street and away from the neighbors.

He had mentioned his wife. He could have remarried. Perhaps that was why he had avoided Ma-ma. But it didn't make any sense. None of it. Why had he abandoned us, but continued to see me? Why hadn't he told me who he was? These were good questions I needed to ask the next time I saw him.

Right now, my mother's words were an anchor I clung to, to stop the world from spinning. I must know her side first so I would be prepared with the right questions for my father. And the harder I struggled to cling to my hatred, the harder it was to grasp, like attempting to squeeze a fistful of water.

I had to continue reading. My mother hadn't finished speaking to me.

I picked up the diary and returned it to my lap. My fingers trembled as I turned to the last page I had read.

> *Mother, you should have been inside.*
> *What were you doing outside of the restaurant?*
> *You shouldn't have gone outside.*
> *If you stayed inside, you would still be alive.*
> *Mother, why did you go out?*

The lines repeated themselves for pages and pages with erratic handwriting. The paper they were written on undulated like waves on a seashore from the enduring moisture of Ma-ma's tears. The rising anxiety from my mother's thoughts vibrated my fingertips. The cat squirmed from the disturbance.

The next entry was dated months after the death of my grand-mother.

> It's strange living away from the only home I had ever known.
> This new apartment in Nob Hill feels like an itchy sweater in the winter.
> I'm happy to be with Thomas, but everything else feels out of place.
> The noises, the people, the buildings are odd.
> I don't want to go outside.
> Mother died going outside.
> I feel more comfortable with my books while I wait for Thomas to come home.
> He's been having problems finding a job and I think moving back into Mother's home in Chinatown is best for us. I can't deny that I want to be back to the only place I've felt at ease.
> I want to go home and this isn't home.

I couldn't imagine Ma-ma living anywhere but here. This entry contained the first signs of her agoraphobia. She had never taken to change well. Moving out to a new place must have been stressful for her.

I gripped the edges of the journal tighter. I'd known about Laolao's death, but the details of my father's departure were unknown.

> One day, my love, you will play for the symphony.
> You need to believe that your seat is waiting before an audience.
> I wish I could banish your disappointment.

I see you come home, time and again, without the job you deserve.

I hope you know that I will always believe in you, Thomas. You will succeed.

Mama once told me that a talent like yours... your erhu can tame dragons. The same dragons that adorn your arms.

You are strong, my love.

Give it more time...

Father or not, Mr. Kuk Wah and his erhu played to the soul. I had never imagined two strings could create a bridge into one's being, the way his playing did. It was his true voice. Even Laolao had acknowledged it. No wonder Ma-ma and I were held spellbound. The erhu spoke every emotion, and its vocabulary was melody instead of words. Even now, I yearned to hear it.

Father. Why didn't you tell me? You must have known I was your daughter because you kept coming back to see me. Or did you not know?

I had too many questions. Questions like marbles poured into a balloon, unsettled, bulging, and threatening to break through the thin latex.

I had one journal left to read and no room inside me for the words right now.

The sky was the darkest shade. The candles on the coffee table had diminished into stumps while the clock ticked, marking the time I had wandered into the forest of my mother's thoughts. My dreams would be restless tonight.

The next morning I invited Celia over for a breakfast of congee with pickled cucumbers and shredded pork. The dried scallop and duck wings added an extra dimension of flavors to the plainness of the rice porridge. Crowned with delicate rings of spring onion and golden bits of fried garlic, the bowls of steaming porridge were comfort food. Our toppings of choice were crunchy pickled cucumbers and sweet shredded pork floss.

"So you're down to the last diary," Celia said. "How do you feel?"

I appreciated Celia being respectful in not asking for details. I wasn't ready yet to disclose my father's identity because of all the questions I still had. I placed my spoon into the empty bowl with a sharp clink. "I can't stop thinking about my father. With all of our family secrets, how does he fit in? I can kind of understand why Ma-ma didn't tell me about Laolao. Their relationship was complicated, but full of love. It was made worse when Laolao didn't approve of my mother's marriage, but after all these years, I think Ma-ma still mourned her mother. It was too painful for her to talk about."

"And your father?"

"I always thought she hated him, but now that I've read the journals, I see that she did love him."

Why had Mr. Kuk Wah left us? Hadn't he loved her as much as she had loved him? Again, questions cluttered my brain, overwhelming in their number and importance. I wanted my father to return so I could speak to him.

Celia turned her head toward the windows facing the street. "It's early. You have time to finish that last book. Good thing it's the weekend. You can read all day."

"Do you mind if I text you if I need something?" I felt silly for asking, but she smiled as she packed up.

"Of course not. It'll be a welcome distraction from playing sudoku."

Celia waved goodbye as she let herself out.

I transferred my attention to the final journal on my lap. Its weight was deceitful. An object so light couldn't possibly contain all of my hopes and apprehension. Taking a deep breath, I dove in.

> *How can I be so happy yet so afraid at the same time?*
> *These emotions didn't comingle like a pair of chopsticks.*
> *They were separate and one came with great shame. So it must be hidden in a box and brought out when you weren't here.*
> *The call finally came this evening. A job opportunity. An audition with an international traveling symphony. Your dream. Our dream. The once intangible was now yours.*
> *You would be gone for a few days. Only a few days. To me, it would feel like years.*
> *You wanted me to come with you.*
> *I wanted to, but I was terrified.*
> *I couldn't leave the apartment.*
> *Ma-ma left the apartment and she died.*
> *No, I couldn't leave. Bad things happened. Too dangerous. The world out there wasn't safe. This was why I stayed. I was safe here, protected, alive.*
> *I didn't want you to leave.*
> *But your dream, which became mine, was too precious. I couldn't deny you this.*
> *The voice of your erhu needed to be heard.*
> *Your seat and the audience were waiting.*
> *But I don't want you to leave.*
> *Don't leave me, don't leave me, don't . . .*

Thus confirmed my mother's transformation into a recluse. The neighbors mentioned that my mother hadn't always been this way. Like her beloved birds, the loss of my grandmother had trapped and caged Ma-ma until she'd been a prisoner of her anxiety.

Oh, Ma-ma. How I missed you. Reading your words lulled me into believing you were still with me. Was this when my father left you? When he went to this audition and never returned?

I searched for the end of the diary, keeping a finger in my place so I could pinch the number of pages left to read. My papery version of a countdown clock. The precious time with my mother was drawing to a close. Thus, I held on, clinging to her final written words and hoping she would provide answers about my father.

> *Where are you, my love?*
>
> *It has been two weeks and you fail to return or call...*
>
> *Did you finally realize I am a broken woman with too many flaws to reconcile?*
>
> *Did I scare you away and into the arms of another woman?*
>
> *I know I'm strange. I don't leave the house, I can't. My demons will never leave me.*
>
> *The neighborhood whispers. I know you must have heard it, my love, yet you show me no signs that the horrible rumors about me exist. But I know. Strange girl. Never comes out. Full of ill luck. Not normal. Broken ever since her mother died. Strange, oh so strange. Not right in the head.*
>
> *They're right. I am broken, but when I'm with you, I feel whole. I feel loved and worthy of love. You don't judge me. You accept me and understand.*

Has this changed?

Have you had enough?

Where are you? Are you coming back?

You can't leave me ... us.

Not now.

This morning, I found out I'm carrying your child.

We're supposed to see your family in a month so they can meet me.

Your daughter, Thomas.

You have to come back to meet your daughter!

Come back ...

I wiped my tears away. He hadn't known I was his daughter because he'd already left us. My mother. My poor Ma-ma. How could he have done this to her? How could he have left her when she'd needed him the most?

Tears streamed down my cheeks, unrelenting, soaking the pages of the diary on my lap and down my bare legs onto the floor. I welcomed the dampness. We'd been abandoned. Nothing he could say could change this.

One entry left and my heart bled ocean blue.

What have I done?

Our child can never know. She would hate me ...

I received a call this morning from a stranger.

Do you know Thomas Kuk Wah?

Yes.

Are you his wife?

Why?

I'm sorry, but he has been in a terrible motor vehicle accident. If you are his wife, you need to come down to the morgue and identify the body.

I'm not his wife. You are mistaken.

I'm so sorry to bother you then, ma'am. We will notify his next of kin. I apologize again for having taken your time.

I denied you, Thomas.

I can't leave the house.

You're dead because you left.

You shouldn't have left. I was right.

And now, you're dead. Like Ma-ma.

I won't leave the house. I don't want to endanger our baby.

Can't leave. No, my baby or I could die.

My love, I'm so sorry. I'm sorry. I'm sorry.

I love you. Always.

Forgive me, Thomas.

Please forgive me.

Forgive me because I can never forgive myself.

My father was dead?

Why didn't Ma-ma ever tell me? She had never said a word. Didn't she think I had a right to know? Ma-ma led me to believe that we had been abandoned. She must have chosen not to tell me he died because perhaps, after all these years, she couldn't accept the truth herself. Ma-ma also grappled with guilt, and if I had been in her situation, could I have told my daughter the truth about how my father's body was robbed of the rituals he needed to enter the afterlife? That she couldn't claim his body in fear of leaving the apartment? Why he still wandered this world as a ghost?

Ma-ma had no one left to help her. She was alone with a baby to care for and crippling agoraphobia. As angry as I felt for having been lied to, I couldn't hold on to that pain. My mother did what she thought was best for me. She could not explain her mental illness to those who would not understand. Her fear and her shame were heartbreaking.

Oh, Ma-ma.

How could my father be dead? I'd spoken to Mr. Kuk Wah most of my life. I had heard him play, just like Ma-ma had described in her journals. But according to this journal entry, he died a long time ago.

Baba. Father. All these years, had I been communing with a ghost? Baba's ghost.

I had thought he had abandoned me.

He must not remember me because he died before I was born. Someone told me once that ghosts can be forgetful. They also choose only to appear to those they want to be seen by. My father had been with me for a large part of my life. He must have loved me, even if he didn't know what our true relationship was.

I closed the final book and hugged it to my chest.

I had to talk to Ma-ma.

I knelt before the shrine.

"If you were afraid that I wouldn't love you after I read your words, Ma-ma, you were wrong. I didn't think it was possible, but I love you even more. You were strong. I wish I was even half as strong as you.

"You fought your demons and won. How else could I be standing here? Your wish came true. I turned out exactly as you hoped, and all because of everything you taught me: to love, to be kind, to be strong. Your strength inspires me, pushes me to be better, and to seek out my dreams.

"I want to thank you for your journals. I now know who my father is. I love him, Ma-ma. I wish he could have come home safely that day. Our lives would have been so different.

"You and Baba convince me to open myself to the possibility of love, that I am deserving of love. I think it could have worked with Daniel if I had been brave enough to try. I think you would like him, Ma-ma.

"I miss you. I will always miss you."

I rose to my feet and placed a hand over my heart.

My parents, Celia, my neighbors, and even Daniel, even though I had pushed him away. I was so fortunate to be loved. Everything I had done to this point had been to fulfill my mother's last request. Now, I had one desire of my own, one I wanted so desperately.

I wished I could speak to my father again.

He came and went without warning—or did he? He seemed to appear when I needed him the most, and I needed him now. I closed my eyes and walked to the windows, sending out my heart's wishes to my ghost father. I envisioned invisible homing pigeons carrying my request in tiny scrolls attached to their legs.

Baba.

I need you.

Please come and see me.

My fingers pressed against the windowsill. My face soaked up the warm sunlight streaming in from the glass of the windows. Wishes were powerful, and I needed that power now. Again and again, I called to my father. If a mother's love could transcend space and time, surely a daughter calling to her father could do the same.

Baba.

Chapter Twenty-eight

Baba.

I opened my eyes. He was here!

Through the windows, my father, with erhu in hand, strolled past the tea shop and was looking both ways before he crossed the street. This made me smile. He was a ghost: a speeding car or the 38AX Geary A Express bus could not have harmed him.

He was here!

Ghosts are strange creatures in that they live in the limbo plane, and while they abide by a main set of rules, they also can create their own. None of the neighbors had ever mentioned him, so it didn't surprise me that he had chosen to appear only to those he wanted to see him—me.

I don't think he knew I was his daughter. He'd died before he even knew of my existence.

I had to tell him. This could be what he needed to hear the most.

As I ran down the staircase, my feet made no sound: I floated down, cushioned by the lightness of my being. My father was waiting for me. Baba.

I had a father. He hadn't abandoned me. He had returned and visited often, enough for me to consider him a dear friend before I'd discovered his true identity.

While Ma-ma and I had shared a love of opera, my father and I worshipped music in all of its notes, chords, arrangements, instruments, and science. I imagined that in a different life, my father and I would be found draped over sofas listening to records, eyes closed, intoxicated by the melodies or tapping on surfaces, dancing to the swing of the up-tempo beat.

If he'd lived, the sound of the erhu would have been a constant presence in our apartment, as natural as the bells of the streetcars, the air brakes of the tour buses, and the vinyl on the Victrola. Even if he'd accepted the job at the traveling symphony, he would have been home in between his journeys, and the three of us would have been a family.

He stood, waiting before the closed glass door, dark cap in one hand and erhu case in the other. The two tattooed dragons on his forearms constricted, undulated, always moving in concert with each other. Dust and errant loose threads adorned his usual gray attire.

I let him inside.

"Xiao Niao," he said with a smile. "I came back as soon as I could."

Tiny bird. My heart clenched as if it were being squeezed by an invisible hand.

He walked to the counter and ran his hand across it. He leaned his erhu case against one of the stools as he took a seat. "My wife told me to tell you that everything will be all right," he said. "Hard times always pass. She and I both know you're strong."

I couldn't help but smile. I knew now that he and Ma-ma were together, and I had helped with that.

Returning to my place behind the counter, I busied myself by arranging and rearranging the stack of dishes and cutlery. "You speak of her a lot now. It's only until recently you said she started speaking to you again. Why is that?"

He squinted and stroked the rough, graying stubble on his chin. "For years, she ignored me. It was like I didn't exist. I suppose it's my fault for not coming back sooner from an audition. It was too easy for her to jump to the worst conclusions."

"What's her name? I realize you never told me." I couldn't resist. I needed to hear him say Ma-ma's name, to acknowledge what I already knew.

"Miranda," he replied with a sheepish smile. "The same name as Prospero's daughter in *The Tempest*. It's a beautiful name, isn't it? I'm embarrassed that I didn't say it earlier."

"What is she like?"

"She's beautiful. The kind of beauty I keep rediscovering every morning I awaken beside her. She is an amazing cook like her mother, and her capacity for kindness is boundless. It was one of those lightning-struck loves for me. Remember when we talked about songs and how each person has their own? I played her song for her: 'Sono andati?'"

"She sounds like your soul mate."

"If I can find mine, you will find yours, but I think you know who it is already."

I blushed.

"Daniel is your match." He chuckled. "The one dressed in wires and blinking lights. The one who keeps dropping by."

"Yes, but I don't know if I can win him back."

"Oh, I'd bet my erhu on it."

"How can you be so sure?"

He laughed, then winked at me. "Trust me, I know."

I giggled. "Do I get to keep your erhu if not?"

"You can, but I know I'm right," he said with a laugh. He placed the case on his lap and stroked the hard shell as one would pet a lover.

The urge to hear my father play struck me. The voice of the erhu was his. It was as if he spoke with two voices. I yearned to hear him play now.

"Can you play something for me, please?" I asked, resting my chin on my hands.

"As you wish." He withdrew his erhu from its case.

I listened, enraptured. The rest of the world gave way to the auditory, the beauty of unseen vibrations enchanting the cochleae. Like the song of a siren. There was nowhere else I wanted to be in this moment than in the company of my father.

I sighed when the music ended. The legend of my father's erhu was a gift I would cherish forever. I leaned over. "I want to ask you for some advice about Daniel."

"Well," he said, returning his erhu into its case. "I would suggest that you should trust your heart and realize that love grows while infatuation fades. Do you remember when you asked me about my wife speaking to me again after all these years?"

"Yes, it seemed strange that she would speak to you after years of silence."

"A few weeks ago, something changed. I had tried many times before, but she refused to see me, but that morning was different. As usual, I stood across the street so she could see me from the windows. I waited for her. Though Miranda never ventured outside of her tower, she paced the windows and occasionally watched the world go by."

Until the day she died, the vision of Ma-ma through the second-floor windows was a constant sight in the neighborhood. My mother viewed the rest of the world like a fish tank—one she was glad not to be a part of.

"I waved to her, and for the first time since I left, she saw me. Her eyes met mine. I thought she would be afraid and run away, but she stayed, with her fingertips to the glass and she spoke one word. Even from a distance, I knew she said my name. That was when Miranda ran outside to join me."

Ma-ma. I closed my eyes as tears sprang from them, spilling down onto the countertop.

"Why are you crying, Xiao Niao?" he asked.

"Because I finally know how my mother died, and she was happy."

He stumbled back. "Your mother?"

"Yes. My mother, Miranda." I wanted him to realize it, to acknowledge me first as his daughter, then claim me. I had been waiting too long, all my life, to hear him say the word.

My father narrowed his eyes and stared at me, the type of visual examination I often employed when poring over old photographs or film reels. Was he discovering the truth? Could he see the resemblance? And what if he didn't? Twenty-eight seconds ticked by, one for every year of my life.

"Nu-er."

Daughter.

My tears turned into crystals, sliding off my skin and singing as they fell onto the countertop. I muffled a sob with a cupped hand. My father reached for my cheek. His fingers hovered over my skin, for the gift of touch was impossible.

"You look like your mother," he said. His dark eyes softened, glistening with tears. "How did I not know?"

"Ma-ma never had a chance to tell you," I confessed. "I love you, Baba. Tell her I love her too."

Then Thomas Kuk Wah smiled. It was an expression of joy mixed with paternal pride. This was my father. I snapped a photograph of the moment in my mind, one to place alongside my mother's. And thus, the thread holding him tethered to the Middle Kingdom was cut. Before my eyes, my beloved father dissipated into fog, much like the heavy earthbound clouds of the bay burned off in the heat of the rising sun.

Baba.

I collected the teardrop crystals off the countertop and counted them. Eight. The luckiest number in my culture. Yes, I was lucky. Though I had lost my father once more, I didn't mourn him, for he was with Mama now.

My elbow brushed against the base of the goddess. Bringing her out into the light had not changed her condition. The pits and scars continued to mar her skin. I had hoped she would be restored to her full glory, since my mother's last request would be fulfilled and the restaurant was set to succeed.

"Will I ever see you smile again?" I asked.

I examined the crack running down the center of her face. Though the fire had spared her, her physical corruption caused me pain. As I ran my hands over her crevices, my fingernails caught the edge of a deep pit near her shoulder. The piece came off, peeling, and its lack of sharpness surprised me, for I had been cut before. With a gentle tug, the small piece came off in my hands, revealing something shimmering underneath. Gold.

Hope coursed through me. The goddess might be transformed. I continued to pick at the exposed edges, stripping away the old skin, excavating the treasure long buried. Soon the discarded pile of peelings rivaled the size of my cat, and the goddess was revealed in her true form: golden, regal, and restored.

Acting on the same childish impulse one had when confronted by a pile of leaves, I leaned forward and blew on the mound. The dark shavings took the shape of tiny birds, soaring for a few inches before crumbling into gold dust. Delighted, I puffed my cheeks, expanded my lungs, then expelled my breath so that the rest of the pile took flight. A mass migration of miniature birds launched into the air, wings flapping, swirling into the space before disintegrating into specks of gold.

My joyous laughter signaled the rejuvenation.

My father was with Ma-ma now—his spirit at peace, and I knew they were both happy because they were together. Love was a powerful force. It made me think of Daniel.

My father had told me that time was the deciding factor. Over the years, love grew stronger while infatuation faded. Baba believed that Daniel would return and forgive me. Older Shen also encouraged me to pursue him.

There was still no response from Daniel.

I needed to find out for myself if he didn't want to see me again.

Tomorrow, I'd cook dumplings and deliver them to his work after my meeting with Old Wu.

Once the restaurant was open, perhaps that would prove to Daniel I'd changed and was putting down roots. Otherwise, what reason would he have to believe my apology? Words weren't as convincing as acts when it came to promises.

Exhaustion crept in, weighing down my limbs. I hadn't realized how little sleep I'd had and how much had happened in the past few days. After sending a quick message to Celia, I settled onto the couch to binge-watch old musicals, where I ended up drifting into a long, deep slumber.

My dreams were happy that day. There were no demons or darkness.

Instead, I pictured myself in the kitchen cooking with Laolao while Ma-ma and Baba and the cat danced to the music in the living room. The apartment overflowed with laughter and family. All of us under one roof.

I awoke to the beautiful voice of the erhu. It was faint, so faint that I thought I was still in a dream. I slipped off the sofa and followed my siren call.

The song of the erhu grew in strength, rising and falling, striking into familiar notes of "Sono andati?" I closed my eyes and followed the source while losing myself in the music. My feet found their way to Ma-ma's bedroom.

I didn't step across the threshold. My fingers touched the wooden doorframe, anchoring me, as I waited for the phantom song to end. The finality of the last note lingered in the air, giving way to silence that ushered in an overwhelming sense of loss.

Stepping inside, I opened my eyes. Something tickled my bare feet. Through the open window, sunlight bathed the room, illuminating a mountain of feathers from every hue of the rainbow: hundreds of them in all shapes and sizes littering the floor. I picked up a bright canary one, reveling in its sunny color. Another was as long as my forearm, snowy white, belonging to a swan. The largest was from an ostrich.

The shelves, where Ma-ma had kept her flock, were empty.

Ma-ma and her birds were free.

Baba was free.

And I was free.

Chapter Twenty-nine

My meetings with Old Wu at his restaurant were set weekly at nine in the morning.

I brought my homework for my first official meeting. My mentor waited for me at his special table. A pot of jasmine tea along with a platter of steamed chili turnip cakes populated the glass lazy Susan. He gestured for me to take a seat and spun the rotating disk so the teapot and the dish faced me.

I poured myself a cup of tea and helped myself to a modest portion. Rings of red chilies and sprinkles of minced green onion decorated the plump turnip cubes. I squeezed my chopsticks and took a nibble. The spiciness of the chilies complemented the creaminess of the turnip.

"The renovations are going well?" he asked.

The concert of hammering and sawing downstairs in my restaurant was soothing. The cat didn't mind it either. She spent her time playing the game of tapping parts of the floor where the sound came from. The scent of cut lumber replaced the permeating smoke. Progress brought hope and new life to the scarred space.

"Yes, Lao Shi. Almost all of the damage has been cleaned up. I ordered the new gas stove and industrial fryer you recommended, and they should be delivered next week."

Old Wu sipped his tea. "Have you given a thought about your seating plan? Do you want three tables or four?"

"Actually, two." I brought out a sheet of paper from my laptop bag with a drawing of the restaurant's layout. I placed the paper on the lazy Susan and spun it toward him. "I'd rather maximize the seats at the counter and make room for a bathroom."

He picked up the design and studied it. "Ah, there is space then. It's a better layout than before."

"I found a way to incorporate it into the existing budget."

Old Wu smiled. "Good, that was my next question."

"How did Laolao manage all this? I'm thankful for the funding, but she started with nothing."

"She bartered. Your grandmother's skill in the kitchen was matched only by her negotiation tactics. She made shrewd deals with the shop-keepers at the market and her suppliers for the lowest prices. Pair that with her cooking, and she became profitable in a short amount of time."

I nibbled on the story and savored it as if it were the piece of turnip cake between my chopsticks. "I really wish I had a chance to know her."

"By reopening the restaurant, you are walking on her path and sharing in her experiences. I'd like to think that she's watching over you as I am." Old Wu checked his watch. "I have to get back to work. I will see you next week, Ye Ying."

"Thank you, Lao Shi."

"Think about your menu and start making a list."

I gathered my papers and tucked them back into my bag. "I will."

The meeting was about as long as I'd expected, since Old Wu was quite busy. This freed up the rest of my morning to prepare the dumplings I wanted to deliver to Daniel's office on Mission Street. I wasn't attempting bribery so much as I was determined to apologize in person.

I missed him.

The risk of being rejected was worth the chance of seeing him again.

I arrived at the Hearttech office on the sixteenth floor two hours later. I'd hoped to get there before the noon lunch hour. Clean lines, bright woods, and glass along with the same red logo on Daniel's lanyard greeted me.

The receptionist was a perky, twentysomething Asian American named Jeanna with a sharp-angled pixie bob.

"Hi," I said. "I have a delivery for Daniel Lee."

Jeanna leaned forward. "Oh, that smells amazing. He always finds the best food. What did he order?"

"Special-order dumplings." I lifted the lid a bit and gave her a peek. "I'm hoping I can take it to him, but if he's busy, I'll just leave it here."

"Let me check if he's in a meeting right now." She picked up the phone. "Mr. Lee, there is a delivery here for you." Jeanna hung up and smiled. "I can take you in."

"Thank you," I said.

She led me through a maze of open cubicles to a corner office. Everyone wore business-casual wear, similar to what I'd seen Daniel in when he visited me. The employees in their brightly decorated spaces seemed in good spirits. As we walked by, there were curious stares, but it wasn't directed at me so much as it was at the box I held in my hands. The tantalizing aroma trail of the dumplings swiveled every head in the vicinity.

"You need to leave me your card or menu. I definitely want to check out the restaurant," Jeanna whispered. "I'll pass them on and you'll get a bunch of us from work coming by."

"It's undergoing renovations right now. I'm hoping in a few months I'll host the grand reopening."

She slipped a card into my hand and winked. "In that case, call me when you're ready."

We stopped at a door with Daniel's name. He opened it before Jeanna had a chance to knock.

"Hi," I said. "I brought you a snack."

Daniel held the door open and I slipped inside. "Come in."

The view from his modest office showed the city and its color palette of neighborhoods. A classic *Lost in Space* poster hung on the far wall along with a couple of family pictures, while a massive desk with dual screens dominated the space.

"I'm sorry. I came in person to apologize." I handed him the box.

He placed it on his desk. "Thank you for the dumplings."

His expression was unreadable. His dark eyes behind the glasses studied my face. I didn't know whether I should stay or leave. He hadn't acknowledged my apologies, and being near him again swept me away with longing.

"I wasn't sure if you got my text."

"I did. I needed time, Natalie." He traced the lid of the dumpling box with his index finger. "I wasn't sure if there was anything left to say after how we ended things. Up until now, I thought you had left."

"I was going to leave, but I decided to stay. I found a mentor, and he's a fixture in Chinatown's business association. He's helping me. I'm going to make it work." I stepped toward him. "I also want to make us work."

He didn't move from his spot by his desk. "I don't know if I do. I still need more time."

My heart constricted. Tears collected in the corners of my eyes, and it took all of my will to keep them from falling. "I see."

"It's great that you're back on track with the restaurant. You should focus on that. I wish you the best of luck . . ."

I nodded and slipped away, closing the door behind me.

As I made my way out of Hearttech's offices, the dams of my disappointment and sorrow crumbled. I sobbed in the empty elevator for what I had feared I'd lost, but was now confirmed: Daniel.

Chapter Thirty

Color had returned to the neighborhood the way the silver screen once transitioned from black-and-white to Technicolor. The faded gray darkened, redefining the shapes and silhouettes of the alleys and architectural details until the buildings emerged from the dim. Reds came back first, bold, bright, the harbingers of fortune and luck, before ushering in the rest of the colors. The giant poster of Melody Minnows had been taken down when she left in search of other prey. San Francisco's Chinatown was known for its vivacity, the heightened, ornate chinoiserie that beckoned to visitors.

My neighborhood was restored.

The cracks on the sidewalk from the Chius' marital discord had healed into fine hairline fractures. When it came to the affairs of the human heart, a scar would still be left after the problem was mended, a physical reminder of survival and hope.

My restaurant underwent a transformation. The rock concert of electric drills, hammers, and band saws from the construction had tested my delicate sensibilities, but even I couldn't deny the wondrous metamorphosis that had taken place downstairs.

At Old Wu's suggestion, the galley kitchen had been widened to accommodate more than one person at a time. Shiny updated appliances were unwrapped from their plastic cocoons and readied for service. Slate replaced the chipped laminate wood of the long countertop, and fresh flowers filled the vases flanking the goddess, who now graced her own niche in the wall. The permits and licenses were displayed prominently. The renovation had been completed two days ago, and now the grand reopening was scheduled for tomorrow. I would open the restaurant to the public before closing early to cook ten courses—with the help of Old Wu—for a private neighborhood party.

I arrived at Old Wu's restaurant for our weekly meeting ten minutes early. One minute longer and I would have been considered late. This wasn't our usual time but, waving to the host, I let myself in, weaving through the crowded tables of the lunchtime rush to reach the table surrounded by folded screens.

My mentor sat with his stack of newspapers and his customary cup of jasmine tea. Baskets of dim sum rested on the glass lazy Susan: spicy phoenix claws, plump purses of har gow, shumai topped with green pea crowns, and airy wu gok.

I had learned from previous meetings that the old man was adamant about following tradition, which meant I had to arrive with an empty stomach. Refusing offered food was an insult Old Wu didn't take lightly.

I helped myself to a sample of each dish. Made of minced pork with a paper-thin wrapper, the steamed shumai was tender, and the har gow was juicy with the shrimp with bamboo shoots highlighted by a peekaboo skin. Then I bit into the wu gok, a fried taro puff with a wispy, crunchy shell and a dripping shrimp and pork filling. The powdery creaminess of the dish made this my favorite of the bunch.

I wiped my mouth with the cloth napkin. "Good afternoon, Lao Shi."

He glanced up from his newspaper and greeted me with a smile. "Are you ready for the grand reopening?"

"Yes," I replied before listing the completed preparations for my mentor. "With all of that done, I'm still left with the decision of what to choose for the first daily special."

The old man laughed. "I thought you were going with the duck. Have you changed your mind back to the shrimp and mushroom dish, Ye Ying?"

I winced and shook my head. "I want it to be perfect. Maybe I should serve both."

"It is your restaurant and your decision. As it should be. You know what is best."

The decision about the two dishes was the last detail I needed to confirm. Everything else was accounted for. I'd even hired and trained one assistant based on my mentor's recommendation. Old Wu had insisted that the restaurant would soon be busy enough and someone needed to take care of the front of the house while I cooked.

"You still have the permit for our special party, yes?" he asked.

"It arrived two weeks ago. I made sure I filed before the ninety-day-window requirement. The neighborhood can't wait to celebrate."

"Good." Old Wu reached under the table and withdrew a small, flat box wrapped in decorative red foil. He placed it on an empty spot on the glass and spun the revolving stand so that the gift arrived to where I was seated. I cleared my spot before pulling the present toward me.

"What is this? You've already sent a beautiful bouquet, Lao Shi."

He shrugged. "Why not open it and find out?"

My fingers found the edges of the slippery foil, tugging it loose from the small pieces of tape. The present was roughly the size of a hardcover book, about two inches thick. I should have known that the old man would have something up his sleeve. The one takeaway lesson I'd learned from my mentorship was never to underestimate my teacher. The box underneath was simple but elegant with an etched lotus design.

I lifted the lid.

A familiar face with my eyes stared back at me from a picture frame, a black-and-white photograph of a woman with a determined brow and angular features. I had seen this woman before.

Laolao.

"Thank you," I murmured. My throat tightened. "The only picture I had of her was claimed by the fire. Her book survived, but the memento didn't. Up until this moment, I thought I had lost her face forever."

"It is not right that you do not have a photograph of her for your family shrine. I believe that is the only surviving photograph of your grandmother. She belongs with you."

"But—"

"Qiao lives on in here," he said, pointing to his temple. "And in here." He patted his chest. "I was a friend, but you are family, Ye Ying. There's more."

I checked the box and, at the bottom, found three sheets of paper. These were recipes written by Laolao's hand: ones I hadn't seen before. "What is this?"

"These were given to me by Qiao. We developed those recipes together. They're now yours. Consider this your graduation gift."

I tried my best not to cry. The show of emotion might unnerve my mentor. Instead, I bowed my head and clutched the rosewood photo frame to my heart. "Thank you, Lao Shi."

I returned home long enough to install my grandmother in her rightful place beside my mother in the family shrine and to give the cat a quick update before heading downstairs to the restaurant to take care of last-minute details, one of which included writing thank-you cards for the flowers I'd received for the grand reopening.

The dining room of the restaurant had been transformed into a tropical garden with its profusion of orchids, birds-of-paradise, yellow gold chrysanthemums, and Chinese roses. I closed my eyes and took in the heady fragrance combination. The Chius had sent a bouquet of chrysanthemums and red roses with two bright yellow banners. From Older Shen, an arrangement of bamboo with yellow gold chrysanthemums, and from Younger Shen, birds-of-paradise and Chinese roses. Old Wu had chosen a garland of Chinese roses along with a red and gold ribbon and banner wishing prosperity.

My neighbors. My community.

I smiled and returned to the task of finishing my note to Older Shen.

A sharp tap on the glass broke my attention.

Miss Yu stood before the door carrying pink orchids. Dressed in a cream shawl and a long blue sheath dress, she was resplendent. She had long since recovered from her concussion from that ill-fated dinner.

I opened the door and let her in.

"I can't wait for the grand reopening and our party later on." She leaned in to give me a quick peck on the cheek. "Congratulations, dear one. You have done it."

"Do you think people will come?" I asked. "I placed an ad in the *Chronicle*. It's buried in the classifieds, but it's a start."

"Celia also placed an ad in the *Sing Tao Daily* for the past month. Your restaurant will have a good turnout," Miss Yu replied. She looked around, taking in all the flowers, until her eyes settled on the radiant, golden Goddess. "Ahh, she is as she should be."

I beamed. "Yes, she is restored."

"Do you know that she's the symbol of prosperity for our neighborhood?" Miss Yu asked. "Things will start to improve again for everyone."

I smiled. "I certainly hope so. I feel comforted by the fact that she is watching over us all."

Miss Yu approached me and enveloped me in a peony-scented embrace. "This is great to hear. You will do well. I better take my leave. I'm sure you'll have more visitors coming."

Celia walked past the windows and waved.

"Thank you," I said to Miss Yu.

"No, thank you." She bowed her head and smiled. Miss Yu held the door open for Celia as she left.

Celia beamed. "Look at all the flowers! Are you excited?" She carried an arrangement of birds-of-paradise and orchids. Her fuchsia lips curved in a crooked smile. Wearing a bright frock of sage green with a pattern of canaries, she was stunning.

She handed me the flowers. "Oh, I have news. Fai has finally found the perfect buyers for his bookstore. It's a young family with a daughter from San Diego who apparently love books as much as he does. Isn't that perfect? I invited them to the party tomorrow."

"Yes!" I replied, setting down the flowers on the counter. "I'll be so happy to see new neighbors come in."

"Well, you'll still see Fai around. He's coming tomorrow and he mentioned bringing his lady friend. I can't wait to see what she's like."

Last month, Older Shen had consulted me about his brave

decision to pursue the woman of his dreams. It turned out to be some-one from his ballroom dancing class. I encouraged him to invite her to the party. He wanted to dance with her and so he should. His fracture had fully healed a month ago.

"We've been hearing so much about her," I said. "I'm dying to meet her too."

"Do you have the menu set for the restaurant yet?"

"I think so. Everything is decided except for the daily special. I'm not sure which dish to pick."

"I'll give you some advice." Celia winked. She threw her arm around my shoulder and lowered her voice. "You need to do another trial run of the choices you're considering. I'm always up for another round of testing."

I laughed. "Perhaps. I have a few ideas on how to adjust the dishes."

She giggled. "I'll come by when I close the store. I hope you're ex-cited. Are you sure the party after won't be too much trouble? I mean, you're already doing so much work to prepare for the grand opening . . ."

"I'll be fine. This is what I'm supposed to be doing. Thank you again for the flowers."

Celia nodded and waved goodbye, disappearing down the street to return to her gift shop.

There had been an overflow of blessings since the devastation of the fire. If I were the superstitious type, I would start worrying about the balancing string of bad luck coming. But I wasn't Ma-ma.

I missed her and I missed Baba.

I locked the door and played *Benvenuto Cellini* on the Victrola. Ber-lioz's beautiful opera echoed within the walls. The Chinese roses swayed to the music, stems bending, assuming the flexibility of undu-lating seagrass. Their petaled heads surrendered to the notes, their movement dictated by the tempo.

I missed Daniel too.

I hadn't seen him since I visited him at work.

Thinking of him unleashed an ocean of regrets. Months later, it still stung, though it was my fault for driving him away. If my grandmother could forget about her love for the Shanghainese hotelier, then perhaps I could do the same with Daniel. I would take the strength of the women in my family to heart. My mother had taught me to let your love make their own choice. My laolao taught that you needed to honor it.

I shook my head, pushed the painful thoughts of Daniel away, and focused on the grand reopening. I still needed to prep for the restaurant's opening in the afternoon and make arrangements for the evening's private feast for the neighbors.

Tomorrow, I could finally fulfill my heart's wish.

Chapter Thirty-one

Chapter Thirty-one

The afternoon of the grand reopening drew in a healthy crowd. As I finished prepping my newest creation to serve as samples, a lineup gathered on the other side of the glass door. These faces were excited strangers: peering in through the windows, whispering with subdued smiles, pointing at the flowers and the decor, and taking pictures of the newly painted sign.

I glanced at the clock. Two minutes left.

I had arranged samples of the ginger shrimp balls on a large tray. Toasted bread cut into small cubes hid a juicy center made of minced shrimp and ginger: bite-size, golden hors d'oeuvres with an addictive crunch.

Ginger Shrimp Balls
(Natalie's Recipe)

Ginger
Black tiger shrimp

Egg

Salt

Pepper

Sesame oil

Cornstarch

White bread

Cilantro

Sauce:

Ketchup

Hot sauce

Grate the ginger until it is fine enough to pound in a mortar and pestle. Discard the pulp and scoop out the juice and set aside. Peel the raw shrimp and mince. Mix the egg, minced shrimp, ginger juice, salt, pepper, sesame oil, and cornstarch in one bowl. The consistency should be sticky like a paste.

Set aside because this will be the shrimp balls. Toast a few slices of the bread lightly. The color should still be pale, but the bread itself, firm. Cut and discard the crust. Chop the remaining toasted bread into small cubes no bigger than your fingernail.

Scoop a tablespoon of the sticky shrimp filling and form it into a round ball. Cover the surface with the bread pieces. Place the breaded shrimp balls on a flat sheet and chill in the refrigerator for at least fifteen minutes.

Heat the cooking oil to the right temperature. If it's too hot, the bread will turn brown and burn. If it's too cold, they will fall off.

Garnish with cilantro and serve with ketchup mixed with hot sauce for dipping.

Note:

When well prepared, this dish should resemble golden, faceted jewels. The visual impact will impress and invigorate. Even the pickiest customer cannot resist its crunch and juicy filling.

Serve this to those you want to sway over to your side. The more stubborn the mind, the more ginger you must add.

One minute left. The murmur outside grew louder, as did the sound of my heartbeat. I reached the door, unlocked it, and flipped the sign. My restaurant was officially open.

Traffic exceeded my expectations. Even though I had rationed my samples well, they ran out three hours before closing. The dumplings sold out and were a hit like the rest of the menu items. I'd made new connections and potential repeat customers, and had set up interviews with food bloggers and the local papers.

On any other day, I would have felt exhausted, but not today. Today I was living my dream.

I closed early to prepare for our neighborhood dinner that night. I'd filed a permit to have the road closed off for a few hours. Tonight would be for us: to celebrate our families and our businesses. We had the street to ourselves for a few precious hours. Younger Shen and Mr. Chiu set up a long table and chairs while Mrs. Chiu and Celia arranged the tablecloth and place settings. I was kept busy in the kitchen putting the finishing touches on the dishes for our meal. Old Wu had come to help so I wasn't too overwhelmed.

Miss Yu gave each of us a red paper lantern, and we released them into the night sky. They floated in the air, miniature dirigibles, sustained by our dreams for the future. Their light provided extra warmth on the cool night. I pulled out the Victrola, and my neighbors supplied their own records for the evening. Dolly Parton, Teresa Teng, and Stravinsky's *The Rite of Spring* filled the air, courtesy of Younger Shen, Miss Yu, and me. The lanterns above our heads bobbed to the music, swaying like drowsy fireflies.

We all rushed back into our apartments to change for the occasion. Celia insisted that pageantry was required after decades of living in gray. She was radiant in a lemon sundress with a purple butterfly print. I wore a short-sleeved, white qipao embroidered with ivory phoenixes. Mrs. Chiu wore a floral black and red poppy dress that I had no doubt was a by-product of Celia's influence. Miss Yu favored her signature pastel palette of creams and robin's-egg blue. The men donned elegant suits: Mr. Chiu in silver and Younger Shen in scarlet. Older Shen had yet to arrive, but had promised to adhere to the dress code.

The Hsu family appeared at the same time as Older Shen and his date. The Hsus had bought the bookstore and were due to reopen it in a month. Eugene and Dorothy Hsu were in their late thirties with a nine-year-old daughter, Vanessa. Eugene was an experienced bookseller and Dorothy, a successful litigator. When I noticed a copy of Philip Pullman's *The Amber Spyglass* peeking out from her backpack, I knew we could be friends.

Older Shen's date turned out to be a stunning clinical psychologist named Sneha. In her late sixties, she was newly retired and had taken up ballroom dancing on a lark. He held her in his eyes as if she were the most precious, fascinating being in his world: a combination of wonder and love. She reciprocated with a level of awe reserved for those who finally found what they sought after a long journey. I couldn't be happier for both of them.

Old Wu was the final guest to arrive. He had changed to a dashing black suit accented with a red silk dress shirt.

I beckoned Celia and Older Shen to join me in the kitchen. Together, we brought out the feast I'd prepared. The looks of admiration and appreciation from the dinner guests filled me with joy and pride. Everyone took their seats, and the dinner could begin.

A formal ten-course Chinese dinner was a deliberate courtship of the senses. The appetizers of cold plate meats gave way to steaming fish maw soup, cold and hot introductions to titillate and delight before the showcase of entrees: beef, pork, chicken, fish, seafood, vegetables. The ensuing textures, aromas, and flavors seduced, fulfilling the promises of the first courses. The inclusion of noodle and rice dishes provided a sense of comfort. The final dessert course of sesame balls stuffed with red-bean paste sealed the engagement on the sweetest of notes.

After the meal, Old Wu and I hovered by the Victrola as couples waltzed before us to the mesmerizing voice of Nat King Cole, a record Older Shen had provided. The Chius danced together cheek to cheek. Their marriage was on more solid ground. Mrs. Chiu had wanted her husband to choose her and he had done so by setting a firm retirement deadline within five years. Older Shen and Sneha displayed their superior skills by engaging in a Viennese waltz. Celia and Younger Shen danced together alongside the Hsus.

"Did you ever dance with my grandmother?" I asked Old Wu.

"Yes," he replied. "She was light on her feet, much more than I was." He tipped his head to the swaying couples. "You're young, Ye Ying. There's still hope."

I blushed. "Perhaps, one day, Lao Shi. For now, I'm content to watch."

"Make sure not to stay on the sidelines too long," Old Wu warned.

"Or I'll end up like my beloved mentor?" I teased.

Old Wu broke into a raucous, rusty laugh.

The evening ended when the red lanterns disappeared into the sky, the table was dismantled, and the Victrola returned to my restaurant. Celia insisted that I take the floral centerpieces from the table. With the night over, I returned my attention to tidying up the restaurant and preparing for the next day.

I had just reached for a new stack of paper napkins to refill the empty holder when I heard the jingle of the bell at the door.

"Did you forget something, Celia?" I asked, wrestling with the sticky adhesive binding.

The visitor cleared his throat.

I looked up.

Daniel.

The bundle fell from my hands. Napkins scattered on the floor.

He'd come back.

He was wearing a red pin-striped long-sleeved dress shirt and fitted black jeans, his signature earbuds peeking from above his collar. His messenger bag was missing. Instead, he carried a dozen roses and what looked like a wrapped gift.

"Hello," he said. "These are for you." He handed me the bouquet.

The heady perfume of the red roses matched their deep, vibrant shade. I resisted the urge to bury my nose in the soft petals. "Thank you," I said, placing the bouquet on the crowded countertop.

He crouched down, picked up the scattered napkins, and arranged them into a pile. He placed the collection on a stool and took note of the extravagant collection of flowers. "Congratulations on the grand opening. I'd better clear my schedule so I can get a good spot in line. You're well loved."

"I didn't think I'd ever see you again."

A soft shade of pink crept into his cheeks. "You opened the restaurant. You did it. I knew you could. I wanted to see you the moment I saw the ads. I wasn't sure if you wanted to see me again, but it couldn't hurt to find out. Honestly, after all this time, all I could think about is the incredible woman in white whom I left in Chinatown."

I felt like I had been launched into the sky on the wings of a thousand birds.

"The time apart wasn't a complete waste. It took that long to find this for you." He handed me the gift. It was flat, and judging by its dimensions, I knew it was a record. "Before you open it, I want to tell you something about me. I love music, and as you probably noticed," he said, touching his earbuds, "I listen to it all the time."

It was another sign of the red thread that connected us to each other. Baba had been right. Daniel was my match. I wish they could have met—they had much in common.

"So do I," I said, smiling. "My earliest, favorite memories center around the sound of the erhu."

"That reminds me, there was a musician with that instrument I spoke to a while ago. Is he related to you?"

My heart soared. It was impossible. "Yes. How did you know?"

"You both have the same smile," he replied with a grin. "I talked to him a few times when I was on my way over here before."

Baba had chosen to appear to Daniel. As if I wasn't completely smitten already. Heat bloomed in my cheeks as I lowered my eyes to prevent myself from revealing too much of the state of my heart.

"So, that," he said, pointing at the gift, "is your song. It's the first track on side one. It took me a while to hunt it down because I wanted the best version. I heard it from the birds in the square that day when we kissed."

I ripped the blue wrapping paper. I realized I had never thought about what my own song would be, but Daniel knew. It was an album by Edith Piaf titled *La vie en rose*. A striking Frenchwoman, someone I had never seen before, graced the black-and-white cover. Being raised by an opera connoisseur, I had limited exposure to other genres.

"Who is she?" I asked.

"An incredible singer from Paris in the forties. Her stage name, 'Piaf,' means sparrow. This song is sung in French and it means 'Life through rose-colored glasses.'" He held out his hand for the record and headed for the Victrola. "May I?"

"Yes, please."

He returned the Berlioz record to its sleeve. The needle lowered and the music began. With the first magical chords, I held out my hand. Daniel accepted and pulled me into his arms, and we began to dance.

The rose petals from his bouquet floated in the air, clustering into patterns of sheet music, dots of rose red, arranging and rearranging in sync with the melody, circling us while we swayed.

Our feet floated above the polished floor, weightless and free.

He leaned in, holding me closer, and whispered the translation of the lyrics into my ear.

And we danced to my song.

Natalie Tan's Book of Luck & Fortune

ROSELLE LIM

Discussion Questions

1. How did the relationship dynamics between Qiao and Miranda differ from those between Miranda and Natalie? Is there a repeating pattern, and if so, what is it?

2. Cultural expectations drove Qiao and Miranda apart. What did Qiao expect from her daughter and, consequently, what did Miranda expect from Natalie?

3. The imagery of birds appears throughout the book. When do they occur and what do you believe is the meaning behind each occurrence?

4. Miranda's agoraphobia debilitated her greatly, from not being able to travel with her husband to not being able to help her daughter after she fell outside. How might her life have turned out differently if she had been able to get help early on?

5. Was Natalie selfish for leaving her mother and traveling all over the world, or is she justified in pursuing her dream?

6. What do you think is the effect of the magical realism incorporated throughout the book?

7. Daniel evokes a strong emotional and physical reaction from Natalie from the very beginning. What makes him different from the previous men in her life? Do his family dynamics affect their relationship in any way?

8. Natalie is used to running away from her problems. At what point does she realize she can't run away from her troubles at home? What external and internal factors is she running from?

9. Food is a huge element of the book, connecting the residents of the Chinatown neighborhood. How does food impact your own life and the way you interact with others?

10. Natalie's father is absent throughout most of Natalie's life, yet clearly he has a large presence in it. How do you think his absence has affected Natalie and the decisions she has made?

11. Were you surprised at the identity of Natalie's father? In retrospect, in what ways did he act like a father to her?

12. After her mother's death, Natalie stays at her home with the intention of reviving the neighborhood, but in turn, its residents end up guiding and encouraging her. What are the small and big ways that they help Natalie?